MW00479822

Santa Took Them

Also by William Malmborg

Novels:

Jimmy

Text Message

Nikki's Secret

Dark Harvest

Blind Eye

Collections:

Scraping the Bone: Ten Dark Tales

Santa Took Them

William Malmborg

Darker Dreams Media
Chicago, IL

Darker Dreams Media
Chicago, IL
www.darkerdreamsmedia.com

Publisher's Note: This is a work of fiction. Names, characters,
places, and incidents are a product of the author's imagination.
Locales and public names are sometimes used for atmospheric
purposes. Any resemblance to actual people, living or dead, or
to businesses, companies, events, institutions, or locales is
completely coincidental.

Santa Took Them/ William Malmborg. -- 1st ed.
ISBN 978-0-9962831-2-0

Dedicated to Betty Smith

A grandmother who used to take great joy in scaring her grandchildren with terrifying tales of horror while sitting around the campfire in the woods alongside the house.

"Death has come to your little town sheriff."
-Dr. Sam Loomis *Halloween*

December 24, 2005

The snow was gentle, but persistent, and had slickened the roads to the point where Marty McKenzie had to focus on his driving more so than on what Chris and Paul were saying, his knuckles turning white as he kept the SUV from skidding. Unfortunately, Chris and Paul didn't realize this, their five and seven year old minds still several years away from understanding the horror of winter driving, which led to a constant chanting of, "Dad, did you see Rudolph?" and "Dad, are we going to be home before Santa?" and "Dad, are you *sure* you sent him my letter about wanting an Xbox?"

Shut up and let me drive!

Ruth, obviously noting his growing anxiety, turned toward the backseat and said, "Paul, honey, why don't you tell Chris about how Rudolph became one of Santa's reindeer."

"Mommmm!" Paul said. "He knows that story already."

"Chris, is that true?"

"No."

"Yes you do!"

"No."

"Mom, he does!" Paul cried, a familiar edge of frustration present, one that was a precursor to an apocalyptic melt down. *"We watched Rudolph on TV last night!"*

"I know, honey, but maybe he forgot so you should tell him again."

"Because it was foggy!" Chris shouted.

"See!"

Marty's knuckles became even whiter.

And then Chris began to sing 'Rudolph the Red-Nosed Reindeer', his young voice poking at Marty's nerves without mercy, almost as if he desired nothing more than to drive his father into the womb-like confines of a padded room.

"Very good!" Ruth said with a clap following the song, Chris having somehow managed all the lines.

Naturally, Paul, not wanting to be out performed, began singing as well, his high pitched voice belting out the lyrics to 'Jingle Bells' at the top of his lungs.

Almost home, Marty said to himself.

He turned onto Route 8, tires sliding a bit on the untreated road.

"Rudolph!" Paul shouted.

"Paul!" Marty snapped. "What have I said about screaming in the car?"

Tears followed, and Ruth gave him an angry glare.

Next year I'm staying home, he said to himself, mind already savoring the two hours of freedom he would enjoy as Ruth took the kids to the Christmas Eve service by herself.

It'll never happen.

Ruth would never condone him skipping such a service, not with the way her family would bombard her with questions and concerns about his salvation. They would bring the children into it as well, questions on what they would think if they knew their father refused to attend service, thus spitting in the face of

God and his gift to mankind. Hell, they already were upset about the children believing in Santa, their feeling being that believing in the jolly old elf was the first step toward offering oneself to Satan.

Many sleepless nights had resulted from the craziness of her parents, nights where Marty tried to put his foot down on how he didn't want his children exposed to their extreme beliefs. Ruth, however, wanted her parents to be a part of their children's lives and, given the back and forth conflict within her own mind on what she believed, often put her foot down as well.

"I see Rudolph too," Chris said.

"His nose is blinking," Paul said, seemingly recovered from the shout Marty had delivered. "Mommy, why is his nose blinking?"

"I don't know, maybe it's a signal to the other reindeer."

Marty turned onto Hawthorn, tires skidding once again.

Ruth gasped and then said, "At least it'll be a white Christmas."

"Yeah," Marty said. "If we don't crash into a tree first."

"Are we going to crash?" Paul asked.

"No, honey, Daddy was just teasing." She shot Marty another glare, one that he could feel rather than see since he refused to look her way.

Merry Christmas! Marty said to himself.

Five more turns awaited them, tires skidding with each. He also went through a stop sign, the brakes simply unable to catch on the snowy surface.

And then he was getting ready to turn into the driveway.

"Look out!" Ruth cried as a cat darted from the bushes.

Marty hit the brakes, tires taking the car into a tree on the edge of the driveway, one that fortunately had been planted for

Mother's Day and therefore didn't provide much resistance as the car snapped its frozen trunk.

Chris and Paul were crying.

"It's okay," Ruth said in an attempt to calm them, and then, to Marty, "That's Popeye, isn't it."

"Is there another one-eyed tabby that runs around digging up my tomato plants?"

Ruth didn't reply to that.

In the back, the crying continued.

"It's okay," Ruth cooed, her voice calming them. Then, to Marty, "He shouldn't be running around like this. It's too cold."

He shrugged.

"If it were a dog, you'd agree," she pressed.

"If it were a dog, I would give a damn."

"Mommy!" Paul cried. "Daddy swore!"

"I know honey; sometimes adults do that by mistake when they're being silly. But it is something that I *never ever* want to hear you doing, because if you do, I'll have to spank you."

"Are you going to spank daddy?"

"Not tonight," Marty said and gave Ruth a grin.

Ruth was not amused, and simply glared back at him, her arms crossed.

Fuck.

"Daddy, why does Michelle hurt Popeye?" Paul asked.

Ruth's glare turned to a look of puzzlement, one that was almost asking Marty if he knew what Paul was talking about. She then turned toward Paul. "Honey, I don't think Michelle would hurt Popeye."

"She does though. She once tried to set his whiskers on fire when I was over there playing with Roger and then -- "

"Rudolph!" Chris shouted, finger hitting the window as he pointed toward a communications tower, one that blinked red every night.

"Mom!" Paul said, worried. "What if he comes and we're not in bed?"

"It's okay honey, he knows to wait until you're asleep."

"But he's coming right now!"

"No, that's just -- " she stopped, obviously not wanting to ruin the Rudolph illusion. "Let's go inside and get some milk and cookies ready, okay?"

"And carrots for the reindeer!" Chris shouted.

"Yes, and carrots for the reindeer," Ruth confirmed. She turned to Marty, "Can you bring Popeye back."

"Ruth, it's a cat, they like being outside."

"He's an indoor cat."

"One that's outside all the time killing rabbits and birds."

"Let's put it this way," she said, taking his hand, voice barely audible so that the kids wouldn't hear. "You help out that pussy, and maybe later you'll find another one showing you gratitude." She took his hand and placed it between her legs.

Marty felt himself stiffen, and quickly looked into the backseat, fear that little eyes were watching getting the better of him. No little eyes were upon them, however, the concern about Santa arriving within minutes keeping their focus on the skies beyond the window.

"Okay, I'll meet you inside," Marty said, pulling his hand away and switching off the ignition.

A moment later, he was approaching Popeye who had decided to seek shelter beneath the porch swing, his one eye watching the family as they went inside.

His body shifted.

He's getting ready to dart inside, Marty realized, his hands quickly grabbing him before he could slip through the door.

"Be right back," Marty said.

"Okay," Ruth said, grinning.

Marty started toward the Harper house, which was about two hundred yards away, his feet instantly regretting the decision to make the trek in his church shoes rather than a pair of boots that he could have easily thrown on.

Then again, Popeye would have probably freed himself from his grip once across the threshold, hiding himself somewhere within the house, which, in turn, would have ruined any chances he had of getting lucky that night.

* * *

Getting the kids changed into their pajamas was fairly easy, their fear of upsetting Santa by being awake and out of bed guiding them into a mode of compliance that was rarely seen during the rest of the year.

Secured within their bedroom, Ruth went into her own to change, a quick dip into the closet to retrieve a bag that she had tucked away being made, her goal being to don the red teddy, stockings and panties before Marty got back, everything being hidden beneath a old pair of pajama pants, t-shirt and bathrobe.

Once the presents were out beneath the tree, she would duck into the bedroom before him, bathrobe, pajama pants and t-shirt coming off, and put herself upon the bed, waiting seductively for him in the risqué ensemble.

* * *

Feet frozen from the snow that seeped into his shoes, and fingers growing numb from the biting cold that ate away at his bare flesh,

Marty carried the purring Popeye across the unkempt expanse of scrubland that separated his home from the Harper home, head angled downward against the wind that had picked up.

Thoughts on the Harper family entered his mind while making the trek, specifically the comment from Paul about how Michelle liked to hurt Popeye.

Concern about letting the children into that house followed; concern that he had felt frequently given the incident that had unfolded two years earlier with Randy Harper. Before that night, Marty had never called 911, but after being awakened by Randy's wife Amy, who had been bloodied by a blow to the face, and whose five children were all crying hysterically, he had pressed the three digits without thought and then watched with satisfaction as the police took the man away. No other major incidents had unfolded. Randy and Amy had divorced, Amy staying in the house with the children, and Randy going off to wherever it was his old rusted Dodge took him. Yet, even so, Marty had always had an odd feeling about the family and never felt comfortable about the friendship that Paul had with Roger and the other Harper children. Ruth, however, thought having friends that were next door was positive, and encouraged it.

"Almost home," Marty said, a sense that Popeye was beginning to grow weary of being held unfolding.

Popeye began to fidget.

Marty quickened his pace, rounding the pine trees that shielded the Harper home from view and stepping upon the unshoveled driveway.

Popeye hissed and tried to get away, back claws catching within Marty's coat, all while a front one nailed his chin, tearing the flesh.

"Son of a bitch!" Marty cried, hands opening up so that the cat could get the freedom he suddenly desired.

Popeye ran off into the trees, disappearing.

"Fuck it," Marty said, hand touching his chin.

He started to turn, but then realized the front door of the Harper home was standing open.

Hesitation arrived.

Fear as well, a sense that something was wrong entering his mind.

Go check.

No, go back and call the police.

It's Christmas Eve.

He turned and looked back toward his house, the bright Christmas lights barely visible through the pine trees, a sense of isolation growing.

Maybe the wind blew it open.

Maybe . . .

He heard something. *From within the house. Crying!*

He approached, heart racing as his feet crunched the snow, a growing sense of dread trying to make him go back.

"Hello?" he called once he was near the door.

The crying stopped.

"Amy, everything okay?" he asked.

Nothing.

"Amy?" he asked a second time.

Nothing.

He stepped inside.

* * *

Ruth waited and waited, but Marty didn't come back. Concern arrived. She went to the window, eyes peering through the glass.

Nothing.

A gust of wind howled, its strength causing the Christmas lights to rattle against the house.

She shivered.

Earlier, the falling snow had made it look like a winter wonderland, now, however, it felt like a winter nightmare-land, one that the Donner family would have recognized.

Maybe Amy welcomed him inside to warm up a bit?

Maybe she helped him out of his wet clothes!

Ruth tried pushing the thoughts away, the rational parts of her mind knowing Marty would never do such a thing, especially with Amy, but the other part of her mind, the part that lived in constant fear of divorce and being left alone so that she had to return to her parents, that part watched as she slowly stripped the clothing from his body and toyed with his manhood, fingers bringing it to life.

She'll put it in her mouth, and then bend over the bed so that he can slide it up into her.

No!

He's just there getting warm, being polite as Amy enjoys his company on what is probably a very depressing time for her.

He'll be back any moment.

* * *

The Christmas tree seemed to be the only source of light within the house, its colorful display illuminating the front room and part of the hallway. Beyond that, it was nothing but darkness.

"Hello?" Marty asked.

Nothing.

"Amy?"

Still nothing.

Go back.

Call the police.

He started back toward the front door.

Above him, the floor creaked.

Heart racing, he turned and looked up the stairway, eyes noting a shadowy movement on the landing above.

"Amy?" he asked.

For a moment, there was no reply, but then, someone above began to cry.

Marty froze, his body unable to move, the eeriness of the situation literally paralyzing him.

And then there was more movement above, a shadow, one that stayed low to the ground, almost as if they were slithering across the landing.

Crawling!

Because they're hurt.

The thought broke his paralysis and he quickly climbed the stairs.

Oh my God!

Amy was curled up on the floor in the fetal position, blood covering her hands and face.

"*Santa . . .*" she said.

"What?" Marty asked, kneeling before her.

"*Santa . . .*" she gasped. "*Santa . . . took them.*"

"Santa took who?" Marty asked, eyes going from her to the blood trail that had marked her path upon the landing, one that came from an open bedroom doorway.

Amy didn't reply, her face scrunching up in pain.

A smell followed, one that had a coppery fecal mix.

She just shit herself!

And there was blood in it.

He then realized her hands were clutching her lower abdomen. *No, not clutching . . . holding!* She was holding her abdomen, more specifically, holding in what was trying to come out.

She gasped and he heard a wet fluttery sound, one that seemed to echo from near her fingers.

A stronger, more pronounced, fecal smell hit him.

He backed up a bit, body standing, a realization that she had just farted from her lower gut arriving.

Someone sliced her open!

He spun around; expecting someone to be standing over him, but no one was there.

He then turned back toward Amy and looked beyond her at the trail of blood that had marked her path from the bedroom.

Don't! he told himself.

Go back and call the police.

He started back toward the stairs, but then stopped and once again looked at the room.

What if they're hurt?

Nothing you can do.

Best to get the police and paramedics out there.

Santa took them . . .

Are the kids gone?

Is that what she meant?

Had Randy come back to kill her and take the children, all while dressed as Santa?

A chill entered his system.

Don't go in there!

Ignoring his better judgment, he stepped over Amy's body and started toward the bedroom, feet careful to avoid the trail of blood that marked the floor.

* * *

Marty didn't come back.   Five minutes turned to ten minutes,
which then turned to fifteen and then twenty minutes.

Something's wrong.

Something's happened.

But what?

She went to the window, but as before, there was no sign
of him.

Call the police.

She picked up the phone, but then hesitated.

What if he is having sex with her?

Better to catch him in the act.

He's not having sex.

Something happened.

Her finger hit the nine and then the one on the dial pad,
but then hesitation arrived once again and she put the phone back
into the cradle.

She went back to the window and pressed her face to the
glass, hands cupped around her eyes to keep all the light from the
room spoiling her view.

Footprints!

In the snow.

They were alongside the first set, which were disappearing from the falling snow, coming back toward the house.

In fact . . .

She heard the door open.

Finally!

She started toward the bedroom door, but then stopped, a
thought on greeting him in the sexy ensemble she had purchased

from the mall entering her mind.

Offer to warm him up after his cold ordeal.

She unbelted the robe and let it fall to the ground, and then quickly removed the t-shirt and pajama pants.

And now Chris will come out of the bedroom, forgetting that it's Christmas Eve and ask for a glass of water.

Chris did not come out as she passed the kid's room, a rush of sexual excitement spreading through her body at how exposed she was outside of the bedroom.

She started down the stairs.

* * *

Marty would have cried out at what he found in the bedroom, but couldn't because he was vomiting all over the floor, his knees giving out halfway through the ordeal, hands landing in the acid-laced eggnog and prime rib mess he had created.

Following that, he got to his feet and tried to find a phone, his unfamiliarity with the house leading him into an unused office / bedroom before he found the master bedroom, which had a phone on the nightstand.

"911, what is your emergency?" a voice asked.

"They're dead, they're all dead!" Marty screamed.

"Sir, did you say they're all dead?" the operator asked.

Marty didn't reply, his hand dropping the phone, a sudden urge to get back home and make sure everything was okay unfolding, the distance between the two houses not enough to take comfort in.

He slipped in blood on his way out, the crunch of his wrist as he landed on it reaching his ears.

The pain was intense, but not enough to stop him.

Blood!

He hadn't noticed it while climbing the stairs, but saw it now, drops of it, almost as if something had been carried.

One of their heads?

The image almost caused him to vomit again, but he managed to hold the purge at bay.

More blood was on the first floor.

How did I miss that? he demanded of himself, the trail leading down the hallway toward the back door.

He left through the front, and started back toward the house, his eyes instantly catching sight of the footprints that ran alongside his own heading toward the house.

Oh no!

He ran home, feet barely registering the snow this time, the pain in his broken wrist disappearing as he sprinted toward the front door.

Locked!

No!

He pounded on the door and then pressed the bell.

Inside he heard it chime over and over again.

No one answered.

"Ruth!" he cried. "Open the door!"

Nothing.

He ran around toward the back, mind trying to think if there was anything strong enough to throw threw the sliding porch door.

In the distance, sires began to echo.

* * *

Ruth heard the pounding and the bell, but couldn't shift herself to address either, not with what she had come face to face with in the family room.

The eight-year-old girl was sitting by the tree, facing it, a Santa hat atop her head, tiny voice reciting the *'Twas the Night Before Christmas'* poem.

The porch door shattered.

"Ruth!" Martin shouted while coming into the room. "Are you -- " he stopped and stared.

"Santa?"

Ruth twisted toward her son who had come down the stairs, a hand rubbing his sleepy eyes.

"Paul, honey, can you please go back upstairs while Daddy and -- "

"'Merry Christmas to all, and to all a goodnight!'" Michelle shouted gleefully while twisting toward them, her blood-splattered nightgown clinging to her body as she shifted.

A tiny head rolled from her lap, its lifeless eyes staring up at them as it came to rest in the middle of the floor.

December 21, 2015

Lucy nearly ripped a chunk of hair from Eliot's head as he ran circles around her clit with his tongue, the little flicks of movement causing bursts of pleasure that were almost painful in their intensity.

"Oh God! Oh God! Oh God!"

"Shhh!" Eliot warned, the word vibrating against her. "We don't want to wake Michelle."

"Fuck me!" she cried, giving his hair a tug, his body crawling up hers to relieve the strain.

His penis slid into her.

She grabbed his butt and pulled down while lifting her own midsection, envisioning their bodies becoming fused together.

And then he did that upward penis curl that always set her off, one where he somehow caused it to lift inside of her, hitting those inner pleasure points that most men didn't even know existed.

He pulled back while still curled, his penis gliding against that pleasure pad of nerves, and then thrust back in.

"Oooooohhhhh!" was all she could utter.

His mouth found one of her nipples, his tongue working on it the way it had worked on her clit moments earlier, all while he continued to slide himself in and out.

She bit into his shoulder, the mouthful of flesh the only way to keep from screaming as her orgasm erupted.

* * *

"You don't think she heard, do you?" Lucy asked, voice taking on a sudden shyness that he had never witnessed from her before.

"I don't know. If she woke up, she probably heard a few things, but..." He shrugged. "Would she even know what it was?"

"How old is she?"

"Eighteen."

"Eighteen!" Lucy said, playfully smacking him on the chest. "Of course she would know."

He thought about that for a few seconds, finger toying with the bite mark on his shoulder, which now stung. It also needed to be cleaned, though getting up the motivation to head into the bathroom after everything they had done that evening was difficult. All he wanted to do was lie in bed, holding Lucy, savoring the first night of his two-week vacation.

"Unless—" Lucy started to continue but then stopped.

"Unless what?" Eliot pressed.

"Well, what was that place like? She wasn't kept in, like, a straightjacket or anything, was she?" This last part was whispered.

"No, no, no. I think it was more like a boarding school than anything else, one that has classes and whatnot, but for children that are troubled rather than rich brats whose snobby parents don't want them tagging along as they travel the world." He paused and thought about something. "They had TV and the Internet and other kids her age, so..." He held up his palms. "I suppose you're right, and she knows exactly what sex is."

"Let's hope so, because—" She stopped.

"Because what?" he asked.

"Those sounds we made, what if that triggered a flashback from that night? What if she thought you were killing me and then were going to kill the children?" A shiver raced through her as she spoke, one that he felt against his skin.

"But we don't have any children," he said.

"I know. I meant that her mind would go back to that night and think it was happening again."

"Ah, well, I don't think Samantha would have let her come stay here if she thought she was that fragile," Eliot said, though deep down inside he wondered. Funding was nowhere to be found, the state so broke that it could barely afford to pay its employees, let alone fund medical facilities such as the one Michelle had been placed in, so there was a chance that her evaluations for release had not been up to the standards one would expect. Then again, he had known Samantha a long time now, and he felt she would have said something if she felt the release was premature.

"You're probably right." She pressed herself against him, her naked flesh and the way she was now angled causing a stir down below. "Again?"

"He's willing if you're willing," Eliot said with a smile.

Lucy took hold of the organ in question and guided it into her, their bodies facing each other while side by side. "Gently," she said. "If we're going to do this every night for the next two weeks, I don't want to be rubbed raw on the first night."

"No worries," he said, his hips starting to move slowly so as to slide in and out without much friction, almost as if they were both teasing each other with the lightest touches possible. "I'll be so gentle that you won't even know I'm there."

"Now where's the fun in that?" she asked and started

rocking with him, their movements eventually synchronizing together in such a way that they moved as one.

* * *

Happiness encased her, her body floating in a world so perfect she never wanted it to end, and she dared not close her eyes for fear that sleep would pull her from this perfect moment and thrust her into the next day.

But then tomorrow night you can return to this perfect world, this time with Eliot on his back and you taking control of things.

"Hmmm," she moaned.

"What?" Eliot asked, sleep having started to overtake him.

"Nothing, just thinking," she said.

"About?"

"How happy I am right now."

"Me too," he said, arms squeezing her.

A grunt of pain followed.

"You okay?" she asked.

"Yeah, just my shoulder."

"Sorry about that," she said, a smile upon her face.

"It's okay. The pain made things even more intense."

"Did you wash it out yet?" she asked, her mind unable to tell if she had drifted away at all, though she was fairly certain she had not.

"Not yet," he said. "I don't want to get up."

"Well, you have to, or else it could get infected and the next thing we know, I'm having to explain to your parents and the school what happened."

"I don't think you'll have to do that," he said with a sleepy chuckle.

"Well, then I don't want it getting infected because that might prevent you from being able to use that arm, which in turn will cut down on the pleasure you promised to provide me with during your Christmas vacation."

"The real motivation comes to light."

"Better believe it."

He slid himself from the bed and fumbled around for his pajama pants. "Now, just remember, you promised to provide pleasure as well."

"Yes, but that was because I know you take pleasure in knowing I'm being pleasured. Thus both thirsts are quenched when you go down on me."

"Ah, I see how this is going to work," he said and let out another laugh. He walked to the bedroom door. "I'll be right back."

* * *

Lucy watched as Eliot left the room and, not wanting to fall asleep while he was away, she scooted herself up into a sitting position to await his return. While sitting there, she began to think about Michelle and the things she had read about after Eliot had let her know that his niece was going to be staying with him for a while. Initially, she had been upset with the situation, though only because she had thought the live-in arrangement would infringe upon the holiday plans they had agreed on, plans that saw her coming to stay with him during his vacation as a sort of trial move-in period. But after learning what Michelle had been through and then meeting the girl herself, who was incredibly quiet and initially didn't interact with anyone beyond a few words when spoken to, she'd had a change of heart. That said, she wasn't fully comfortable with it, her digging into the tragedy all those years ago having alerted her to the fact that some out there thought Michelle herself

was responsible for the murders of her family. One person in particular, Detective Hines, had been adamant about his theory that
Michelle had been the killer that night, but others felt there was no
way an eight-year-old could go so far as to sever the heads of four
people, especially her own siblings, and then stab her mother. It
just wasn't possible. Instead, they felt that Michelle had been the
lone survivor of a Christmas Eve slayer, one who had never been
apprehended—at least not for the crime that night. His having
never struck again on subsequent holidays was attributed to his
having been captured and imprisoned for some other crime.

A yawn ended her thoughts on this, as did the intrusion
of a new thought, one that brought a smile to her face.

You know he is going to do it.

It wasn't a question of if, but when.

This week?

Before Christmas or after?

Maybe during the New Year's celebration?

Please not during an actual holiday!

This was her only request, though she hadn't voiced it to
him. She wouldn't either because it seemed weird dictating terms
on how one should be proposed to. Instead, she hoped he would
realize that linking their engagement with another holiday
wouldn't be right, simply because they would then have to balance
two celebrations for the rest of their lives, engagement anniversa-
ries always seeming to take a backseat to the more established
holiday celebrations.

* * *

Walking to the bathroom alerted Eliot to the soreness he felt, which
hadn't been there before he and Lucy had entered the bedroom
several hours earlier.

Maybe I should have stretched first, he thought to himself with a smile.

He grabbed the peroxide and then dug around within the bathroom drawer, looking for something that would allow him to dab the disinfectant upon the wound. Nothing was present, however, so instead he went into the shower, deciding to simply dump a handful into his palm and then splash it onto his shoulder.

Beyond the bathroom, the hallway creaked.

Lucy? he wondered. *Or maybe Michelle?*

Had they awakened her to the point where she came to investigate the sounds, or was she simply wandering around, unable to sleep? She had done that the other night, her steps pulling him from his own sleep, and when she didn't return to her room on her own, he had gotten up and helped her back to bed, his presence seeming to bring her back to her present situation.

Questions on her staying with him and whether or not it was a good idea had followed, his mind wondering what it was that had possessed him to say yes to the request.

"She can't stay here much longer," Samantha had said that morning. *"And she shouldn't be in one of the adult institutions."*

"But..." he had replied, unable to think up a legitimate reason why it wouldn't be a good idea.

"And you've been visiting her so often that she has bonded with you in a way that she hasn't with anyone else, which makes you the ideal person to help her find a place within society."

The conversation had gone on for nearly an hour, Samantha slowly but surely breaking down the hesitation he felt.

Two days later, after cleaning his house and putting a room together for Michelle, he had picked her up, a tiny bag clutched in her hands as they left the home and went to his car. A moment of hesitation had gripped her, one that reminded him of the time many years earlier when he had decided it was time to bring Gizmo, the stray cat he had been feeding for two months, into his home so they could live together. Several hesitant footsteps toward the open door had taken place, each one punctuated by a look backward into the yard. Eventually, however, Gizmo had crossed the threshold and begun exploring the house, much the way Michelle had done upon her entry.

Will she die from cancer too? he asked himself, memories of how sick Gizmo had become two years later bringing sadness to his eyes.

He splashed the peroxide onto his wound, teeth clamped down against the pain.

Outside the door, the floor creaked again.

Grabbing a towel, Eliot wiped away the peroxide that had run down his arm and chest and then tossed the towel into the hamper before walking up to the bathroom door.

"Michelle, is that you?"

No answer.

"Lucy?"

Still no answer.

Someone's out there.

He could feel it, the years of being alone in the house having tuned his senses to the point of knowing when someone else was near.

"Michelle, if that's you, you know there's a bathroom next to your room downstairs," he said, unease growing. "You have your very own."

Nothing.

He put his hand on the knob and twisted.

"Ho! Ho! Ho!" a voice echoed from beneath the Santa hat.

Eliot let out a startled cry while jumping backward.

* * *

Lucy laughed at the pathetic scream that left Eliot's mouth while he jumped backward, his hands flopping in a way that looked like he was trying to wave away mosquitoes that were coming after him.

"Jesus Christ!" he gasped. "You scared the shit out of me."

"Really? Ugh, then maybe I'll use the bathroom downstairs instead." She made as if to turn.

He let out a weak laugh.

She grinned.

"Where'd you get the hat?" he asked, snatching it from her head.

"Forgot that it was in my bag," she said. "They had us wearing them at work until someone complained."

"You serious?" he asked.

"Yep. But I'm totally going to keep wearing mine while working. I'm Lucy Sanders, who from this point onward will always be known as the Rosa Parks of the bank teller struggle to wear a Santa hat during the Christmas season," she said, snatching it back.

"Um...I'm not sure the two are really comparable, unless you're an anchor on Fox News."

"Good point," she said. "Now move it so I can use the bathroom. I really gotta pee."

"Okay," he said, smiling.

The two slipped by each other through the door, her boobs brushing his chest through the T-shirt she had thrown on, the contact causing her nipples to stiffen.

We could probably go another round after this, she told herself, realizing desire was still present within her.

Then again, he might be out cold and snoring when I get back.

Tomorrow night.

She closed the door while thinking this and scurried over to the toilet.

* * *

Eliot headed back to the bedroom, a yawn removing the smile that had been present due to Lucy's antics. Back in bed, he looked at the empty spot next to him, one that he was enjoying having filled with her presence. In fact, on nights when she wasn't here with him, he longed for her, which was something he had never experienced with prior relationships.

She wants you to ask the question, he said to himself.

He had a ring, one that he had gotten from the Kay's at the Park Place Mall. The trouble was he didn't know if asking her now was a good idea, not with the Michelle situation having come into play.

Will she be here a long time?

Samantha had called it a trial period but hadn't specified any time frame for that period, or what exactly would unfold afterward. Making things worse, he was starting to suspect the term "trial period" had been a way of saying, "Let's see if things work out with you so that she can stay there forever."

Forever.

No, that wouldn't work.

But where else would she go?

Getting a job and moving out on her own wasn't going to happen anytime soon, not with the communication issues she had.

Her background would also hinder her, the sad reality being that no matter what name was given to the hospital, everyone would always view it simply as a mental institution for children.

And then there was the question of whether she had killed her family. Eliot didn't believe she had, his sister's death and the deaths of her children having been the result of either a drifter or someone she had fallen for who wasn't what he seemed—of this he was certain. But others didn't believe this, and it wouldn't take long for that information to be used against her at whatever job she found herself working. People were cruel, and the integration of social media into the everyday workings of America had turned the adult world into one that resembled high school. People were bullied for whatever reasons were available, and Michelle would be no exception. Life outside of the home she had been in, and outside of this one, would be difficult for her, which in turn made him think that joining him in marriage would be difficult for Lucy. Before Michelle, it wouldn't have been; now, however, it would be, which was why he was going to wait and see what happened with his niece before asking the question.

* * *

Lucy heard a sound outside the bathroom door and wondered if Eliot was going to try to get her back for scaring him a few minutes earlier.

If so, it wasn't going to work. She was too prepared for it. In fact, she was going to try to get him again, and rather than flushing the toilet after finishing, she carefully stood up and crept to the door.

It was locked, but that didn't matter because she knew that by holding her thumb against the button she could keep it from making a popping sound while twisting the knob.

Lock unlatched, she pulled the door open as fast as she could.

No one was there.

Huh? she asked herself while leaning out the doorway to peer both ways down the empty hallway, eyes catching sight of a faint shadow disappearing into the dark office to the right, which was on the opposite side of the landing from the master bedroom.

Aha! Got ya!

Hesitation followed, and she once again peered toward the master bedroom.

It might not be him. It might be Michelle.

Earlier, she had introduced herself to the teen but hadn't gotten much of a response beyond a soft "Hi," followed by a question on if she was Uncle Eliot's girlfriend. Lucy had explained that she was, which earned a nod and a statement about how Michelle had a boyfriend too but hadn't been able to meet him yet.

Nothing else had followed, though it wasn't for a lack of trying to engage the girl on Lucy's part. Instead, Michelle had simply stopped talking, her focus seemingly elsewhere, even though she was staring straight at Lucy.

Maybe try to talk to her again?

Lucy looked at the master bedroom one more time and then started across the hallway toward the office.

* * *

"Lucy?" Eliot asked, somewhat startled by something that he couldn't pinpoint, his eyes having drifted away for a second before being yanked back into waking reality.

The bedroom door, which had been partially closed, eased open with an eerie groan.

"Lucy?" he asked again more forcefully while sitting up,

noting that she was still wearing the Santa hat.

Not Lucy!

"Michelle?" he asked. "Is that you?"

She didn't say a word.

"Michelle, are you okay?"

Nothing.

A chill raced through him.

Why is she wearing Lucy's hat?

"Lucy?" he called.

Nothing.

"Michelle, where's Lucy?" he asked.

Nothing.

Concerned, he reached over the edge of the bed, blindly trying to find his pajama pants while keeping an eye on Michelle, who was simply standing there in the doorway, body encased in shadow.

Is that Michelle?

He couldn't find the pants.

He risked a glance over the side.

Something thumped onto the bed.

He turned and gasped as he came face-to-face with Lucy's head.

The figure screamed and came at him, his eyes catching a reflection of the knife blade as she lifted it over her head.

Panicked, he tried to deflect the blade with a pillow, but it simply sliced through the feathers and into his palm, a cry of pain leaving his lips.

And then she stabbed him, the sensation as the blade entered him and scraped against bone unlike anything he had ever felt before.

She pulled it free and stabbed again.

And then again, and again, and again, his mind losing count as a dull fogginess came over him, one that was welcomed given that it took away the pain.

Not the sound though, his ears somehow feeling rather than hearing each entry of the blade, the vibrations racing through his body, almost like ripples in a pond..

December 22, 2015

Samantha heard the musical ring from her phone and patted the nightstand several times before she could find it, her finger hitting the snooze button twice before realizing it was a call, not her alarm.

"Dr. Loomis," she answered, her voice unable to mask the fact that she had been asleep.

"Sam?" a familiar voice asked. "It's Mark. Sorry to wake you, but, well, something has happened."

Mark was on the administrative board at the children's home she did rounds for, a board that was always focused on things that could affect the image of the hospital and its funding.

"What?" Samantha asked, fully awake now, and then, somehow knowing, "Michelle?"

"I'm afraid so," Mark confirmed. "Can you come down here? I'm calling an emergency meeting to discuss our response."

"Is Michelle there?" Samantha asked.

"No, um, they haven't located her yet."

Then why the fuck should I be there? she asked herself, anger unfolding over the fact that they would be more concerned with image than finding Michelle. Into the phone, "Where'd the incident take place? Was it at her uncle's place or somewhere else?"

"Um…we really need you here," Mark said. "The media is going to come down on us given the timing and how similar this is to the incident ten years—"

Samantha disconnected the call and started scrolling

through her contacts until she found the number for Eliot.

Please pick up…

No answer.

Fuck!

Her phone rang.

"Mark, I'm not—" she started.

"This is Detective White with the Elm Grove Police Department," a voice said, cutting her off. "Are you aware that you just tried calling a cell phone that is part of a crime scene?"

"Detective White," Samantha said, unfazed. "My name is Dr. Samantha Loomis. My patient, Michelle Harper, niece to Eliot Bakerson, was staying with Eliot Bakerson through the holidays."

"Do you know where Ms. Harper is at this time?" Detective White asked.

Samantha's heart dropped. "No, sir, I don't. I was hoping you could tell me that."

"You're her doctor?"

"Yes."

"Well then, I think you better come down here." He gave her an address that she didn't need to write down. "Is this a good number to call you at should we need to reach you?"

"Yes, and I'm on my way."

"Good, oh, and Doctor?"

"Yes?" Samantha asked, hand reaching for the closet door.

"To the best of your knowledge, is Michelle Harper dangerous?"

"To the best of my knowledge…" *She never displayed any violent tendencies while under my care,* was going to be her answer, but she stopped herself when she realized it was exactly the sort of thing Mark would want her to say. "I don't know. Yesterday at this time, I would have said no, but if I'm hearing you correctly, something horrible has happened and Michelle is missing, so…"

"You're right. Something horrible did happen here and your patient, Michelle, who a neighbor told us was staying here, is nowhere to be found, so any information on where she may go or who she might be with would be very helpful."

* * *

"He was about fifteen when his sister and her children were murdered," Samantha told the detective after arriving on the scene and being asked about Eliot. "Apparently the two were close despite the age difference, and following the murders, he was the only one who would ever visit her daughter Michelle."

"And you felt that because of this connection, it would be okay for her to live with him?" Detective White asked.

"We really didn't have any other choice," Samantha said, somewhat defensively. "Given her age, she could no longer stay at the children's home, and given the progress she had made, going into an adult institution didn't seem like the best route to take."

"What do you mean by progress?"

"When she first came to us, she appeared to be catatonic; her movements were slow, facial reactions muted, body positions rigid as if she were sculpted into them. If we led her to a chair in the TV room, she would likely stay in the chair all day, hands folded in her lap, eyes staring forward, until someone came to move her for a meal or take her to the bathroom. What was interesting was that if we didn't take her to the bathroom, she wouldn't have an accident. She would simply wait until we did eventually come to take her. And she didn't speak, the only exception to this being that we would sometimes find her reciting the words to the

"Twas the Night Before Christmas' poem when it was dark out. Never during the day, and it wasn't secretive. She wouldn't stop when we came upon her, nor hesitate. She would simply keep going."

"Is she psychotic?"

"Though initially it would be easy to say that she was, the answer is no. She wasn't disconnected from reality, but instead kept herself distanced from everything that was going on around her, mentally, not physically, though she would sometimes tuck herself as far away from the other children as she could. No pattern of that behavior developed, so it seemed to be a decision she made on her own for unknown reasons depending on what she was presented with when she entered the common area."

"You said that she made progress," Detective White noted. "How so? What is she like now?"

"Now she simply appears to be a quiet teenage girl who doesn't make a big splash in her environment. To some this may seem concerning, but given how she was when she first arrived, it is a marked improvement. She also will talk to people. Not much, and she won't elaborate on things unless pressed, but she will communicate and make her thoughts known. What's difficult with this is that most of the time she won't display body language or facial expressions when communicating, so all you have are her words."

"And her mobility?"

"Fully functioning," she said and then, sensing his impatience, added, "She doesn't have any trouble going from room to room, taking herself to the bathroom, going to the kitchen to get a snack—things like that."

"So heading to the kitchen to grab a knife and then going

upstairs to kill her uncle and his girlfriend, that wouldn't be be-yond the realm of possibility?"

Samantha didn't like where this was headed but knew she had to answer. "No, it wouldn't be. Like any human being, Mi-chelle is fully capable of such an act. That said, I wouldn't know her motivation for doing such a thing and, like I said earlier, she never displayed any violent tendencies while under my care."

At that moment, a stretcher with a body was wheeled out through the front door and taken to a waiting ambulance.

Samantha was a bit startled by this and, once she noticed them, by how many people had come out to watch, the area just beyond the police tape seemingly in high demand as spectators stood shoulder to shoulder, phones held up, snapping pictures and video of everything that unfolded.

A second body followed the first, the ambulance leaving the scene once everyone was secure within, no lights or sirens needed as it navigated the quiet neighborhood streets.

A gust of wind arrived, chilling Samantha.

"Snow's coming," Detective White said. "Big storm. Win-ter weather advisory has already been issued for the area starting tomorrow night, and they said areas to the northwest may have a blizzard on Christmas Eve."

Samantha had caught something about that on the radio while driving over but hadn't paid much attention.

"That night, ten years ago..." the detective started and then paused momentarily, a finger beneath his lips. "They were experiencing a blizzard as well, weren't they?"

"I...um..." She thought about it for a moment, unable to visualize the period of time from her own point of view since she and her then-husband had been elsewhere for the holidays that year. "Okay, yeah, I don't know if it was a blizzard, but there was certainly a snowstorm hitting the area, according to the police investigation."

"And according to that investigation, Michelle was found wearing a Santa hat at the neighbor's house."

"Yes."

"Was it ever determined where that hat came from?"

"Um...no."

"Michelle never talked about it?"

"No."

"Did you know she was wearing a Santa hat when she left here?"

"No, I didn't." Then, "How do you know she was?"

"The neighbor that called nine-one-one, she saw Michelle leaving the house after hearing screams and said she had on a Santa hat."

"And what, she just walked away?"

"Right down the sidewalk." He pointed toward the left. "Turned at that stop sign and disappeared. No one has seen her since."

"You've done a search though, right?"

"Of course," he said. "We've had dozens of officers patrolling the area since the call came in, but we haven't found her."

Samantha thought about that and the fact that it was only forty degrees out, which, while warmer then it had been during the previous week, was still cold enough for a person to have issues if they tried to stay outside overnight without the proper clothing.

"Tell me, Doctor, what are the chances that Michelle would try to go home?"

"Home? You mean back to the children's home, or..." She

let her voice fade.

The detective stared at her, waiting.

"Rockwood's what, like a hundred miles from here?"

"More like fifty," Detective White said. "Does she know how to drive?"

"No, that isn't something we're equipped to teach at the children's home."

"Did she have any friends, someone who might have been able to drive her somewhere?"

"Friends?" she asked, voice raised a bit. "No, no one. The only person who came to visit her was Eliot."

"What about a web connection? Was she able to go online?"

"Um...yeah, but she didn't do it too..." Samantha stopped, a memory of talking to Michelle about how she was doing at her uncle's place coming back to her. *"I have a boyfriend,"* Michelle had said, smiling. *"We talk at night."*

"What is it?" Detective White asked.

"Not sure. Um...are you able to access the computers inside?"

"Yeah, we can have a tech take a look at them."

"Okay."

"What are you thinking?"

"Not sure. I spoke to Michelle after her first week here, and she mentioned she had a boyfriend, one that she spoke with at night. I didn't think much of it at the time, but now I wonder if she was talking to someone online."

"She wanders a lot at night," Eliot had reported.

Samantha had asked if she seemed troubled, but Eliot said no, she simply seemed like she couldn't sleep. Samantha had then suggested that maybe the new situation was the cause and she simply needed time to adjust.

* * *

"Santa took them."

It was written in blood on the wall in Michelle's bedroom, the giant letters looking as if two fingers had been required to make them.

"This is what her mother said before dying, correct?" Detective White asked.

"Yeah," Samantha said, though she was certain he already knew this and didn't need her to confirm it. "And it was also written on the wall just like this in the children's bedroom."

"Right," he said with a nod. "According to the report, it was her mother that wrote it, and the blood used came from her children."

"That's right, they confirmed three DNA strands."

He nodded again. "She had five children, four of whom were beheaded, but only three strands were confirmed, meaning..."

She waited, his words making it pretty clear that he had studied the case before she arrived, but when he didn't continue, she said, "They concluded that the mother was under some type of duress while writing it and that she didn't realize she dipped into the same pool of blood twice."

"Duress because someone else had just killed her children, or because she had just killed her children?" he questioned.

Samantha nodded, somewhat relieved that this detective understood the uncertainty of the crime. Detective Hines had not and spent his entire time on the case trying to find ways of proving that Michelle had committed the horrific acts.

"Of course, that brings up the question of who killed her?" he mused. "They found Michelle's fingerprints on the knife."

"That's right," Samantha said, once again thinking that he wasn't really asking for her confirmation on this, yet answering all the same.

"So that brings us to the questions of did Michelle hide while her mother was killing her siblings, while watching someone else who was killing her siblings, or did she kill her siblings herself, then her mother?"

"If she killed them herself, why would she wait for her mother to write on the wall before stabbing her? And why leave her to bleed out rather than beheading her like her brothers and sisters?"

Detective White put a finger to his bottom lip and thought about that. No words followed.

* * *

Five missed calls and a voicemail were noted on her phone screen when Samantha returned to her car, all but one from Mark, who, given the voicemail he had left, was not happy with her right now, his implication being that she had abandoned them to the press.

Not really, she said to herself, a vision appearing within her mind of neighbors with their phones held up documenting her as she talked with Detective White. It wouldn't be long before those shots appeared online. And the ones of the bodies being wheeled out...those would surely be purchased by the news networks in Chicago and played over and over again.

Should I call him back, or let him sweat a bit longer?

Her phone buzzed.

It was Detective White.

"Dr. Loomis?" he asked.

"Yeah?"

"Forgot to ask, will you be staying in town or heading back?"

"Heading back," she lied. "The administrative board at the hospital is pestering me to be with them when the media arrives, so..."

"Ah, yes, well, good luck with all that."

"Thanks. Let me know if you need anything or if you find her."

"I will, and you do the same, okay?"

"Okay," she said, somewhat puzzled by his words. "I will."

He knows.

Samantha wasn't heading back to the hospital but to Rockwood to see if Michelle would, in fact, go home.

But she doesn't know how to drive a car.

Boyfriend.

The two thoughts weighed heavy upon her mind, as did her certainty that Michelle had not been responsible for the horror ten years ago.

And she isn't now!

The certainty she felt wasn't as strong as she wanted it to be, simply because when three people were within a house and two of them were murdered, the only real logical answer was that the third person had done it. And when one of those individuals had witnessed a similar crime ten years earlier, and then was part of one that had the same characteristics, the likelihood of being responsible nearly doubled.

That said, it almost seemed too similar, almost as if it was supposed to lead everyone to the conclusion that Michelle was to blame.

Santa took them.

Though she had seen pictures from the scene ten years ago, nothing about them had prepared her for what it was like to see such a display in person, blood still damp, coppery smell hanging in the air.

It was...

She felt a tickle in her throat.

NO! her mind cried, quickly rolling down the window to let in some cold.

She took a deep breath and then another and another until the sensation passed.

Her phone buzzed.

Mark, again.

She hit the *ignore* icon and began to program a route to Rockwood.

Fifty-five miles.

Detective White had been right.

THUNK! THUNK!

Samantha shouted with surprise!

A woman was standing by her passenger window, ready to hit it again.

Samantha pressed the button to lower it and asked, "Yes?"

"Are you with the police?" the woman asked.

"No," Samantha said, suddenly concerned. "But if you need to talk to them, the detective is still over there."

The woman looked over toward the scene, hesitation gripping her.

She doesn't want to go over there, Samantha realized.

She's nervous.

What if she knows something important?

"I can relay a message to them if you need?" Samantha said. "Did you see something last night?"

"No, well, maybe. I don't know."

"What was it?"

"Um…well…I think I saw that girl, the one everyone is talking about. I saw her walking down the street."

"Ah," Samantha said with a nod. "Wearing a Santa hat."

"No, see, that's just it," the woman said. "She was just walking like she did on other nights. See, well, I live right there"— she pointed to a house two down from where Samantha had parked—"and I'd see her walking at night around nine or ten, all bundled up against the cold, but no Santa hat or anything. She did it every night."

"I go for walks sometimes," Michelle had told her.

"Oh, that's good," Samantha had said. *"Helps clear the mind while also keeping you in shape."*

Nothing had been said about the time these walks were taken, and if Eliot had known she walked at night in the dark, he hadn't said anything.

"Did you see her walking at all later with a Santa hat on?" Michelle asked.

"No, not at all," the woman said, arms now crossed against the cold, "but I might have been asleep when everything happened." She started going from foot to foot. "Do you think that's important?"

"It might be, and I suggest you tell the police about it."

The woman squeezed herself tighter and looked over toward the scene, then back at her. "Do you think I should do that now, or wait until they come by asking questions? They will come by asking questions, right?"

"Um...I don't know," Samantha said. Canvassing the area to see what people had seen did seem important, but...well...she didn't know what the actual procedure was and thus couldn't say for sure. "How about I do this, I give them your name and address, so they can come talk to you, okay?"

"Okay," she said. "My name's Barbara Hill, and I'm at that house." She again pointed to the house on the corner. "When do you think they will come talk to me? I have to be at work at four."

"Oh, um, that I don't know, but I'll be sure to let them know about you needing to be at work."

"Okay, thanks."

"Yep."

With that, Barbara returned to her house, glancing back a few times toward the scene as she walked.

Samantha watched as she went, a question unfolding within her mind about how many details were lost to investigators simply because people were too shy to report them.

* * *

"Steve, no, come on, let's go to Freddy's or something," Renee pleaded. "Or back to your place."

"Kyle would tell my parents that you were over, and we wouldn't get any privacy at Freddy's," Steve said. "Besides, it's cool. I have the key, and my Dad wanted me doing some touch-up work here anyway during break."

"Touch-up work?" Renee asked.

"Yeah, like painting and shit. Says that a kid my age shouldn't get to lie around for two weeks, and that when he was a kid his father made him work the fields when he wasn't in school."

"That's so bogus," Renee said, uncertainty still present in her eyes.

"Yeah, and even if he did work the fields, I'm sure he got paid. I'm not making a dime helping with this."

"Are you serious?" Renee asked. "He's not paying you at all?"

"Nothing."

"That's…" She shook her head, seemingly lost for words.

Steve had felt the same way when his father informed him of his "job" during break, but after letting it sink in, he had managed some words, ones that simply stated that if his father wanted him working on the house during his break, he had to pay him ten bucks an hour. An angry exchange had followed, his father eventually stating that his payment would come in the form of being able to stay in the house they currently lived in and have food on the table, thanks to the money that would arrive from selling the house he was trying to flip. Steve, unable to stop himself, had replied if that truly was his payment, then that meant he should be able to make his own rules for himself within the house since he was helping with the mortgage.

"I thought he was going to hit me after that," Steve said with a fake laugh, the fear of the moment coming back. "Instead, he smashed his plate against the table and stormed off. And then my mother started screaming at me, apparently thinking my attitude was responsible for the marriage problems they've been having these last two years."

"She said that?" Renee asked.

"No, but you can tell she thinks it when she gets angry at me." He gave a dismissive wave.

"I'm sorry, that really sucks." She put a hand on his arm, causing a tingle to race through his skin.

"What can you do?" he said with a shrug and then, not wanting the mood to be so down, added, "And if worse comes to worst and we lose the house, at least we have this one to move into, right?"

"I'd rather live on the street," she said.

He gave her a look.

"I'm serious," she added. "I mean, can you imagine living here after what happened?"

"That was ten years ago."

"So? Still bad juju, especially with four of them being kids. All that youthful energy, cut short like that without warning…"

"You think it's haunted?" Steve asked, unable to hide the amusement he felt.

"What? No way!" She then grew serious. "All I'm saying is that all that energy cut short like that, that shit doesn't go away."

Steve nodded.

"Fuck you," she said with a laugh.

"You know, with so much bad energy in there, maybe it wouldn't hurt to go and put in some good energy—sort of balance things out."

"And how exactly are we going to do that?" she asked.

"I'm sure we can figure something out." With that, he opened his car door and started toward the house.

"Steve, no, stop," Renee said.

"What?" Steve asked, a hand to his ear while walking backward toward the house. "I can't hear you."

"I said no!"

Steve kept walking slowly.

Renee got out of the car and shouted, "You're so going to pay for this!" while hurrying toward him.

* * *

"See, it isn't so bad," Steve said once they were in the sunroom, the key he had grabbed being for the back door rather than the front.

"Steve," Renee said, gooseflesh on her arms. "Please, I really don't want to be here."

"Oh come on, chill out. I've been inside a hundred times since my Dad bought it, and nothing weird has happened yet." He took her hand. "Come on, let me show you around."

"No, no, no," she said, resisting his pull for a moment before giving in and letting him lead her deeper into the house. "Okay, I'll look around here, but I'm not going upstairs at all!"

"But that's where I need to do all the touch-up," Steve said. "Cover up all the bloodstains."

"What!" she cried.

He laughed. "I'm just joshing you. There aren't any bloodstains. The guy that owned this place before us painted over them once the police were done with the house."

Renee didn't reply to that, a new chill racing through her body at the thought of what had occurred here.

This is where he stood when first entering the house, she said to herself, imagining the man next door, Marty McKenzie, walking inside to see if anything was wrong. *And then he heard the noise up—*

Something crashed upstairs!

Renee screamed.

* * *

"Fuck was that?" Steve asked.

"I don't know, but—"

He felt her yanking at his hand, which he hadn't realized

he was still holding.

"—let me go!"

"Sorry," he said and released her hand.

With that, she started toward the back door.

"Renee, wait."

"No!" she cried and continued out the back.

Steve didn't follow, knowing his father would kill him if something horrible had happened here—something that resulted in a need for more than just painting and other trim work to be performed.

* * *

Renee ran all the way to the car before she realized Steve was not following her. Even worse, he had the keys and the car was locked.

Not going back in, she said, hands stuffed in her pocket. *Not after—what the fuck is he doing?*

Anger arrived.

* * *

Steve hesitated on the stairs, a sudden realization unfolding that this was the first time he had been in the house all by himself. Yesterday, one of his father's electrical contractors had been there, his work occurring in the basement where something had gone wrong with the wiring that had been installed months earlier. Steve had been up in the bedroom at the time, one that required painting due to the walls that had been replaced, walls that, while having been painted over, had still shown faint traces of blood where the stains had somehow seeped through the paint the landlord had used nine years earlier. Rather than trying to paint over it again, his father had had him and Kyle tear out the wall so that he could put new drywall in, the two enjoying the work since hammers and putting holes in things were involved.

Until Kyle cut himself on a nail.

After that, Steve's mother had put a stop to Kyle's presence within the house, and she didn't want Steve doing any demo work while unsupervised, despite the fact that he was seventeen.

Now, however, it seemed okay to have him unsupervised in the house when it came to painting, which he had spent hours doing yesterday, nearly completing an entire bedroom.

And you left a fucking window open!

The realization struck as a gust of wind hit the house, the cold air actually reaching him on the stairs as he walked up to investigate the noise.

The paint fumes were the reason he had opened the bedroom windows, a horrific nauseous feeling in his gut encouraging him to let fresh air in while working. Being somewhat cold hadn't really concerned him, the new furnace his father had installed that fall doing a fantastic job of keeping the room warm while he painted. Plus, any moments when he did get a chill from cold air seeping in were nullified by the fact that it was that or spend several moments vomiting into the new second-floor toilet, the latter of which was something he didn't want to endure.

Another crash echoed, followed by the sound of feet pattering against the floor.

"*Oh fuck!*" he said to himself, now knowing that some creature had gotten in through the open window, one that was knocking shit down.

* * *

"Hey, Renee, it was just a cat," Steve said, coming around the front of the house.

"A cat?" she asked.

"Yeah, must've gotten in through the window I left open

to air out the paint fumes."

"Is it still inside?"

"Yeah, poor guy doesn't want to leave. Made himself a nice warm bed in the drop cloth I put down."

"What was the crash we heard?"

"He must have knocked over the paint roller. I had it leaning against the wall."

"That loud noise was NOT a paint roller!"

"Well, it's the only thing I can see that has fallen over." He shrugged. "The only thing that makes sense really." He shrugged again. "Anyway, I need your help getting it out."

"What? No. I'm not going back in there."

"Oh, come on, it's just a house."

"No. Steve, please!"

He waited, arms crossed, giving her a look that seemed to carry a mix of pity and anger.

Embarrassment began to build.

It is just a house, she said to herself, looking up at the windows and then over to the overgrown pine trees that touched the roof and acted like a border of sorts.

The silent statement did little to curb her fear of the place, fear that wasn't unique given that no one had rented it following what had happened.

And no one will buy it, even after they fix it up.

Steve's dad was going to lose money on this place and it would ruin him. After that, she and Steve wouldn't be able to be together because he would have to move.

Here?

Steve had joked about it earlier, but honestly, that was probably the reality they would face if they couldn't sell it.

"Okay, let's go," Steve said, pulling out his keys.

"Where?" Renee asked, relief arriving.

"Home for you, then I'm back here getting the cat out and finishing the work I have to do." He started to walk toward the driver's side.

"But you said we could spend the day together."

"Yeah, but we have nowhere we can go. If we hang out at Freddy's, my dad will eventually find out I wasn't working here, and we can't go to my place or your place because of Kyle and Katie, so…" He gave her a look that asked, *Any suggestions?*

She had none.

Worse, she knew that if they left now, he would realize that her fear was stronger than her love for him, which might make him question whether they should really be together.

"Okay, we'll stay," she said.

"What?" he asked.

"We'll stay."

"No, you don't have to do that," he said.

"I know, but I want to." She paused and then added, "I want to spend time with you, and if this is the only place we can do it, so be it."

Steve smiled and then, once he came around the car, leaned in to kiss her.

Lips met, her knees weakening with a pleasure-laced happiness, and then his arms were around her, squeezing her against him, winter clothing doing little to hide the excitement he projected.

"Inside," she said, mouthing the word against his lips, the sudden euphoria of the moment knocking away the unease she felt about this place. "Now!"

He didn't argue, his hand once again guiding her inside, this time without any protest from her.

* * *

They went to the couch in the family room, Steve pulling free the sheet that had been put over it to protect it from the remodeling work.

"Did you bring anything?" Renee asked, her hands undoing the first couple of buttons on her shirt, but not all.

"Always," he said, grinning, pulling out the condom from his pocket before shrugging his jacket off and onto the floor.

Her hands went down and cupped the front of his pants before undoing them, his own hands touching her while she worked, his fingers finishing the work she had started on her buttons before toying with her nipples through her bra.

She groaned and then gasped.

"What?" he asked, startled.

"Someone's outside."

"What?" he said, twisting toward the window. He didn't see anyone. "Where?"

"I just saw them walk by the window toward the front door," she said, pulling her shirt closed. "Oh God, what if they saw us?"

"They would have had to peek into the window to do that," he said, zipping up his pants. "Wait here. I'm going to go see if I can see who it is."

Jesus, I hope it's not my dad.

She nodded.

Steve cautiously went to a window but didn't see anyone and then started toward the front door, a face appearing against the glass just as he reached it, causing him to cry out.

An equally startled shout echoed from beyond the door, followed by a voice that loudly proclaimed, "My name is Dr. Samantha Loomis." She held up an ID. "Can I talk to you for a moment?"

* * *

"Sorry to bother you," Samantha said, struggling to regain her composure from the window scare. "I was hoping I might be able to look around a bit. I was going to wait for the sheriff to arrive, but once I saw the car, I figured you might be able to help me out."

"Sheriff?" the young man asked. "Is something wrong?"

Samantha smiled. "No, nothing. Just wanted to look around." She could tell she had caught the young man doing something he wasn't supposed to be doing, the "thing" obvious when the girl appeared asking if everything was okay, her mismatched buttons displaying how frantic she had been while trying to make herself presentable.

"Why?"

Though he was obviously flustered, Samantha could tell it hadn't kept him from recognizing that one didn't simply look around a place like this without there being a reason. And mentioning the sheriff…that had been a mistake.

"My name is Dr. Samantha Loomis, and I'm actually just here to verify that a patient of mine isn't here."

"Patient of—" the young man started, then stopped, looking over her shoulder.

At the same moment, Samantha heard a vehicle coming to a halt behind her and turned.

The sheriff had arrived.

* * *

"I thought you were going to wait for me," Sheriff Burke said as they stepped away from the young man and his lady friend, both of whom seemed confused and somewhat startled.

"I was," Samantha said, "but then when I saw the car here I thought maybe I should check and make sure nothing was amiss inside, you know, just to be safe."

"Just to be safe?" he questioned. "Fifteen minutes ago you said that you were almost positive your patient wasn't responsible for the murders of her uncle and his girlfriend, and that it was incredibly unlikely that she would return here given that she can't even drive a car, yet here you are."

"Unlikely, but not impossible," Samantha said.

Sheriff Burke crossed his arms.

Samantha waited.

"I want an honest answer," Sheriff Burke said. "If Michelle had come back here today and found those two inside, what would she have done?"

Samantha thought about this for several seconds and then said, "Honestly, I don't know." She paused. "Like I said to Detective White at the scene this morning, Michelle never once displayed any violence toward anyone at the children's home, nor did her uncle report any issues during her time with him."

"Yet two people are dead, and if what Detective White said was true, they were killed in a manner very similar to what unfolded in there ten years ago." He pointed toward the house while saying this. "How do you explain that?"

"I can't," Samantha said. She wanted to add more, wanted to give a reason why Michelle wasn't behind this, one that would make the sheriff nod his head with agreement, but nothing was there. Her gut told her it wasn't Michelle, but such a statement wouldn't be enough. She needed proof. She needed to be able to point to the real murderer and explain why he did it. Or better yet, catch him in the act.

* * *

"How did you know I was heading to Rockwood?" Samantha asked into the phone.

"I'm a detective," Detective White said. Then, a few seconds later, "Honestly, I don't know. My gut told me that's what you were going to do, and since I always trust my gut, and figured you were trusting your gut when it told you Michelle was heading there, I decided I better let the sheriff know what happened so he could keep an eye out."

"Your gut, my gut, we all seem to be having gut feelings on this, though I'm thinking I'm the only one whose gut is telling her that Michelle didn't do it." Samantha looked over at the house where the sheriff was talking to the young man and his girlfriend.

"Honestly, of everyone involved in this, you knew her the best, so I trust your gut. That said, I also have to trust my gut as an investigator who has worked hundreds of crimes. Right now, the evidence is all pointing toward her. Now, in the movies, this would likely be because someone planted the evidence to make it look like her, but in reality, things like that just don't happen all that often, and when they do, the fact that it was staged is almost always obvious."

"And because of this, she's your main suspect right now."

"Only suspect, really," he muttered.

"Yeah," she muttered back.

"But that doesn't mean she's already convicted and sentenced," he said, the statement obviously a response to whatever it was he thought he heard within her reply.

"Most won't realize that, though. They'll see her as a killer, one that needs to be stopped at all costs."

"Which is why we need to find her, not just to protect society from her if she does turn out to be the one responsible, but to protect her from society regardless of whether or not she is responsible." He sighed. "I know you know this, but I'm going to say it anyway. If you get the feeling that you know where she is, it would be best to bring law enforcement in. Don't try to approach her yourself."

"I won't," she lied, watching as the sheriff started back to his car.

He stopped and looked at her, a debate over whether to approach apparently taking place within his head. And then he started toward her but stopped again, possibly because he saw her phone.

"Detective," Samantha said. "I think the sheriff needs to talk to me."

"Okay, let me know if you find anything, or if she makes an appearance up there."

"Will do, and let me know as well if you find her."

"Trust me, you'll be the first to know."

Trust me, she repeated to herself while pocketing the phone. Typically, such a statement was said in hopes of convincing one to trust someone she really shouldn't, yet in this case, Samantha actually believed what he said. She trusted him.

"That was Detective White," Samantha said as the sheriff resumed his approach. "They haven't found her yet."

"And they haven't seen anyone lurking around here," Sheriff Burke said, thumb pointing toward the two teens. "Though, given what they were likely doing while inside, I doubt their focus was on anything but each other."

"Well, now they know to keep their eyes open."

Nothing else was said for several seconds.

"Do you really think she would come back here?" Sheriff Burke asked.

"I don't know," Samantha said, an inner sigh echoing through her mind. "If not here, then where?"

"Well, maybe she went to ground somewhere, holed herself up in a house down the street from the scene."

"They're checking that," Samantha said. She didn't actually know whether or not this was true, but it sounded legit.

What if she did do it?

What if she snapped and now is holding some terrified family hostage?

Samantha tried to picture Michelle in such a situation, body bloodied from the murders, her mind a mess from the psychosis that would have taken over, face twisted from the strain of the activity she was engaged in and the stress her mental state was causing, fingers wrapped around a large kitchen knife, all while wearing a Santa hat.

A chill slithered through her.

"Getting cold," Sheriff Burke said, noting her shiver. "Why don't we wrap this up so you can head...are you going to be staying in town or going back?"

"I'm going to stay in town for a while, see if Michelle returns." A snowflake fluttered past her face. *You might get stranded here during the blizzard, during Christmas.*

The thought weighed heavy for a moment, but then she shook it away and asked, "What exactly is going on with the house here? You said earlier that someone was fixing it up."

"Yeah, Steve's father"—he pointed toward the young man

who was standing on the front porch, watching them — "bought the place last year and has been fixing it up to sell."

"Flipping it?"

"Yeah, though he has had it longer than would be considered typical for a flip."

"Why?"

"Hard to say. I think there've been some problems."

"What kind of problems?"

He shrugged. "Problems that seemingly don't require law enforcement getting involved, since he hasn't made any requests for help."

Samantha stared at him for a moment, the wording of his statement making her think that the problems *were* something that law enforcement could get involved in, but that Steve's father hadn't gone that route, probably in an effort to avoid negative attention toward a property he wanted to eventually sell.

Already has quite a bit of negative attention.

But after ten years...

If the price was right, she doubted the events from a decade earlier would prevent a sale. However, if something new were to happen, something that would make it seem like the property attracted the wrong kind of attention, then that probably would hurt the likelihood of someone wanting to buy it — well, at a price that would make the work put into it worthwhile.

"So if you don't think Michelle is responsible for the murders back then, or the ones that took place last night, who do you think is responsible?" Sheriff Burke asked.

Another snowflake went past her face, followed by a second and third one. She watched each while thinking, but no legitimate answer arrived, so she simply said, "I don't know."

Sheriff Burke nodded. "That was the issue ten years ago as well. If Michelle didn't do it, and if her mother didn't do it, who did? No one could ever answer that."

"Detective Hines spent all his time trying to pin it on Michelle," Samantha said.

"And…" he asked. *Your point?* seemed to be his question, though he didn't voice that part of the statement.

"I just think that if he'd spent some time trying to figure out who else could have been responsible, he might have uncovered something that has remained hidden from everyone."

"In the same light, if Michelle had told us what happened that night, maybe Detective Hines could have given his investigation a new angle."

"She was traumatized," Samantha said. "It took years for her to recover from what she saw."

"Even so, she was the only living witness to what unfolded, so the fact remains she could have told us what happened."

Samantha didn't reply to that.

"I know what your next question is going to be," Sheriff Burke said.

"Oh?"

"You want to know if anything unusual has happened here that might have a connection with the murders, or if anyone has been inquiring into the murders all those years ago."

"And your answer will be no, right?"

"Bingo," he said. "The only one who has ever shown any interest in the case is Detective Hines's daughter, and that's because she obviously feels his inability to solve the case is what broke him, and that she can do his memory justice by solving it herself."

"Hanna," Samantha said, weighing the name. "She called me once right after her father died. "Wasn't a pleasant conversation."

"Well, the girl went through a bit of a rough patch following his death and, believe me, you weren't the only one that she aimed at when venting her grief. Sheriff Powell was constantly receiving calls from her and about her from others who were either concerned or upset, depending on her interaction with them. And much to the man's credit, he never lost his cool with her."

Maybe it would have been better if he had, Samantha said to herself. *Let the little brat know that even though she was grief-stricken, she had no right to scream at people over the phone, or to leave threatening messages on their voicemail when they refused to pick up.*

* * *

"So…" Steve said with a smile, hand reaching for her shirt buttons. "Where were we?"

Renee pulled away.

"What's wrong?" Steve asked.

"'What's wrong?'" she asked back, disbelief distorting her face. "Were you listening to anything they just said, or was your mind completely focused on fucking me?"

"Um—" he started.

"You know what, don't even answer that." She crossed her arms.

"Renee, come on, don't be like that."

She turned away from him.

Jesus Christ! "Renee," he said.

She didn't reply.

"Fine, let's go." He pulled out his car keys and started toward the door.

She didn't move.

Frustration-laced confusion echoed through his body, as did a voice that told him not to lose his cool because that was exactly what she wanted. Ninety percent of the time, Renee was a rational sixteen-year-old girl who seemed ready to embrace adulthood, the other ten percent of the time...*holy fuck, look out.*

Now was a *holy fuck, look out* moment, one that had obviously been triggered by the sheriff and that stupid doctor.

Triggered, but not the root cause.

After four months of dating Renee, Steve was wise to the fact that these moments, though seemingly sudden, were anything but and took days, even weeks, to reach the point they were at now. If it hadn't been the unexpected visitors, it would have been something else. Probably just the sex itself, which now he was glad they hadn't engaged in because who knew what kind of fury it would have caused within her. It wouldn't matter that she hadn't protested the act at all leading up to it, or that they had had sex several times in the past. She would have cried foul, maybe even rape while in her rage, and then within a few days, acted like everything was totally fine between them.

And you knew this going into the relationship, so don't act all victimized because of it, he said to himself. *Just take her home and wait for it to pass.*

* * *

"That's what you'd like, isn't it?" Renee said while yanking away from the hand that had started to touch her shoulder. "Get rid of me so you can call up Hanna or another one of your fuck buddies and have her meet you here."

"Renee," he said, voice starting to elevate. "I just suggested it because you obviously don't want to be here."

"Yeah, and you're using that to trick me into leaving so you can fuck someone else." She twisted away as he tried to face her.

"What?"

"That's why you're still friends with her on Facebook, and that's why you hide the things you two talk about from me."

"What are you talking about?" he demanded.

"I saw what she posted on your wall, and so did Molly, and then you hid it so we couldn't see what you were talking about."

"I didn't hide anything." Anger was now showing on his face. "Fuck, I don't even know what post you're talking about, and I'm sick of you always throwing—"

A crash echoed upstairs.

"Fuck, I need to get that cat back outside before he pisses all over the place, if he hasn't already." He started toward the stairs.

"Hey, aren't you going to take me home?" Renee asked, not liking the idea of being alone on the first floor.

Steve turned and looked at her for a moment and then, without saying a word, started toward the front door, keys in hand.

* * *

Once home, Renee's worry about Steve and Hanna getting together to finish what *she* and Steve had started got the better of her, and she decided to see if any evidence supporting her worry appeared on his wall—not through her own viewing of his wall since he would obviously block her from anything they were doing, but through her friends, who he probably hadn't thought to block.

I DON'T SEE ANYTHING, Jenny texted in reply to her

request.

NOTHING, BUT I'LL KEEP AN EYE ON IT, Andrea replied.

GIRL, CHILL, YOU KNOW HE ISN'T INTO HER ANY-MORE! Maggie said.

DIDN'T YOU THINK THE SAME THING ABOUT MARIA AND BRIAN BEFORE HE DUMPED YOU FOR HER? Renee texted back, pissed that Maggie would reply like that.

FUCK YOU!

OH, THAT'S MATURE!!

Five minutes later: HEY, WHAT'D YOU SAY TO MAGGIE? Kelly texted.

NOTHING, Renee said. BITCH IS BEING UBER SENSI-TIVE.

Nothing followed from Kelly.

In fact, nothing followed from anyone for about ten minutes. Then her phone echoed with a new message. Her mother: ARE YOU AND YOUR SISTER HOME?

YEAH.

OKAY, LOCK THE DOORS AND DON'T LEAVE THE HOUSE.

WHY?

THAT GIRL THAT KILLED HER FAMILY TEN YEARS AGO ESCAPED TODAY.

Oh great. If word on that was spreading, then word on the fact that she and Steve had been at the house together might spread as well, and if her parents found out about that…

Fuck! Fuck! Fuck!

* * *

The cat was gone by the time Steve got back, which was great because he wasn't really feeling up to spending any more time within the house, not after all the shit that had unfolded thirty minutes earlier. Nope. Even better, he had a feeling that the mental patient situation would keep his father from having him slave away within the house during his break.

Don't be so sure.

But Mom won't stand for it.

With her on his side, even if it were for a ridiculous reason (*how would that girl get all the way back into town?*), he wouldn't have to worry about his father trying to enforce the issue.

Window closed, he started toward the front door, a grumble from his stomach suggesting that maybe he should stop by Freddy's on his way home and grab a burger.

One for Kyle too, he told himself, the sad fact being that he would actually feel bad if he showed up back at home with his own burger and nothing for the little twerp.

* * *

"Can you do me a favor?" Renee asked.

"Um...maybe..." Molly said.

"Can you check and see if Steve and that Hanna bitch are together?"

"Wait, I thought you and Steve were spending the day together."

"I was, but he got mad at me and now I'm home while he's at that house his dad bought."

"And you think Hanna's with him," Molly said. "Girl, that's the last place Hanna would go, especially to see him. All she'd think about was her dad."

"Yeah, well, she might suck it up if it means getting to suck him up."

Molly laughed, which irritated Renee to the point of calling her out on it.

"Sorry," Molly said. "It's just, well, I think you're way off on this. I mean, I don't doubt Steve would totally drop everything to have sex with her—or any girl for that matter. He's a guy and you're simply his rebound girl, so any twat will do. But not her in that house. Nope. Not happening."

"Well then, can you go and see if he's there with someone else?" Renee asked, an obvious plea present within her voice.

"Why don't you just swing by yourself?"

"Because my mom has put us under house arrest."

"Seriously? What'd you do?"

"Nothing, it's because that girl escaped."

"What girl?"

"The one who killed her family in that house ten years ago."

"Holy fuck, you serious?"

"Yeah!"

"And you want me to go there by myself! What're you out of your fucking mind!"

Irritation arrived.

She took a deep breath and said, "I want you to be a friend and help me out. You're always telling me I shouldn't be with him, so maybe now you can get some evidence and prove to me why you think that."

"Girl, I don't need evidence, and you shouldn't either. You know what he's like and need to pull your head out of the sand."

"You know what, never mind. I should have known you wouldn't help me."

"What?" Molly said, startled. "I've been trying to help you since the day you decided to go out with him."

"Help me?" Renee snapped. "You're just jealous."

"Jealous!"

"Yeah," Renee said and then, knowing it would really get to her, added, "Jealous that guys always pick me over you!"

"Guys pick you because they know you'll drop to your knees if they say hi to you in the hallway. No offense, but I'd rather find a guy who wants to know me rather than just shove his dick down my throat."

"Go fuck yourself!" Renee shouted, tears starting to roll.

Molly didn't reply.

Renee disconnected the call, a mix of anger, sadness, and embarrassment getting the better of her—the latter because of what had happened at the homecoming dance during her freshman year, the dance that had started the "drop to her knees for any guy" imagery that now seemed to be synonymous with her name.

All because of that drink.

Drinks…

Rumor had it that there was a video of her as well, though she had never actually seen it. This didn't make her doubt its existence, not in today's world. Plus, she had awakened in a dress that was covered in cum stains, one that she didn't dare try to have cleaned because she knew everyone would know what the stains were. Instead, she had thrown it out, the beautiful gown double bagged and buried in her closet until garbage day, when she carried it to the trash and tucked it beneath another bag of kitchen garbage.

She wiped her eyes as the memories unrolled, the looks she had gotten that Monday following the dance, and the whispers she had overheard in the classrooms and hallways, alerting her to the fact that not only were her suspicions of what had happened correct, but everyone knew about it as well. In fact, everyone seemed to know more than she did, which was terrifying.

And Molly just threw it at you.

How could she do that?

Snot joined the tears, her sleeve growing more and more disgusting as she kept wiping at her face.

The two were best friends, had been since kindergarten, and until now, Renee had been able to count on her support.

Not anymore!

We're done!

And to make it official…

She signed onto Facebook and removed Molly from her friends list. She also unfollowed her from Twitter and Instagram and blocked her number from her phone.

After that, she checked Steve's Facebook to make sure they were still friends and listed as in a relationship together. They were. She then checked to see if Hanna was interacting with him at all, not through her own Facebook, of course, but through a sock puppet account she had created to keep tabs on the bitch.

No updates since the morning before.

Unfortunately, given how crafty the bitch was, and the possibility that her cover with this profile had been blown, Renee wasn't convinced, which was why she had her friends checking up on Steve to see if Hanna was posting anything on his wall.

Nothing so far…

She went back to Hanna's wall and, though she warned herself against it, clicked on the photos icon and began scrolling down until she found the picture from when the bitch and Steve had been a couple.

Her stomach tightened.

Panic followed.

It wasn't simply due to them being together in the pictures, but because she could see how happy Steve was with Hanna
and vice versa.

She also knew he had a folder of pictures of them on his
Facebook, one that her legit account couldn't see but which was
visible to her sock puppet account. Why he blocked her from it was
a mystery, but she suspected it was because he didn't want her
seeing that he still had feelings for Hanna.

And since she dumped him...

Dating a dumpee was always risky because if given the
chance, he would go back to the one who had dumped him.

You're his rebound girl.

No, I'm not!

*If he can't get sex from you, he will just hook up with someone
else.*

But...

She tried pushing the thoughts from her mind, but they
wouldn't budge, so instead she shifted her focus to the fact that he
had already gotten sex from her—*good sex!*—so why he would feel
he needed to go elsewhere would be a mystery. Today it just
hadn't been right. Not in that house. He had to know that.

Maybe he doesn't.

*Maybe he is now so pumped up with sexual energy that he
won't be able to function until it is released.*

Maybe—

"*Renee,*" Katie called from the hallway, her footsteps on
the stairs having gone unheard.

"What?" Renee asked, nearly a demand.

"*I'm hungry!*"

"There's cereal in the cupboard."

"That's breakfast food. I want lunch food. Can you make a pizza?"

Renee sighed. "Okay, can you turn the oven to four twenty-five for me?"

"Mom says I'm not supposed to touch it."

Jesus Christ! she shouted to herself. Out loud, "When she is gone, I'm in charge, and I'm telling you it's okay."

"But she'll still get mad at me!"

"How will she know?"

Katie was silent for about fifteen seconds and then said, "Okay, I'll do the Home Run Inn one because I know you like sausage!"

Renee nearly lost it but then caught herself because she knew Katie wasn't implying anything based on the homecoming stories.

You hope.

Does she know what a blow job is yet?

"Renee?" Katie called, concern present.

"Yeah, do that one. Start the oven; I'll be down in a bit."

"Okay."

She stood up and started toward the door but then stopped and turned back toward her computer. The screen was still showing a picture of Steve and Hanna, one where they were at the Bristol Renaissance Faire, her slutty wench outfit making it impossible to look away from her impressive cleavage.

Wonder if she's wearing something similar for him right now.

* * *

Molly Mason sat in her car for fifteen minutes, debating with herself over whether or not she should do as Renee had asked. The
angry side was screaming *no*, but the side that had maintained a
friendship for nearly ten years, the side that cared deeply for her
friend and hoped they would get to go to college together and be
roommates, that side wanted to do everything she could to help
her.

And you can't take what she said to heart, her friendship side
said. *You know she gets emotional.*

Guilt followed, guilt for making the comment about
Renee dropping to her knees for any guy that knew her name.

She insulted you first!

*But you should have been the better half and not let it get to
you.*

Sadness arrived.

Give her time.

*Find out what, if anything, is going on at that house, tell her
about it, and then let her come back to you once she cools down.*

This wasn't the first blowup to occur between them and
wouldn't be the last. Renee was hotheaded and emotional, but
once she realized she had gone overboard and the embarrassment
filtered in, she would come back, apologize, and all would be well.

A gust of wind rattled the car as Molly sat within it, the
cold air seeping inside and chilling her to the bone.

Do you really think he's there with someone else? she asked
herself,

The answer was no, not because she didn't think he
would cheat on Renee—he would—but because she didn't think it
was plausible for him to have someone on standby like that.

Even so, she would go check in hopes of putting Renee at

ease, which would then begin the process that would eventually lead to her reaching out and smoothing over the little hiccup in their friendship.

* * *

Michelle was leaning against the post in the attic, mind free of thought, when she heard the screech of brakes outside, the present returning to her with its own screech as she crawled over to the tiny round attic window to look outside, horror unfolding at the thought of more people coming to the house.

* * *

Molly couldn't help but feel a tiny bit of apprehension as she drove up to the house, not because of the events that had occurred there ten years ago, or because of the information about the mental patient having escaped. Instead, it was from the memories of a Halloween night four years earlier when she had been dared to go inside and take a picture of herself in the bedroom where the murders had unfolded—a dare that many kids in town had been faced with during the last decade, usually around Halloween, but also during Christmastime and sometimes just at random moments throughout the year. Most failed to get the picture; she had not.

A selfie in the bedroom where it had happened, one that showed the faint traces of bloody writing that had seeped through the paint. She'd taken about thirty pictures with her phone, just to be safe, and then headed back outside to rejoin her friends in the yard, all of whom were impressed.

And then they had seen it.

A face peering at her from the partially closed closet door to the left of her body as she stood with her back to it, phone held high so the picture would show both her and the faint writing.

Terrified, they had fled the area, a debate on what to do

about the picture arriving as they sat around a table at Freddy's.

The psycho girl is locked up!

Then maybe it really was someone else.

We should tell the sheriff!

And what, get arrested for trespassing?

Maybe it was just someone else who was trying to take a picture and got scared...

Eventually, they all agreed on this latter point, mostly because it allowed them to leave the situation unreported. Molly, however, had never felt satisfied with the answer, nor had she ever gotten over the chill of knowing that someone had been in that room with her, someone who could have easily sprung forth from the closet and killed her.

How long would they have waited outside for me? she wondered while sitting in front of the house.

Five minutes? Ten?

Would they have come inside to make sure I was okay, or simply decided I ditched them?

Though she wanted to point at the former, she knew the latter was probably the more likely scenario.

Renee wasn't there that day.

We were having a tiff then too!

She shook her head, amazed at the coincidence.

And then it faded away.

Someone's watching me.

She couldn't see anyone, and from all appearances, the place was empty, but something tingled within her mind, an instinct of some kind, causing a static-like feeling to course through her body, gooseflesh rising along the surface of her skin.

* * *

Michelle stared at the car from the tiny attic window, willing whoever was inside to stay within the car and drive away.

Don't get out!

Please!

PLEASE!

The car door opened, a girl stepping out.

Go away!

She wanted to scream at the girl, tell her to run, but
couldn't, and then she caught a momentary reflection in the glass,
the red of the Santa hat clearly visible.

NO!

She went to pound on the glass, her hope being the sound
would reach the teen, but stopped and stared at the blood that covered her hands.

Horror followed.

The knife!

Grunting!

*Blood hitting her in the face, stinging her eyes, while her skin
absorbed the dying warmth.*

No! No! No!

*Heads everywhere! Tiny ones! Sitting by the fireplace, waiting
for Santa to take them!*

Why?

The movement of the teen in the front yard brought her
back for a moment. Questions on what she was doing there followed, questions similar to the ones she had asked about the other
two who had been here earlier, the two she had tried to lure up
into the attic by smashing an old flowerpot that had been sitting in
the corner.

And Dr. Loomis!

Seeing her had brought a momentary comfort that had faded quickly after Dr. Loomis's departure. Michelle had wanted to run to her, wanted her to take her back to the children's home where everything made sense.

Or back to my uncle's place!

She liked it there. It was quiet, and she could have food whenever she wanted, rather than having to wait for mealtimes or make a special request. And he had lots of books that she could read, and an Internet connection so she could talk to people.

No! You can't go back there!

The horror of last night came back to her.

The knife! Blood! Santa!

NO!

Tears sprang to her eyes and started rolling down her checks, dampening the blood smears that had dried during the early morning hours.

She needed to take a bath.

Needed to wash herself clean.

Needed—

The teen below left the front door and started around the house, her body disappearing around the side.

* * *

Just go, Molly told herself as she stepped away from the front door. *They're not here.*

But someone is.

Just your imagination.

Is it?

She decided to circle the house, just to make sure, curiosity getting the better of her.

After that, once she could say for sure that Steve wasn't

here—*you can say that now!*—she would head elsewhere to see if he and Hanna were together at his place or her place.

Her place for sure, her mind stated as she walked up the back porch steps to peer into the back through the sliding glass door, the one she had used to get inside all those years ago.

Hanna's mother worked full time to keep the house for her and her daughter, rumor being that the pension her father should have gotten for his years of serivce had been held up due to the circumstances of his death.

Drinking had been a factor, drinking that, if what she had heard was true, began shortly after the Christmas Eve murders and got worse and worse as the years passed.

"*Nothing,*" she said to herself while her face was pressed against the glass, the rooms beyond the door completely deserted.

She pulled away...

...and screamed as movement within the glass alerted her to a figure behind her, a figure wearing a Santa hat.

Ax!

The word registered in her mind just as the blade planted itself into her gut with a wet *thump!* that she both heard and felt, the pain of the impact itself more impressive than the splitting of her skin and stomach—*initially.*

She tried to talk, but all that came out was blood, her ruined stomach spurting it up in its panic, clogging her throat and making it impossible to breathe.

Her attacker grinned, the blood that had landed upon her face matching the red of her Santa hat and coat, a coat that Molly suddenly wanted as an icy chill encased her.

The ax blade came free and with it a splash as her stomach contents rained down upon the wooden porch.

Molly tried to take a step but instead fell down to her knees, hands fruitlessly trying to hold everything in, sensing that her bowels were slipping through her fingers.

And then a foot was pressing her face down onto the wood, a splinter piercing her cheek.

Something crashed into her neck, the blow giving her a crushed, choking feeling, followed by a sensation of flying, thousands of thoughts flowing through her mind, all while her eyes came face-to-face with her attacker, registering but not processing the image before darkness overtook everything.

* * *

Michelle stared at the lifeless head of the teen girl where it sat atop one of its own ears, the edges of the shattered spine protruding from the base in such a way as to make it impossible to balance upright, which, she remembered, had been a problem all those years ago as well—the tiny heads not balanced upright in front of the fireplace but on their sides like this one was.

You took one!

Why?

The memories were unclear, the events of that night only available in little snippets rather than a full narrative, something she had once tried to explain to Dr. Loomis by referencing ancient scrolls found in caves and how the bits and pieces had to be worked back together, and the missing words guessed at based on the other visible words.

Dr. Loomis had been pleased with her for expressing such a comparison, a huge smile on her face, which caused a smile to appear on Michelle's face as well...until she thought about her brothers and sister.

The smile always faded when that happened.

Frustration followed, a strong desire to remember what had happened that night going unfulfilled. Making it worse, she knew Dr. Loomis was frustrated as well, though she tried not to show it.

She looked down at the head again, her mind back in the present, and noticed that the eyes were barely open, the lids looking as if they were ready to close from exhaustion.

Is that what they've been like this entire time?

Or are they slowly closing?

She tried to think back to the first moment when the head was still fresh and warm but couldn't pull up any images of the eyes, her mind obviously not having noted their state. Instead, all she recalled was the horror of seeing the head.

Why did she come here?

And why kill her?

No answers arrived, and soon she was leaning against the brick column that was the central feature of the attic, a blanket pulled over her legs, her mind completely empty, eyes staring toward the window but not really seeing it, the only sounds within the attic those of her stomach growling from hunger.

* * *

Using an app on her phone, Samantha navigated to the Pinewood Lodge, which was the only motel in the area. It sat off the main road from the interstate and backed up into a wooded scrubland that looked as if it connected with the same wooded area that Michelle's childhood backyard led into.

Not that one would want to walk from here to there, she noted while looking at the Google Earth image on her phone, the distance between the two locations one that only experienced outdoors people could safely trek in these cold winter conditions. Heck, even during the warm summer months she would probably have a difficult time walking the distance if there wasn't a marked path she could follow.

But what about someone else, someone hell-bent on murdering a family one dark and snowy Christmas Eve?

Anger toward Detective Hines and his relentless attempts at pinning everything on Michelle arrived. Had it not been for him and his focus on Michelle, they may have uncovered leads that led to a different perpetrator, one who could very well be the same fiend responsible for what had unfolded the night before. But no, Detective Hines had decided Michelle was responsible, and once that happened, he had been able to twist and manipulate the evidence to point toward her, very much like the people who had kept using vague prophecies and drawings to state the apocalypse would occur in 2012. Without a date in their minds, the prophecies would never have brought the year 2012 into consideration, but with it already in their minds, it was easy to interpret the prophecies as pointing toward it. The same was true with Michelle. Had Detective Hines not already viewed her as a suspect, the evidence he found might have pointed elsewhere, but instead he always saw it as pointing toward her.

"Of course there was trace evidence!" Samantha had said into the phone, voice elevated. *"Michelle lived there, for Christ's sake!"*

"Family members are the most likely to be responsible for killing other family members!" Hines's daughter had screamed.

"Not eight-year-old family members, and if your father had been worth even half his weight as a detective, he would have known that!"

"My father solved hundreds of crimes!"

"That's easy to do when you arrest innocent people."

"You're going to regret that one day when Michelle is cutting

off your head like some camel-fucking sand nigger."

"And you're going to regret all these calls to me when I press charges against you for harassment."

CLICK!

The calls had not stopped, and while Samantha had toyed with the idea of pressing charges, she had never taken the necessary steps. It was because of Hines's death. It wasn't easy to lose a father, and as much as she had despised the man, she knew he probably meant the world to his daughter. Thus she had let the calls slide, first by ignoring the calls when they came and deleting the messages when they were left, and then, once she figured out how, by blocking the numbers Hanna called from so that her phone never even rang. Same with the email addresses the girl messaged her from and on Facebook—the girl having once tagged her in dozens of porn-like pictures. And then there had been the time with the dating site—

A face looked at her through her window.

"Are you here looking for a room?" the man asked, voice muffled by the glass.

Samantha rolled down the window. "Yes, sorry, was going to come into the office but got lost in thought."

"Okay, well, I'll be inside when you're ready. Just ring the bell."

"I'm ready now," she said, pushing aside the indecision she had felt earlier about staying in town through the holidays.

"Okay, just go through that door right there and I'll meet you behind the counter."

Samantha did just that and soon found herself in a room tucked into the far corner of the motel. *"Lucky seven,"* the proprietor had said with a smile, one she tried to return without much success.

Her phone buzzed.

"Dr. Loomis," she answered.

"Hey, it's Detective White. Just wanted to let you know, we couldn't find any prints within the writing on the wall."

"Meaning?"

"Whoever wrote it was wearing gloves."

"Gloves? You mean like winter gloves, or the type you use to prevent fingerprints?"

"That remains to be seen, but on the surface, there doesn't seem to be any evidence of fibers from cloth gloves, so they were either leather gloves, of which we've found three blood-free pairs within the closet, or the latex type, of which we haven't found any."

"So someone was either bundled up against the cold while writing with the blood, or they wore latex gloves in hopes of hiding their prints?"

"Yep."

"Why would Michelle hide her prints?"

"Why indeed?"

Silence settled.

"Have you found any interesting online activity?" Samantha asked.

"Not yet. We won't have anything from our techs until tomorrow at the earliest."

"And what about the neighbor who saw her walking earlier in the night than when the murders are thought to have happened?"

"It seems she is not the only one who routinely saw Michelle walking at night. Given the semi-publicity that her entry into the neighborhood caused, mostly thanks to a young mother of three who protested her being allowed to live there and printed up fliers, many of the neighbors kept a wary eye on things."

"So if a neighbor saw someone leaving after the murder, dressed up with a Santa hat and coat, there is a chance that it wasn't Michelle but someone who they assumed was Michelle, due to the fact that they've seen her walking so often during the nights that she has been there and were aware of her history."

"Exactly, and it's something we're looking into."

"Okay."

"Have you uncovered anything out there?" Detective White asked.

"Nothing in terms of evidence that Michelle is here, but I did learn odd things may have been going on at her house over the last few years."

"What do you mean?"

"I don't have anything specific yet, but while talking to the new sheriff, it does seem like there have been incidents that have gone unreported—probably in an attempt by the owner, who is trying to flip it, to keep it from having any recent negative publicity."

"But nothing has been documented?"

"Unfortunately, no."

"Okay, I'll see if maybe I can get more info on that from Sheriff Burke. In the meantime, if you learn anything while there—"

"Call you right away," she said before he could finish.

"Yes."

"I will."

* * *

"What took you so long?" Martha Burke asked as Richard walked through the side door of the house, accusation audible within her words.

"I was working," Richard said while hanging his jacket on the back of the door. His hat followed.

"I called the station over an hour ago to see if you could pick up some creamer on the way home, and they said you had left for the day." She crossed her arms.

"I stopped by the old Harper place on my way back," he said, eyes staying focused on her in hope that the answer would placate her.

"Why?" she demanded.

"To make sure everything was okay there."

"And that took you an hour?"

"I was pretty thorough," he said. "Making sure that girl isn't back and holed up there."

She squeezed her lips together while staring at him, her eyes telling him that she was trying to believe him but couldn't. "I tried calling your cell, but it wasn't on."

He sighed. "You know I turn it off while investigating. Don't want it going off as I come upon someone in the act."

She continued to stare.

"Come on, honey, don't be so suspicious all the time." He reached out his arms to embrace her. "That's my job."

Verbally, she didn't reply, but she did step into his arms so he could hold her.

She made no effort to hug him back, which, for some reason, pleased him, though he wasn't sure why. Likely, it had to do with his suspicions that she knew exactly what was going on but wouldn't say anything—not because she wasn't upset, but because she feared losing him.

Having such power was a trip, though at the same time he knew he had to be careful. If pushed too far, she would have no choice but to leave, the fact being that they both controlled his position within the community, and if things ended between then, then so too would the position.

Does she fear losing you or the power she gets from being the sheriff's wife?

The question hovered in his mind for a long time, and while he tried to dismiss it with a reminder that he hadn't been sheriff when they married, just a lowly deputy who had ambitions to be an investigator, it wouldn't go away. Power corrupted, not just those who were in power, but also those who profited from being close to those with the power.

* * *

With the early darkness came hunger, which made Samantha realize she hadn't eaten more than a few high-calorie sugary snacks from a gas station that day, her last meal having been nearly twenty-four hours earlier.

Wish I could go back in time and eat it again.

Nothing remarkable had occurred during the dinner for her to wish this, nor after as she sat alone in her tiny house watching TV, but it had been a period before the call about Michelle had arrived, and thus the stress of this horrible situation.

You don't really have to stay here.

You can let the authorities handle this.

As appealing as the suggestion was, she knew she couldn't really do that. No. She had to do everything she could to help Michelle. If she didn't, she would regret it forever and feel that she had failed her.

Is this really helping? she asked herself while staring at her laptop screen, her Internet browser a mess of windows from newspaper stories detailing the murders from ten years ago and events within the town that had piqued her interest. One in particular was the death of Detective Hines, which, prior to reading the article, she had known a few details about, but nothing like what she had learned from the papers. And these new details were probably nothing compared to the info she could learn from local residents if they opened their mouths when she asked.

Images of going around acting like an investigator played across her mind and then faded as she realized how absurd they were. She wasn't a detective or a journalist, and her only investigative abilities involved digging into the minds of those sitting across from her, many of whom wanted help and just needed to be guided toward helping themselves.

Still, being here rather than at home felt productive, and it would be good to be able to talk to Michelle right away once she was caught.

But will she be caught?

Or is she already being detained?

The latter was her theory, the reality being that there was no way she could have eluded capture on her own, not without a car, the ability to drive a car if she came upon one, or the resources to provide for herself.

Plus, she wouldn't have killed her uncle.

Hell, she didn't kill her family.

Her certainty of this was unbreakable.

Equally certain, she wasn't going to be any help sitting in this room starving to death. It was time to head into town, first to get some food, and then back to the house to take a look at what, if anything, was occurring there now that the sun had set.

* * *

Though he wasn't hungry, Richard ate a good portion of the meal Martha had made while complimenting her skills as a chef and then retired to the TV room for the evening, his thoughts torn between the time he had spent with Sarah after leaving the office and the idea that the mental patient might be on her way here.

Or already here.

Probably should do a more thorough investigation of that house.

His earlier "investigation" had simply consisted of walking around the property for a few minutes after finishing with Sarah, his hope being that people would see him in the area, should questions arise from Martha on where he had been.

Unfortunately, no one had been around, the dead-end road being one that few journeyed down, given the lack of destinations. In fact, up until recently, the only people who ever really visited the area had been teenage couples who needed a private place to express their love for each other, or kids who wanted to prove their bravery by venturing near the Harper home.

As a deputy, he had been required to patrol the area two to three times during each shift in an attempt to disrupt immoral behavior, but as sheriff he never bothered with trying to keep teens from being teens and focused his deputies on other more important tasks, like catching speeders near exit 217 who thought it was okay to maintain their expressway speeds while on the county road. Though dull, his deputies knew that writing such tickets was an important financial contribution toward the county and its ability to keep its law enforcement personnel employed; thus no one complained. Even the townsfolk felt it was a worthwhile endeavor, especially those who lived out near the exit who had lost pets to the speeders or were frequently disturbed by the sounds of engines going by their homes at night. Mostly, however, they liked the idea that the deputies were busy ticketing out-of-towners rather than people from the community. This wasn't to say they wouldn't ticket those within the community—Sheriff Burke actually encouraged that as well, so everyone knew his deputies were doing what they were supposed to via venting from those who'd been stopped—just that the majority of those who did receive citations were from beyond the town limits.

Now, however, he was going to have to turn his attention toward the Harper house and the potential for things to get ugly as the mental patient tried to hack her way through the town—if she was really heading this way.

Even if she didn't show up, once word spread the town would want to know that he took the threat seriously and that he was up to the task of protecting them during such situations.

Public perception was everything, and the worst thing he could do was lose the trust of the town. It wouldn't matter how well he had performed in the past, present-day screwups always overshadowed things and were the most visible when it came time to vote.

His phone buzzed.

He looked down.

Sarah.

He stiffened, the rule between them being that she never, ever contacted him while at home, thus eliminating the possibility that Martha would see the name on the phone before he had a chance to grab it if it had been left sitting somewhere.

He thumbed the touch screen and, once the picture appeared, knocked over his beer in an attempt to kill the TV so that he could mentally process the image, the sound of the bottle hitting the floor echoing through the room.

"Richard?" Martha called, concern present.

"It's okay," Richard said, eyes going from the picture to the door as she appeared. "Just knocked over my beer while grabbing the remote." He tried to smile.

"Let me get some paper towels," she suggested and then asked, "You didn't ruin it, did you?"

"Ruin what?"

"Your phone," she said while nodding toward his hand.

"Oh, no, no, it's fine." He attempted another smile. "I'll take care of this." He motioned toward the beer. "Go on back and enjoy your show."

"Okay, but please don't just soak it up. You need to clean it too, or else it'll be all sticky and moldy."

"I know, don't worry."

She didn't leave the doorway, her eyes still looking at him and, more specifically, at his phone.

She wants me to set it down while I go and get the paper towels, he realized.

Instead, he pocketed it and headed toward the kitchen, his body going through the motions of cleaning up the spill without much thought, all while turning over the picture in his mind and the reasons why she would send it.

And without any message.

What does it mean?

Not long after that, once the beer was cleaned up and the bottle tossed in the trash, he had another thought, one that chilled him to the core.

Who took the picture?

After all, it was an image of her riding him in her bed. Thus someone must have been holding the phone to snap it.

* * *

Once in town, Samantha found a place called Freddy's that served burgers and hotdogs. It also appeared as if it might be the hangout place for the local youth, given that the rear was decked out with gaming activities in the form of old-school arcades and pinball machines that would have been all the rage in her days as a teen. Now, however, they seemed to spend most of their time collecting dust. Then again, it might have simply been the time of year and the chilled air that were keeping people away.

A young man named Zack was running the place that evening. Given his age, she figured he might have interesting bits of information on the Harper home that adults didn't know about or understand.

Wrong.

He shrugged when she asked him about the house and needed several details before he realized she was talking about the home where the Christmas Eve slayings had occurred.

"That's all ancient history," he said.

"Ten years ago isn't ancient," she replied with a laugh.

He dismissed her comment with a wave and said, "It might not be ancient, but it's old news around here. Sure, people sometimes talk about it, but not really."

Samantha nodded and then asked, "What about Detective Hines, anyone ever talk about him or his daughter?"

"Him, not really. Committed suicide after rumors began that a state trooper pulled him over while drunk. It's pretty bad when you have to watch out for police who are drunk behind the wheel, right? His daughter, um, she's still in school, I think. Like a junior or senior. I don't know. I've been out of school for two years now, so I'm out of the loop on what's going on with that crowd."

"I see, well—"

"Are you interested in buying that house or something?" he asked without warning.

"Um...I don't know. Seems to have an interesting history, so I'd need more details before I commit to anything."

"Yeah. The guy that owns it, he may have more info, or the guy that used to own it. Not sure on their names, but they shouldn't be too difficult to find."

"You're probably right," she said. "Thanks."

"Yep."

Samantha didn't ask anything else after that and simply ate the food he had brought her. Afterward, feeling a bit useless at the lack of progress she had made, she drove by the Harper home to see if anything was going on there, but the place was dark and all the doors locked.

Now what?

She didn't want to go back to her motel room but didn't know what else she could do that would help uncover anything.

You need to talk to people.

Find out if anything odd has been going on.

She pictured herself sitting in a bar, wooing men into telling her secrets about the town. In a movie, such a trick might help move the plot along, but in real life, she would simply end up spending the entire night fending off advances from men and their proposals to go back to her motel room, or their home if they didn't have anyone else waiting for them.

Nope, it would be better to go back to her room and get a good night's sleep. Tomorrow something might happen that would reveal Michelle's location, something that would help bring a close to this horrific experience.

She started back toward her car while thinking this, but then stopped halfway across the yard and turned back toward the house.

A shiver raced through her, one that wasn't due to the cold winter night.

Someone was watching her.

Michelle?

She stared at the windows, eyes trying to pierce the darkness, but it would not yield.

Call the sheriff.

And what, tell him you have a feeling someone is inside?

He would want more—would *need* more to legally go inside.

Break a window!

She would then tell him that she had come to take a look at the place and found the glass broken and thought Michelle was inside.

That would surely get his attention.

But what if you're wrong?

What if the place is empty?

She considered this while crossing her arms against the cold and circling the house once again, hoping that something would be noted that proved Michelle—or someone else—was inside.

Nothing.

She walked up to the front door.

Credit-card it?

Though she had seen it done in movies many times, and

in books when she got the occasional chance to read, she had never before tried to slip a lock with a card and had no idea what, if any, technique was involved.

Shivering, from both the cold and her growing anxiety, she pulled out a credit card and eased it through the crack between the door and the frame.

It hit something.

She pushed.

Nothing.

She twisted the knob while pushing.

Still nothing.

She pulled the card back a bit and then tried sliding it in while twisting the knob.

It worked, the knob turning in her hand.

The door did not open.

Dead bolt.

Five minutes later, her card ruined from the attempts she had made against the dead bolt, and her fingers numb from the cold, she gave up and walked back to her car, frustration at her uselessness getting the better of her.

Never should have come here.

Your job is to help them after the fact, while in your office, or their room, not to try to apprehend them while on the run.

As true as this was, she couldn't shake the feeling that this was the right thing to do and tried to push the feeling of uselessness from her mind.

Tonight she had failed, but tomorrow...maybe her involvement in things would help bring a peaceful end to the horror that had begun that morning. Maybe it would be because of her that more lives were spared and Michelle was brought back safe and sound to the home.

She can't go back to the home.

She's too old.

They would put her elsewhere, in a mental hospital or jail, neither of which Samantha would have privileges in. She only worked with children, and while they would probably allow her to be involved with Michelle early on as they got her settled — unless they sent her straight to jail — she would not be a permanent fixture in the girl's life and would eventually be pushed out so that Michelle could be treated by those who worked in such institutions.

Visibly shaking from the cold, Samantha took one last look at the house, wondering what exactly had occurred within all those years ago, and then got into her car to head back to her motel room.

Maybe hit the local bar.

If she learned something about the house and Michelle, great, but really, her goal now would be for companionship, something she had not had in a long time.

No.

She headed back to the motel.

* * *

Fear and anger mixed together within Richard to the point where he couldn't even sit down, his mind demanding to know why such a picture had been sent. Unfortunately, his demands for this information, which he expressed with several texts to Sarah, went unsatisfied.

Nothing.

The silence stretched from minutes into hours, during which Martha eventually went to bed, a question on whether or not he was going to join her earning a vague answer that implied he had some work to do first.

What exactly that work was, he had no idea, but it took all the resistance he could muster not to leave the house and go to Sarah's place.

If it were from her, she would have said something, so…

The only other person he could think of was her daughter, but why would she watch the two of them together, and why send the photo? Did she want to try to blackmail him? If so, he figured a demand would follow, but nothing had, which was almost worse. Getting a picture like that, one that had been taken that very afternoon, with no words and no follow-up replies to his texts, was pure torture.

He didn't know what to do.

One thing was certain: he would be getting no sleep that night. Hell, he couldn't even sit still.

You have to go over there.

You have to find out who sent it and why.

December 23, 2015

"Hello?" Steve said, voice heavy with sleep.

"*Why'd you invite her and not me?*" Renee screamed.

"What?" Steve asked, startled.

"*Hanna! To the party!*"

Confusion arrived, momentarily silencing him. He rubbed his eyes, removing the crustiness. Then, "What party?"

"What party?" she asked. "*What party!* Fuck you!"

The call ended.

Steve stared at the phone, mind unable to process what had just happened.

It buzzed in his hand.

Renee: IT'S OVER!

What the fuck? he asked himself.

And then he saw that this wasn't the first message she had sent him, the original one having arrived at two in the morning.

He tried calling her back, but she didn't answer, so he sent a text that read: I HAVE NO IDEA WHAT YOU'RE TALKING ABOUT.

Read: 7:46 a.m.

She hasn't blocked you.

That was a good sign.

(…)

Seeing the dot bubble, he waited for her reply, but nothing appeared. Thirty seconds passed, then a minute, the dots still there.

Anxiety began to build.

Is she still typing, or did she set the phone down?

If she was still typing, the message was either going to be a novel, or she kept hesitating, unsure what to say.

Or, knowing he would see the dots and anticipate a message arriving, she had typed a few letters just to taunt him and wasn't really going to reply.

The more he considered this, the more he realized how likely it was for her to do something like that.

Anger toward her immaturity followed, as did a question on why he had ever started dating her.

Memories of her mouth on him during their first time together arrived, ending the question of why but doing little to answer the one about the party.

* * *

Renee was so pissed off that she could feel hatred and anger oozing from her pores.

"What party?" he had dared to ask as if he didn't know, his ignorance toward the fact that she could still see the party even though he had hidden it from her, thanks to her sock puppet profile, adding a level of fury that wouldn't have arrived had he simply fessed up to it. But no, he wanted to play games with her. He wanted to act like they were still a couple even though he really wanted Hanna and had invited *her* to his Christmas party rather than Renee. Well, she could play games too. She could act like she had overreacted once he gave whatever bullshit explanation he was going to give, one that was likely to detail how someone must have been mistaken about a party he was supposedly hosting at

the old Harper house. Then, once he was there enjoying his time with Hanna, she could crash it so she could ruin their night.

And his life!

With pictures and that video he had sent her during Thanksgiving.

Post it online and then share the link on his wall right before crashing the party.

*Or...*her mind said as she began to brainstorm, her train of thought cut off when she saw the phone vibrate.

He had sent her a new message.

* * *

The party Steve had apparently created the night before was to take place at the Harper house on Christmas Eve at seven o'clock in the evening. The description read: *Have we been naughty or nice? Santa will decide at midnight!* Dozens of people had been invited, several of whom had already declined, stating that they had family commitments. Others had joined, and some were listed as a maybe and posted that they would try to swing by after they went with their family to the Christmas Eve mass. None of them seemed to realize that he hadn't created the party, his account having obviously been hijacked while he was asleep.

By who though?

The only one who would do such a thing was Renee, but given her reaction to the party and the fact that she wasn't on the invite list, he was almost positive that she wasn't to blame.

One of her friends?

Though he knew she had a few overprotective friends who didn't like that the two of them were together, he didn't think they would go this far. Then again, if one of them had and then told her about it, their goal of separating them seemed to be playing out nicely.

Now what? he asked himself.

Delete it?

No.

If he did that, Renee would surely believe it was because she had caught him and that he was trying to hide it. He also knew that whoever had access to his account would probably just create it again, or do something worse. At this point, his best course of action was to leave it up and find out who had created it and why.

You need to change your password.

And let everyone know the party isn't real.

Or should I?

Such action might cause even more damage as the person who had created it went even further and created more events and posted stuff on his wall. No, first things first, he needed to figure out who was behind it. Once he did that, he could put an end to it.

* * *

"But, Mom!" Renee pleaded. "We can't stay inside all day!"

"I don't want you two leaving the house, not with that killer on the loose."

"But there's nothing to do here!"

"There're all kinds of games and puzzles, not to mention hundreds of books you two can read."

"Read!" Renee cried. "On my vacation! I might as well just be in school."

Arms crossed, her mother stared at her for several seconds and then asked, "What's out there that's so exciting?"

Renee huffed.

"She's got a boyfriend she wants to make out with."

"You butt munch!" Renee shouted.

"Hey!" her mother snapped.

"They were together all day yesterday," Katie continued.

"We were not!"

"Were too!"

"No!"

"Enough!" their mother cried. "My God, listening to you two, you'd think you were both in kindergarten still. Am I going to have to call a babysitter to watch you during the day?"

Horrified, Renee looked up at her mother and said, "You can't be serious!"

"Keep this up and you might find out how serious I am."

Renee and Katie didn't reply.

Their mother eyed each of them and then said, "I don't care what you do today, as long as you stay inside with the door locked and don't kill each other." She held up a finger, anticipating Renee's protest. "If I find out you didn't stay here, or that you two fought all day, then after Christmas, starting Monday, I'm going to have your grandmother stay here with you two while I'm working. Understand?"

Humiliated, Renee nodded, lips squeezed tight so she didn't make things worse by screaming at her mother.

"I don't mind staying inside today," Katie said, her excitement overemphasized. "I think I'll read my new Nancy Drew book."

"That sounds like a lot of fun," her mother replied. "I wish I could stay home and do that too."

Renee couldn't take it, the comments, which were obviously pointed at her, too much, and without a word, she twisted around and stomped off to her room, heels making sure to express her anger with each step before she slammed the door.

Following that, she looked around her room for something to smash, but after a moment realized that wouldn't accomplish anything and might even push her mother over the edge to the point of having her grandmother come today.

Deep breath!

Tears appeared, the stress of everything starting to get the better of her.

And then her phone buzzed.

She looked at the screen.

Maggie: HEY, ARE YOU GOING TO STEVE'S PARTY TOMORROW?

Seeing that, it took everything she had not to smash the phone screen with a fist.

* * *

Much to Steve's surprise, his mother didn't put her foot down on him not being able to work at the house his father was flipping, and she brushed off the possibility of the mental patient coming all the way back to Rockwood as rubbish.

"She's probably curled up in someone's shed right now, less than a mile from that house she was staying in," she said.

"And the police would have found her by now if all the liberal civil liberty groups weren't all up in arms about the rights of criminals," his father muttered, teeth chomping down onto a piece of buttered toast that had been prepared for him while he showered. "You didn't tell the sheriff about the break-in last week, did you?"

"No, just that we hadn't seen anyone in that area."

"We?" he mother asked.

"Me and the furnace guy," Steve said, mentally smacking himself for the slipup.

"Good," his father said. "Last thing we need is for people to get spooked by that place again all because your friends don't know how to respect people's property."

"My friends didn't break the window," Steve said.

"Excuse me?"

"You always say it's my friends," Steve said, anxiety rising. "I don't like that you disrespect them like that."

"Disrespect them?" he asked, voice rising. "And what have they done to earn my respect."

"About as much as you've done to earn theirs, yet you expect them to respect you, so—"

This time the plate broke when he slammed it, shocking his mother, who lashed out at Steve with words that were difficult to comprehend but carried statements like "don't talk to your father like that" and "ungrateful spoiled brat."

Steve got up from the table and started toward his room.

"Don't walk away from me!" his father snapped.

Steve ignored the command and continued toward his room, his heart racing, fear that his father might follow him and kick in the door weighing heavy until he heard the man leaving.

Relief followed.

Not long after that, his mother left as well.

Steve left his room to get some coffee, which he made fresh, and then, cup in hand, headed back to his room.

A message was waiting on his phone. It was from Hanna. He felt his heart flutter a bit, his feelings for her still strong, as was the hurt he had felt when she ended things with him.

YOU'RE HAVING A CHRISTMAS PARTY?? AT THE HARPER HOUSE??

Hesitation arrived.

Tell her the truth, or go with it?

I AM, he typed.

IS RENEE GOING?

I DON'T THINK SO. SHE AND I AREN'T SEEING EYE TO EYE.

WITH HER, IT'S USUALLY EYE TO BELLY BUTTON.

HA! SO TRUE.

NOT A BAD VIEW THOUGH, ONE THAT I WOULDN'T MIND SEEING AGAIN SOMETIME SOON.

The text stopped him in his tracks.

Nothing followed.

"Say something!" he shouted at himself.

But what?

He didn't know how to reply to that, his fingers frozen over the letters.

Is she being serious or teasing me?

Did dating Renee finally work?

In the beginning, his time with Renee had simply been an attempt to make Hanna regret her decision to end things, the blow jobs and sex that Renee delivered being a bonus. As time passed and Hanna didn't say anything or show any interest in his time with Renee, he had decided that it wasn't working and written Hanna off, but he stuck with Renee because he enjoyed their time together.

"Steve?" Kyle asked from the hallway.

"Yeah?" Steve asked.

"Are Mom and Dad going to get a divorce?"

Hope so, he said to himself. Aloud, "Don't know."

"He isn't very nice to her."

"I know."

"I don't think he loves her. Or us."

That's not true, Steve was about to say but then hesitated, a realization that Kyle was right echoing in his mind. Their father didn't love them. Never had.

Me especially.

Steve's birth had been an accident, an unwanted pregnancy that had resulted in an unwanted marriage. He had learned this a year earlier, during what had been a drunken birds and the bees talk his father had decided to give him one night—about five years too late. He had been asleep at the time, his father shaking him awake before taking a seat on the bed. The talk had followed, a handful of condoms being dropped by his legs for him to use if he ever found himself "unable to resist the siren call echoing from the bitch's moist center."

"*Remember,*" his father had continued. "*Mouths and butts can't get pregnant, but if she demands it and tries to hold you in place with her legs, you'll be happy you put a hat on.*"

What followed had been a detailed account of how he had been trapped by Steve's mother when they were teens, her desire to keep him from achieving his goal of owning the largest construction company in the Midwest so that he wouldn't leave her for someone better having succeeded. "*All because I didn't have a raincoat,*" he said. "*And then years later she did it again when she found out I was talking to a lawyer about leaving her by getting me drunk and fucking me every night until she was pregnant with your brother.*"

No explanation of how that had trapped him had followed, though Steve figured it had something to do with how he would have to pay even more child support after a divorce.

"But then she always sides with him," Kyle continued.

"I know," Steve said. That was always the worst part. Her

fear of losing him was so strong that she always jumped to his side and defense. It was sickening and had made Steve lose all respect for her.

His phone buzzed.

Hanna: DO YOU NEED MY HELP GETTING THE PARTY READY?

SURE, he typed in reply while his mind asked, *What are you getting yourself into?* And, *So you're actually going ahead with the party?*

"When you move out and get a house, I want to come live with you instead of them," Kyle said.

WHAT TIME? Hanna asked. YOU HAVE A KEY FROM YOUR FATHER, RIGHT?

I DO, he typed and then followed it with, HOW ABOUT AROUND NOON?

OKAY.

"Who're you talking too?" Kyle asked.

"Hanna," Steve said.

"Oh." Then, switching topics, "Can you make me some French toast?"

"Sure."

With that, the two headed to the kitchen.

* * *

"Richard," Martha said, giving him a good shake. "Richard, wake up!"

"Huh?" he mumbled, room slowly coming into focus.

"Becky has been trying to reach your cell," Martha said. "Molly Mason never came home last night. Her mother called the station this morning when she realized she was still gone."

"Molly Mason?" Richard asked, trying to picture who that

was.

"You know Molly Mason," Martha said, as if repeating the name would help. "High school girl. On the volleyball team."

Richard shook his head, the last tendrils of sleep finally falling away. "Can you tell her I'll be right in?"

"Yeah," Martha said and started toward the door.

Richard rolled over and rubbed at his eyes while searching for his phone, his mind and body wanting nothing more than to close his eyes and go back to sleep. Such was not an option, however, regardless of how much he had tossed and turned, first in his chair and then in bed after he had zonked out a few times in the chair. That was one of the downsides of being sheriff. When calls came, he had to respond. If he didn't, it wouldn't matter how many times he had been present during past incidents, the citizens involved in this particular situation would remember that he hadn't come out to *them* when they needed him and use it to define his police work.

* * *

The first thing Samantha did that morning was check her phone to see if Detective White had called during the night, and seeing that he hadn't, she called him to find out if there were any updates. He didn't answer. She left a message.

Next, she called the children's home, her hope being that Mark wasn't in his office so she *would* get his voicemail. Luck was on her side this time around. She left a message, letting him know there were no new developments and that she was in Rockwood waiting to see if Michelle showed up.

Calls complete, she looked around the tiny room to see if there was a complimentary coffee set up. There wasn't. Needing coffee, she got herself ready and headed toward town, her thinking being there had to be some place that would be a "morning coffee" gathering point.

Her phone rang.

"Dr. Loomis," Samantha said.

"Dr. Loomis, Sheriff Burke. Are you still in town?"

"Yeah, at the Pinewood Lodge and heading into town right now. What's up?"

"Okay, well, just thought you should know, we have a local teen who is missing. Seventeen-year-old girl. Last seen yesterday morning when her mother left for work. No one knows what happened to her."

"And...you think Michelle is responsible?"

"Don't know, but figured it might be something you'd want to know about, especially since they still haven't found her."

"Okay," she said. Then after a moment's hesitation, "Sheriff, I'm not going to hide her if that's what you think."

"I know you wouldn't," he said.

He was lying, but she didn't press him on this. Instead she asked, "Do you want me to meet you at the...um...scene, see if I notice anything?"

"No, we've got that covered."

"Okay."

She waited, thinking there was more, but he didn't say anything else and ended the call.

Maybe she just ran away.

Two days before Christmas?

As unlikely as it sounded, it was still a possibility—unless there was evidence that said differently.

But if there was evidence, and if it pointed toward Michelle, he would have said something.

Maybe...

Does he trust me?

She had a feeling he didn't, at least not fully, and that any information he gave her would be designed to see how she reacted to it.

That's his job.

For all he knows, I'm in cahoots with Michelle.

Had the situation been different, the thought would have brought a smile to her face, but having seen the bodies being wheeled out yesterday and the writing on the wall, she couldn't find any amusement in what her mind had suggested.

A stop sign appeared, her foot easing the brake pedal toward the floor until the vehicle came to a halt.

Indecision gripped her.

Going straight would take her into the downtown part of Rockwood. Going right, she would come upon Michelle's childhood home.

She went right.

* * *

Back at the station, Richard tried to focus on the missing girl situation, but given the lack of direction with that, he couldn't help letting his mind drift over to the photo that had been sent to him the night before.

You have to call her.

His mind would not be able to focus on anything else until he did—the time spent with Molly Mason's parents a perfect example of this, as he had nodded with their words and uttered statements of assurance, but didn't really process anything they said.

He scrolled to her name and hit the call button.

It didn't even ring, just went straight to voicemail.

Is she working?

Sarah worked at the high school doing clerical work. It was a part-time job, one that she technically didn't have to go in for during the two-week winter break, but she may have offered herself for if anything came up since it wasn't paid time off they had given her.

But wouldn't she have said something?

Though Sarah didn't give him a schedule of her day-to-day plans, it seemed odd that she wouldn't have said something like, "By the way, I have to go in tomorrow to do some extra work" before he left. Such pointless comments were common between them, so much so that not making such comments seemed off.

She seemed off.

Something had been bothering her.

At the time, he hadn't realized it, but now, looking back, he could tell that she had been upset.

And didn't want to share it with me.

Why?

Because it was none of my business.

At the time…

Now that a picture of them had been sent from her phone, and no replies to his questions on why had followed, it was obvious that she was upset with him for some reason, and he had to know what that reason was. She couldn't keep it from him any longer, and if the picture was any indication, she didn't want to keep it from him.

But then why not say something yesterday?

Why send the picture?

No answer arrived, nor would one if he continued to sit

there thinking about it.

"Becky," he said, stepping from his office, "I'm going to head out for a bit. Hold my calls, okay?"

"Even if they're about Molly Mason?"

"Um…no, send those and any pertaining to Michelle Harper."

Becky nodded. "Will do."

"Oh, and keep looking for those files on the murders. They've gotta be around here somewhere."

"You don't think Hines had them, do you?" Becky asked. "I mean, he often took them home, and toward the end, he was pretty obsessive."

"If he had, you'd think that Sarah would have given them back."

"If she knew about them," Becky said. "No telling where they might have ended up, especially if he was hiding the fact that he was still investigating things."

"Hmm."

"And given how distraught they were, they might not have even realized what the file was when going through all his things. You don't expect to find active case files tucked away with personal stuff in those situations."

Richard thought about that for a second, questions on if she was speaking from personal experience going unasked. Instead he said, "Well, let's hope it wasn't tucked away like that, because if it was, it's probably gone. And if that is the case and if it turns out she really did come back here, that could be a huge embarrassment to the department."

It was her turn to nod.

A few seconds later, Richard was slipping behind the

wheel of his car, hat set upon the seat next to him, mind back to wondering about the picture of him and Sarah.

* * *

Samantha stared at the house for about fifteen minutes before she finally got out of the car to walk around it, thoughts on what had happened all those years ago and the conversations she and Michelle had shared about it dominating her mind.

Why couldn't Michelle remember? she asked herself.

How did she block it so well?

No answers followed, the human mind and its workings something that science and the medical community had barely scratched the surface of.

But after ten years you should have been able to help her open up and share everything that had happened, she chided herself.

"We were trying to stay up to see Santa," Michelle had always said. *"In our secret hiding spot."*

"The one that your mother didn't know about."

"Yeah."

"And then what happened?"

"I think I fell asleep and then Brian decided to go to bed because when I woke up he wasn't there."

"And why did you wake up?"

"Because I heard noises."

"What noises?"

Michelle could never produce anything credible after that, her mind always throwing up shields that they could not break though. Even an attempt at hypnosis hadn't worked, an attempt that had not been fully sanctioned by the hospital and had caused quite a bit of conflict between her and the board of directors.

It was very—

Samantha stopped, her journey around the house having taken her up onto the back porch, where she noticed what appeared to be fresh paint upon a large section of the wooden planks that made up the porch, only there didn't seem to be a starting edge. Instead, it looked as if someone had begun in the center of the porch and worked outward, almost in a circular motion. And it didn't match the old wood at all, though maybe upon drying it would.

Or they're not finished.

But why start off-center like that?

A noise in the woods behind her caused her to spin around, heartbeat quickening.

Nothing seemed amiss, her eyes unable to pinpoint what had caused the sound.

If a tree falls in the woods…

She turned her attention back to the oddly painted wood and this time noticed what appeared to be a notch taken out of a plank, almost as if something heavy and edged had been dropped upon it.

Or struck?

A horrifying thought arrived, one that involved having to paint over a bloodstain.

Call the sheriff.

No, not yet.

Instead, she took a picture of what she had found, though she wasn't sure why—documenting it seemed important—and then continued to look around the porch area to see if there was any other evidence that could help point a finger toward what she was thinking might have unfolded.

Nothing else jumped out at her, but then she realized

there could be more to see beneath the porch, especially if blood had seeped through the cracks. After all, if this was a quick fix, which it appeared to be, then it seemed unlikely that someone would have done anything to touch up the underside.

Fighting the cold, which was stiffening her joints, she stepped down from the porch and walked around it to see if there was an opening in the lattice trim. There wasn't, so after testing the resistance of the thin crisscrossed strips, she made a decision to cross a line and pull a section away.

A moment later, she was on her hands and knees, working her way toward where the evidence should be.

The sound of a car appeared, one that screeched to a halt on the street in front of the abandoned house.

Startled, Samantha began to crawl back toward the opening but then stopped as a pair of booted feet stepped into view.

* * *

Seeing that no one was home, Richard called the school to see if anyone was working but didn't get an answer, so he drove over to see if Sarah's car was parked in the lot. It wasn't. He tried her cell again, but like before it went straight to voicemail. He didn't leave a message.

Indecision gripped him.

Where could she be?

And where was Hanna?

He drove back to her house.

Once again, no one answered the door.

He stepped back and looked at the house from the driveway, a bit self-conscious about his presence there and the fact that he could tell people were watching from their own homes.

If anyone asks, you're here looking for the missing files.

Better yet, he wouldn't wait to be asked and would simply put out word himself that he was looking for some old files, which would likely spread and help answer any questions locals had about why he was often seen at her place. What wouldn't be voiced by him, or anyone else, were which files he was looking for, thereby making it seem like it was a simple clerical thing that was being taken care of rather than a frantic search for the files pertaining to the worst crime Rockwood had ever seen.

The sound of a mailbox clanking shut echoed.

Richard turned and saw Sherry, the local mail carrier, coming his way.

"Sheriff Burke," Sherry said.

"Morning," he said, finger making a hat-tipping gesture toward her.

She smiled and headed over to the mailbox, easily slipping in the bundle, and headed back his way. "Trouble?" she asked.

"No, no trouble," he said. Then, seeing his opportunity to start the explanation, added, "Just trying to find out if some old files were left here after...well...you know."

"Ah, yeah, horrible what happened."

He nodded.

She didn't start toward the next house.

"What is it?" he asked, her hesitation obvious.

"I heard talk that the Harper girl escaped the mental institution. Is that true?"

"Escaped, no," he said with a shake of the head. "She was staying with her uncle for the holidays."

"And he was found dead, him and his girlfriend."

"Yes."

"Do you think she'll come back here?"

He shook his head. "No. If she murdered them, then she's probably hiding somewhere out there, and even if she wanted to come this way for some odd reason, she can't drive and wouldn't make it very far if she tried."

Relief spread across her face, yet she still didn't start toward the next house.

Richard waited.

"Do you think she did it, that little girl, all those years ago?" Sherry asked.

"Hines was pretty sure she did," Richard said.

"Yeah, and look what happened to him."

"What do you mean?"

"Just that it's not normal for a kid to do something like that, and knowing she had and trying to prove it, well, it drove him to the brink of madness and then beyond."

Richard didn't reply to that.

"And just think, if she would do something like that at eight, what would she do at eighteen?" Sherry shook her head. "It's not natural for a child to have such evil within them, not without an outside force guiding them."

Richard continued to stay silent, while his mind began to predict where this was going.

"If I remember correctly, that mother, she never brought her children to church." Sherry shook her head with sadness. "And there was never a strong father figure to control the household."

"It was a sad situation," Richard said.

"Children in those situations are open doors for Satan's power, and now today more than ever before because we have families that aren't bringing their children to hear God's blessing.

You would be wise to start noting which families those are so that you can keep an eye on their children and be ready to act."

"I'll keep that in mind." He started toward his car.

"Sheriff, I know you think I'm crazy, but that's what people always say when God's message is delivered. No one ever believes until it's too late. His prophets are always condemned."

"Then maybe he needs to pick better spokesmen," Richard said, regretting his words the moment they left his lips. That statement, rather than the fact that he was looking for some old files, would be what she spread.

His radio squawked.

He looked at it and then at Sherry, who was staring at him, before asking Becky what she needed.

"Sir, Henry Jenkins called, said he caught a prowler on his property. That is, the Harper home property."

"Okay, I'll be right there."

* * *

"Blood my ass," Henry Jenkins snapped. "My idiot son probably dropped a can of paint that splattered all over the place."

"And caused a chunk to be cut out of the wood?" Samantha asked, arms crossed, body still feeling the horror of his hands yanking her from beneath the porch.

"Have you ever lifted a can of paint?" he demanded. "Since the answer is going to be no, I'm going to let you in on a little secret. They're heavy sons of bitches, and if you drop one from, say, ten feet up, which is about the right height for the touch-up work he was doing *right up there*" — he pointed — "then that would easily take a chunk out of the wood while also splattering all over the place."

"Was there any blood beneath the porch?" Sheriff Burke

asked.

Samantha looked at him for several seconds and then said, "I couldn't really see anything under there. Not enough light."

The sheriff looked between the two of them and then said, "Okay, we'll clear this up right now." He pulled his flashlight from his belt and walked down from the porch.

"Oh, you can't be serious," Henry snapped. "Call up my son. He'll tell you what happened."

The sheriff ignored him and got down on his hands and knees.

Seconds turned to minutes.

"Well?" Henry asked upon his reemergence.

"Nothing but paint."

"What'd I tell you?" Henry said, throwing up his arms.

"Call your son," Sheriff Burke said.

"What?" Henry asked, suddenly subdued.

"I want to hear from him that he dropped a paint can."

"You can't be serious."

"I've never been more serious."

"You really think he's going to admit to dropping it?"

"Just a moment ago you wanted me to call him. Now you don't."

"I wanted to call him so that you didn't have to crawl around under there, ruining the uniform my tax dollars pay for. Now it's just a waste of time."

"Waste of time or not, I want to cap this situation for good."

Arms still crossed, Samantha watched as the man registered defeat and pulled out a cell phone. About twenty seconds later, he said, "Steve, this is your father. Call me as soon as you get this."

Silence settled.

Samantha looked around, a shiver slithering through her as she looked upon the edge of the old one-car garage and the woods that brushed up against the far side.

A padlock secured the side door.

"Mr. Jenkins," Samantha said.

"What?" he demanded.

"The padlock on the door, is that because you've had issues with people on the property?"

Sheriff Burke followed her gaze and then turned back toward Henry to await an answer.

"Yeah, I have. Kids mostly, but sometimes I find adults here as well, crawling around where they shouldn't be."

"What have they been doing?" she asked, ignoring the jab. "The kids, to warrant a padlock like that?"

He didn't reply.

"Henry, we both know you've had problems here," Sheriff Burke said. "People talk."

"Yeah, they do talk, mostly about you and Sarah Hines spending quite a bit of time together at her place."

Samantha turned toward Sheriff Burke but didn't say anything.

"Sarah's husband was one of my friends, and she and her daughter have been having a difficult time with things since he passed. I've also been trying to find some missing case files, ones I believe Detective Hines had taken home with him since he was the type of detective to work things twenty-four seven."

"Well, I think the good townspeople would be more interested in the details of what happens when you're there, especially if case files are missing, than what goes on here."

"And what exactly goes on here?" Samantha asked.

"None of your goddamned business." He turned to the sheriff. "I'd like her arrested for trespassing."

"Sorry, no can do. You don't have a sign posted, and furthermore, she's helping in a case and thus has my permission to venture onto properties like this one if she deems it necessary in looking for her patient."

"Fine, if you're going to play like that then I will too, and you can be sure that I'll be at the next county meeting. There are some concerns I have about the present state of our law-enforcement efforts and the conduct of those who wear a badge."

Sheriff Burke nodded and turned to Samantha. "Was there anything else you wanted to look at while here?"

"Um…no, not at this present time."

"Very well." He turned to Henry. "If you can let your son know I'd like to speak with him as soon as he has a moment. I have questions I'd like to ask him."

"Fine."

With that, Samantha and Sheriff Burke headed back around to the front.

"He's hiding something," Samantha said, voice low so it wouldn't carry to the back.

"I know, but it isn't what you think."

"What do you mean?"

"He's on the verge of bankruptcy and is about to lose his house."

"And?" she asked.

"Flipping this place is his last hope at staving off disaster, and from the start he has had nothing but trouble, first with all the structural and wiring problems he found and then from people who don't respect his property."

"You alluded to that second part yesterday," she reminded him. "What kind of trouble?"

"Same trouble we've had for years with this house. People, kids mostly, but older individuals as well, like to get inside. Every town has their haunted areas, and this is ours. Lately though, I think something else has been going on, something a bit more problematic than kids trying to get inside. But like I said yesterday, whatever it is, he isn't talking about it, so..."

"So..." she voiced, "...you're just going to leave it at that and not investigate."

"There's nothing to investigate, not without a complaint from him."

"What about his son? If he's working here day in and day out, I'm sure he knows what's been going on."

"Yeah, well, I get the feeling he doesn't really spend all that much time working while here, at least not on the house."

"Still, he's here, which means he should know what goes on here."

Sheriff Burke nodded.

"And the door is open for us to pay him a visit since we need to find out what caused that paint spread."

"We?"

"You said it yourself, I'm part of this investigation."

He shook his head. "I'm going to go talk with Steve, and if what he tells me gives some bearing on where your patient might be, I will share it with you."

"And if I learn anything that will help in figuring out

what has happened here, or where that girl Molly ended up, I'll be sure to let you know."

"Just don't push it with him," he said with a sigh, nodding toward the house. "Henry is a foul man when everything is going his way, and when it isn't..."

Samantha nodded.

"Where're you heading from here?" he asked, concern present.

"Hopefully somewhere that has coffee."

"If coffee is truly what you seek right now, then I suggest heading over to Kathy's Place, which is on the far end of Main Street."

"Good deal."

"And if you're hungry, the omelets are to die for."

She nodded, the mention of food striking a chord within her belly.

* * *

The hunger Michelle was experiencing was the worst she had ever endured, and for most of the morning, her thoughts were solely upon it and the question of how she would get something to eat.

The head.

Cheeks, tongue, and eyeballs—she had watched a man eating such things many times on the TV in the rec room at the children's home, though the parts had never come from a human. The edibility, however, would be the same.

Brain too.

But...

She had no way of cooking it, not unless she went downstairs to the kitchen, which she couldn't do right now. She also didn't know if the fact that the head had sat out for several hours would mean the meat was spoiled.

Such things didn't last long in the open air. She and many other children at the children's home had experienced the consequences of this one day when meat had been left out in the kitchen too long before it was cooked. Almost everyone had gotten sick, even staff members who ate the meal, and the kitchen crew had been reprimanded.

Eventually, the commotion outside distracted her, though she couldn't see what was going on due to the window in the back not being angled correctly to look down upon the area that the three were in.

She could hear them, however, and quickly knew they were talking about the bloodstains that had been painted over.

If they come inside to look around...

Santa will get them.

As a kid, she had always thought Santa only came on Christmas Eve, but then she had learned differently.

No, that's not Santa.

But...

Her mind went into a tailspin as the horrific reality of what was going on unfolded, a reality her mind didn't want to accept and tried to push away.

You have to face it! a voice within screamed, one that sounded like Dr. Loomis.

NO!

YES!

On and on it went until she realized that no one was talking in the back any longer. In fact, everything had gone quiet.

And then she heard it; someone was inside.

They were walking around, the sound of boots clumping

on the floor marking the route they were taking within the house.

What if they come up here?

She looked at the blood on her hands, blood that she couldn't seem to get off no matter how much she tried, and then over at the head.

Everyone will think you did it, just like before.

No, they won't, a voice replied, hands reaching up to her throat.

They will learn the truth.

This time she would be able to explain what had happened, and the fact that she was covered in blood and had a head in her possession wouldn't matter.

Santa took them.

And this time I know who Santa is.

But...

NO BUTS!

"HELP ME!" she screamed.

* * *

Henry Jenkins was starting to panic, mostly because he didn't buy into his own suggestion that Steve had dropped a paint can on the porch. The reason for this was simple: he had not instructed Steve to do any touch-up work outside of the house, not with winter promising to be nasty. Nope. Inside was one thing—he could spend the cold snowy months getting everything ready for the springtime housing market—but outside, he needed to wait until spring was upon them so that everything looked fresh for the prospective buyers.

Someone else was to blame, the same someone who had left all the beheaded animals upstairs and wrote on the walls with their blood.

And now with that local girl missing and the teenage lunatic having murdered her uncle and his girlfriend...

Henry shook his head.

No one was ever going to buy this house.

Not with all that going on.

Bad timing.

Story of my life.

If he had bought the house two years earlier, he would have been able to sell it last spring, but no, he had bought it last year, just when some freak had decided the place would be a good location for torturing animals. A young serial killer in the making, one that he knew he should report to the police but couldn't because it would ruin him. If he didn't sell the house, they would lose theirs, and if that happened...

At least you could then get a divorce without having to worry about paying much support.

That thought was the only saving grace, the only positive thing about the potential that was quickly becoming a reality as more and more shit unfolded.

"*Help me!*"

The voice echoed from above, scaring the piss out of him—literally.

Frozen, he didn't know what to do, and then she screamed again.

"*Help me! Please!*"

Feet unglued, he hurried to the front window to see if the sheriff was still there. He wasn't. Next, he grabbed his phone to place a call but then realized maybe his luck was changing. If someone was up there, trapped or, worse, imprisoned while awaiting the return of the young serial killer, he could save her and come out looking like a hero. Such an image might not help him sell the house, but it surely wouldn't hurt his other endeavors.

What if it isn't a victim?

What if she's trying to lure you up there?

Silence settled.

He waited, his hesitation getting the better of him.

And then, irritated with himself for the hesitation, which was fear induced, he reached into his pocket and pulled out a folding knife that he thumbed open.

A gun would be better.

But no, the liberal masses wouldn't allow that. They'd rather everyone be unarmed and defenseless because guns were scary.

He was stuck with the knife.

Or…

He had tools stored in the garage, but grabbing a weapon-like one from the collection would require going to his truck for the key, then to the garage, and then back inside, all of which might prove costly for whoever was upstairs.

Plus, he had a feeling the killer wasn't here and the person upstairs was simply a prisoner, one who had been locked up temporarily for some reason.

And you'll be her rescuer.

Knife in hand, he started up the steps and then navigated his way to the bedroom with the closet that had a steep stairway going up into the attic, the smell of piss, shit, and decay enveloping him as he neared the top.

* * *

Quite a bit of time passed before the horror of what had unfolded within the attic was edged away by her hunger, thoughts on cannibalizing parts from the head returning to the forefront of her mind.

This one is fresh.

If you hesitate, it will go bad.

Michelle looked at the knife the man had given her before the ax had been planted in him, noting that the blade was sized perfectly for cutting out parts from the face.

What about the brain?

That would have the largest edible portion of all, but getting through the skull...

She looked at the brick support column that ran up the center of the house. The edge would work for cracking the head against, and if she bashed it with enough force, hopefully the skull would split without too much fragmentation.

Thoughts of cracking eggs into a skillet while trying to surprise her uncle with breakfast a few weeks ago arrived. Shell pieces had rained down upon the cooking proteins, her fingers unable to get all of them out before the whites firmed up with the heat.

Skull pieces will be worse, she said to herself, thinking of how the tiny sharp fragments might pierce her stomach and bowels.

What about eating the brain raw?

She still didn't know if that was okay. On TV, when the bald guy ate brains, they were always cooked. But then, she hadn't seen all the episodes, so maybe sometimes he ate it raw, like fish in Japan.

Tongue?

That was different from the brain, and she had watched the bald guy eating other types of raw meat from time to time.

Try that first.

Grabbing the head by the hair, she twisted it around so she could get the mouth open and pull the tongue far enough out to cut it free, a shiver racing through her at how odd the unshaven face felt against her fingers.

This brought to mind the cheeks, and how eating them would be awkward, given the texture the stubble created.

You eat it or you starve, she reminded herself.

Many other people had to endure far worse.

Earlier she had pissed on her own pants and squeezed it out into her mouth to quench her thirst, so eating cheek with stubble couldn't be much worse.

You could make a bowl with the skull if you crack it right!

The thought brought a smile to her face, mostly because she was proud of the ingenuity it had required, but also because drinking her own urine was bad enough without having to taste the rot of the clothing it was squeezed from. A bowl would be better.

Tongue first, she told herself and began the process of cutting it free, first with an attempt at prying open the mouth so she could pull it out, but then, when that didn't work very well, by cutting up through the underside of the chin and pulling it out from the throat.

It wasn't as slimy as she thought it would be, but even so, once it was removed, she couldn't bring it to her lips right away, her disgust too much to overcome.

But then her hunger chimed in with a force she could not deny.

One bite.

It's not about the taste, but survival.

You need to eat.

She brought the tongue to her mouth and, without giving it another thought, closed her teeth upon it and pulled.

Though disgusted by the thought, the actual taste wasn't bad. In fact, there was no real flavor at all, and if it weren't for the chewiness, she would have downed the entire thing within minutes. Instead, she had to work through each bite, teeth grinding away until each chunk was safe to swallow, and then rest her jaw before taking another. It took the better part of an hour to finish half the tongue, at which point she'd had enough, her hunger temporarily sated.

Santa won't even know, she told herself, looking at the head.

But if you crack it open to get the brain and make a bowl...

She had no idea what Santa wanted with the heads, but she knew there was a reason they were collected and that ruining one might not be a good idea after all, especially now that she was no longer hungry.

You have a knife now.

You can kill Santa once and for all.

Could she?

Confusion filled her mind, the mythical Santa clashing with the Santa that had slaughtered her brothers and sister all those years ago and come back for her the other night.

Adding to the confusion was the Santa coat and hat she had on, questions on why she was wearing them when Santa surely needed them to keep warm ruining her thought process.

* * *

Renee spent the entire morning checking the Christmas party Facebook page, her mind unable to distance herself from it for more than five minutes at a time, horror, anger, and disgust always mixing together whenever she saw that another one of her "friends" had checked the *I'm going* tab.

Friends that don't care to find out why I'm not going, her mind snapped.

Maggie was the only exception, but given that the two only really hung out with each other through mutual friends, it didn't mean much. In fact, Maggie had probably asked simply to rub it in. She had seen that Renee wasn't on the invited list and, knowing something had happened between her and Steve, asked about the party just to be a bitch.

Bitch!

Probably hopes she can get together with Steve now.

Maggie and Molly. Both had always been jealous of her man, so much so that they would do anything they could to ruin what she had. If they couldn't be happy like she was, then they didn't want her to be happy.

Well, I'll show them.

Nothing followed.

She had no idea how to show them. With Steve, she could do things to hurt him, thanks to the pictures and video she had, but with them, she didn't have anything.

I wonder if Molly has tried to contact me?

Thoughts on the dismay Molly must be feeling at the lack of replies to the text and emails she was sending brought a smile to her face. Panic was probably present as well. After all, given how unpopular Molly was, seeing that she was suddenly short a friend on Facebook would be noticed and investigated right away. The realization that she, Renee, one of the most popular girls in school, had been the one to break the connection would hit like a brick to the face. Texts and calls about why would follow, all of them going unanswered. Molly was probably staring at the phone right now, waiting, her social life at a complete standstill, regret over the things she had said the day before dominating her mind.

Thought you would be riding my coattails through the social circles your entire life, but nope.

See ya, wouldn't want to be ya!

DONG!

Renee twisted toward the hall.

A knock followed.

"Katie!" she shouted. "Go get the door!"

"Mom said not to answer the door," Katie shouted back.

"I don't care. Go answer the door."

"No!"

DONG! DONG!

"Jesus fucking Christ!"

"I'm telling Mom you swore!"

Renee held back a reply as she got up from the couch and headed toward the front door, peeking through the window before reaching toward the knob.

It was Sheriff Burke.

She unbolted the door and started to turn the knob.

"Renee! Mom said not to—"

"It's the sheriff!" Renee snapped, cutting her off. Then when the door was open, "Sheriff Burke, hello."

"Hi, Renee," Sheriff Burke said. His eyes glanced over her shoulder. "Hi, Katie."

"Hello," Katie said, suddenly shy.

His eyes returned to Renee. "Is Steve here?"

Renee stiffened. "No."

"Do you know where he might be?"

"No."

Sheriff Burke looked at her for several seconds. "You two have a fight?"

"No, well, no, not really." She looked down.

"Renee, what happened?" he urged.

"Well, yesterday he, like, wanted to do things with me at the house when we were all alone, after you left, and I told him no, so he got, like, all mad at me and threw me out."

Though she wasn't looking at him, she could feel his eyes upon her, almost as if he were weighing her statement.

Probably thinks I'm lying.

Everyone always sees me as a whore.

"And you have no idea where he might be?"

She shook her head, frustration at the lack of sympathy he displayed edging its way into her system.

"Think about it. Where does he like to hang out when he isn't with you, at his home, or at the house his dad bought?"

With Hanna! she wanted to say but instead simply shook her head again.

"Renee," he encouraged her.

"I don't know."

Silence settled for several seconds.

Renee waited, a desire to bid him farewell and close the door going unfulfilled.

"Speaking of yesterday," he finally started, "did you notice anything unusual at the house?"

"You asked that yesterday," Renee said.

"I know I did, but now that you've had some time to think about it, was there anything odd going on there?"

"No."

"Has Steve ever mentioned odd things?"

"No."

"Renee, actually think about it, okay? This is important."

She looked up at him, wishing she could put tears into her eyes to show how distraught she was about the breakup, but none would arrive. "No," she said. "He never talked about the house."

"What about your friends, any of them ever talk about the house?"

"No."

A crease appeared in his forehead, one that probably meant he was getting annoyed with her answers.

Though she wasn't sure why, this actually pleased her.

"Okay, well, if you hear from Steve at all, or hear anything about the house, let me know right away."

"I'm not going to hear anything," she said.

The crease became more pronounced.

"If you do," he said.

"But I won't."

He sighed. "Okay." With that, he turned from the door and started toward his car.

* * *

Jesus Christ, was all Richard Burke could think once he was back in his car, the contradictory stance Renee had used toward the end of his questions something he hadn't seen in a while from anyone. It was weird and annoying. Simply saying no hadn't been enough for her; she had needed to get last word in every time.

He shook his head and then shifted his focus back to Steve Jenkins and where the kid could be.

Nothing.

He had checked the local teen hangouts, but all had been a bust. And his little brother Kyle had simply said Steve was heading out to see a girl, which had prompted Richard to seek out Renee, but apparently he had others on standby.

All because of a splatter of paint, he said to himself with a sigh.

The radio came to life, asking for him.

"This is Burke. What is it?" he asked.

"Sir, Molly Mason's mother called. She wanted us to know that she logged on to Molly's bank account with Molly's computer and can prove to us that the debit card hasn't been used since the twenty-first."

"What was it used for on the twenty-first?" he asked.

"She didn't say, but if it was to withdraw a large sum of cash to use while on the road heading to Hollywood or something, I think she would have mentioned it."

"Okay, let her know that I'm going to head over to her place right now so I can take a look at that. While I do that, if you could put out word that I would like to speak with Steve Jenkins and that he needs to head down to the station as soon as possible."

"Do you want him brought in, or is it a voluntary visit?" Becky asked.

"Voluntary, but very important to the point where he doesn't really have a choice. I need to speak with him."

"Will do." Then after a few seconds, "Anything else?"

He considered having her put out word that he needed to speak with Sarah as well but held back on that. "No, that's all for now."

"Okay, over."

Setting the radio aside, he took one look back at the

house, his eyes catching movement in the window as Renee stepped away.

Or was it her sister?

No, he had a feeling it was Renee.

Are the rumors true?

Was she gang-raped during the homecoming game last year?

No complaint from Renee, or anyone else, had ever been filed, so no investigation had unfolded. Rumors, however, had spread, rumors that stated there was video of the act. Unfortunately, if there truly was a video, it had never surfaced, making it impossible to pursue those who had taken part in it. Adding to the trouble, many said that Renee had instigated the entire thing, which most in the area viewed as giving consent, so unless she disputed that and filed a complaint, or unless anyone in the video was over eighteen, there really wasn't anything he could do.

* * *

"Where're you going?" Katie asked.

"Nowhere," Renee said while putting on her shoes, the stupid sheriff having finally left the driveway.

"Mom said we have to stay inside," Katie said, arms crossed, an attempt at sternness failing.

"I don't care," she snapped, her desire to find Steve and see who he was with overwhelming the fear of the threat their mother had leveled upon them that morning.

She finished putting her shoes on and grabbed her keys.

"I'm calling Mom," Katie said.

"You touch that phone and I swear I'll come over there and beat your ass until you can't sit for a week!"

Katie froze.

Renee waited a second to see if she started pressing buttons to make the call, and when she didn't, grabbed her coat and started toward the door.

"Wait," Katie said.

"What?"

"Can I come with?"

"No."

"Then I'm telling Mom."

"And if you do that, you'll be stuck with Grandma all next week too."

Katie considered that for several seconds and then turned to go back to her room, seemingly defeated.

Renee grinned and headed to her car.

* * *

"She didn't run away!" Lydia Mason said, anger replacing the panic that had been present earlier.

"I know, but until we get some evidence that says otherwise, that's what we have to go on right now," Richard said. "That's why it is so important for you to gather as much information as you can on who she is friends with, drama she may have been involved in, boyfriends, things like that."

"I don't know. I spent all morning on her computer"—she pointed toward it—"but couldn't really find anything on there that seemed important."

Richard looked at the screen and saw the Facebook timeline.

"May I?" he asked.

Lydia nodded, an odd look of exhaustion having enveloped her.

Richard sat down and navigated his way onto her friends list. He then typed in Renee's name.

No search results.

"That can't be right," Lydia said, looking over his shoulder.

"What?"

"Molly and Renee have been friends since kindergarten. There's no way they're not friends on here."

"Did something happen?" Richard asked, typing in Steve's name. This time he got a result.

"Nothing that I know about, though, honestly, she and Renee have been on-again, off-again so many times, I wouldn't be surprised if they had a tiff over something."

"A tiff big enough to unfriend each other?" he asked.

"Probably depends on who did the unfriending. It would have to be pretty serious for Molly to remove someone."

He nodded and then asked, "What are your thoughts on Renee?"

Lydia hesitated for several seconds before saying, "When she was younger, she was really sweet and a pleasure to have over during sleepovers and birthday parties."

"But..."

"I don't know. I haven't really seen her in quite some time. The girls don't really get together here anymore now that they all have cars, and the only time I really hear about her is when the kids are fighting about something. Molly vents."

Richard could tell there was more she wanted to say, but nothing else followed.

He waited, an inner debate on asking about the Renee homecoming rumor echoing within his mind. *Could something with that have played a part in Molly disappearing?*

It was over a year ago.

Still...

"I don't like him," Lydia said, indicating Steve, who was pictured on-screen.

"Oh, how come?"

"He's a bully, just like his father. When they were younger, Molly came home from school crying because he said something to her about being able to see her bra strap."

Richard gave her a puzzled look.

"Molly matured quicker than the other girls and was wearing a bra toward the end of grade school. Kids made fun of her, especially Steve. Things got to the point where he actually came up behind her and pulled her bra strap so that it snapped back against her skin. For me, that was the final straw."

"What'd you do?"

"I called his parents, and you know what his father said?"

Richard waited.

"He said that if Molly was going to dress like a harlot, she should expect to be treated like one."

Richard nodded, the response sounding on par with the type of person Henry Jenkins was.

"Dress like a harlot, my daughter, all because she had boobs before everyone else did." Anger appeared. "And that son of his is no better, a product of rape culture through and through. For all I know, he..."

Richard waited, but she didn't continue. "For all you know, he..."

"I was going to say he might be responsible for what happened to Molly, but I really don't have any reason to say something like that and don't want to muddy things up simply because I'm angry about things that happened six years ago."

"If you have reason to suspect he —"

"I don't," Lydia said, exhaustion returning. "I wish I did, but I don't." Tears started to fall. At first, they were gentle, but then the floodgates opened. "My daughter didn't run away. Someone has her. Hanging in a basement somewhere, like that kid in Ashton five years ago. You have to find her."

"We will," Richard said with a nod, his doubt hidden from her. A statement of "Don't worry, she probably just got turned around with friends and will be home soon," nearly followed before he caught it.

She isn't lost or with friends, he said to himself. *Something's happened, something involving that house and that girl.*

And Steve?

He thought about the town of Ashton Creek, which wasn't far from them, and the horror that had unfolded within that small community five years earlier as first one girl and then a second girl disappeared. Both had been kept prisoner in the secret fallout shelter beneath the shed of an old abandoned house, the perpetrator a high school boy who had harbored dangerous fantasies his entire life, ones that his family and friends hadn't known about. Could the same thing be unfolding here? Could there be a secret area within the old Harper house that they didn't know about, one where Molly was now being kept prisoner? Could a high school student be responsible?

* * *

WHERE ARE YOU? Renee typed into her phone but then hesitated, her fear being that asking the question might make Steve realize she was desperate and needed them to be good again.

I'm not desperate; I just want to find out where you are so I can beat the shit out of whatever fuck buddy you're with.

Steve wouldn't realize this, however, and would start to think he had the upper hand in this situation.

So let him think that.

Let him think everything is cool between you two so that tomorrow night is a huge shock.

Fuck it!

She hit send and watched as the message was added to the conversation thread.

* * *

The call from Detective White arrived while Samantha was sitting in a rear corner booth at Kathy's Place staring at her phone screen, trying to figure out what it was about the paint splatter that was bugging her. Something wasn't right, but whatever it was, she couldn't put her finger on it.

Frustration was present, both at her lack of progress with the paint splatter and in figuring out where Michelle was.

You're not a very good detective, she muttered to herself seconds before the call came in, eyes going from the screen to the mug of coffee that was no longer appealing.

And if Michelle did kill them— she began, the inner statement going to focus on her abilities as a doctor.

The call cut off the thought.

"Detective," she said, a sense of relief unfolding.

"Doctor," he replied.

"How's the case coming?" she asked. "Have you found Michelle?"

"No, have you?"

"No."

Dismay started to take root, but then she realized he was calling for a reason and asked what he had found.

"You were right about her having a boyfriend," he said. "One who decided it was finally time to meet."

"And?" she asked.

"They have quite a few 'I can't wait to see you' and 'I'm so excited for tonight' messages going back and forth, the latter ones being from two days ago."

"Just before the murders," she said.

"Exactly, and then the messages stop, which is huge."

She sensed excitement in his voice but couldn't figure it out. "Well, yeah," she said. "Michelle disappeared."

"But why would that stop him from sending her more messages? Did he know she wouldn't be able to reply?"

"Maybe she stood him up?" Samantha suggested, playing devil's advocate.

"If she did, where are the messages asking if they were still getting together? A guy in that position wouldn't just wait in silence, not after all the messages they sent back and forth."

"Okay, I see what you're saying," she said.

The waitress came toward her. Samantha tried waving her away, but she came up to the table.

"I'm sorry, we have a no cell phone policy," the waitress said.

Startled, Samantha covered the speaker part of the phone and said, "I'm talking to the police about an investigation."

"Owner doesn't care, wants you to take the conversation outside. It's disruptive."

Only three other people were in the diner, and none of them seemed bothered by her cell phone conversation, which they probably couldn't even hear given the distance.

"The owner can come talk to me himself if he wants me to

stop," Samantha said.

The waitress looked at her for a moment, somewhat unsure of herself, and then turned and headed back to the front register where the owner was waiting.

"Sorry about that. What were you saying?" she asked Detective White.

"What happened?" he asked.

"Uh, they don't want me talking on the phone while in the empty restaurant, say it's their policy."

"Ah, seems that's becoming more and more common these days. Anyway, we're trying to figure out the identity of the young man she was supposed to see that night. There's something fishy about the entire thing and the fact that he went completely silent once she disappeared." He paused. "Just doesn't add up."

Michelle watched as the owner started toward her.

"You think he might have done something to her?" Michelle asked. "And her uncle and girlfriend?"

"Either that, or Michelle did something to him. Whichever is the case, we really need to figure out who this young man is so we can talk to him."

"What's his name?"

"Miss," the owner said.

Samantha held up a finger for him to wait.

"Put the phone away or take it outside."

"I'm talking to the police," Samantha said, irritation present.

"And you can talk to them outside," he said.

Samantha didn't move.

"At this point," Detective White continued, "we simply have a screen name, and he kept calling himself—"

The manager reached for her phone.

"Hey," Samantha snapped, pulling back. "Don't you fucking touch me."

"If you don't leave right now, I will take that phone and smash it."

"And then I will press charges against you for destruction of property."

"This is a private establishment, and I'm well within my rights to remove you and your phone."

"Not by touching me or my property," Samantha snapped.

"What's going on?" Detective White asked.

"The owner is threatening to take my phone and smash it."

"He can't do that—"

From behind, the waitress yanked her phone from her hand and handed it to the owner.

"Give that back!" she shouted.

He didn't say a word and started toward the front of the restaurant, another waitress stepping aside as he passed her.

Samantha hurried after him but couldn't catch up before he opened the door and threw the phone as hard as he could into the street.

And then he grabbed her by the arm as she tried to go through the door to retrieve it. "Nope, not until you pay your—"

Her fist cut him off, his lower lip deflating beneath her knuckle.

"Oh my God!" the waitress cried as the owner dropped backward against the counter, coffee mugs and rolled-up silverware crashing to the floor.

Without a word, Samantha stepped through the door and hurried to her phone, mind pleading that it wouldn't be broken.

It was.

Anger and dismay arrived, as did a horn from a driver that was nearing her.

She didn't move, and eventually the driver slowly went around her, the lack of traffic making it possible to take the wrong lane without a problem.

Now what? she asked herself.

Go home, a voice said. *Let the police handle all this.*

As tempting as it was, she dismissed the option and headed to her car, a newfound desire to talk to Sheriff Burke arriving.

* * *

WHERE ARE YOU?

Steve stared at the text from Renee while waiting for Hanna to show up at the Harper home, questions on whether or not he should reply playing through his mind.

Give her a dot bubble, a voice suggested.

It's immature, another replied.

Yeah, well, so is she!

He clicked on the message box and typed a few random letters before setting the phone down.

Where is she? he asked himself, eyes needlessly checking the clock.

Hanna had said they would meet up at noon, but it was almost one o'clock and she still wasn't at the house. She also wasn't replying to his texts asking where she was, which in turn had made Renee's text even more frustrating because he had initially thought it was finally a reply from Hanna.

At least she isn't giving you a dot bubble, the voice said, his eyes looking at the Hanna conversation.

Whatever relief the inner statement was supposed to generate, it failed, his anxiety and dismay at the growing realization that she had stood him up getting the better of him.

Was it intentional? he wondered.

But why? After all this time?

The question of *why* could be frequently asked when contemplating Hanna, their time together having made it clear to him that one could never know what to expect from her. It wasn't a *hot and cold* situation like he experienced with Renee. Hanna never went bitch with the flip of a switch. Instead, she just did things that he didn't understand, things that she wouldn't explain. The breakup had been a perfect example of this. One day things had been great and they were getting along and enjoying their relationship. The next day she had sent him a text telling him they couldn't see each other anymore. Nothing else had followed. In fact, despite all his messages and calls to her, this morning had been the first time she had communicated with him since that breakup text.

And now she stood you up.

He shook his head, unable to comprehend what would drive her to do something like this.

A message arrived.

It was Renee.

ARE YOU DOT BUBBLING ME?

JUST PASSING THE TIME WAITING FOR HANNA TO SHOW UP, he typed but then decided against sending it.

Instead, he deleted everything he had written and exited out of the conversation so the dot bubble would go away.

Following that, he looked at the Hanna conversation, but

nothing new had arrived. He then shifted his focus to the Harper house, thoughts on the message his father had left him about needing to speak with him dominating his mind.

Try calling him again.

Though he didn't want to talk to the man, he knew his father would be pissed if he didn't call him back, the number of times he had tried and just gotten the voicemail not being enough in his father's eyes.

As before, it went straight to voicemail.

Fuck it, he said to himself and set the phone down. *Ten more minutes.*

After that, he would text Hanna one more time, wait another five minutes, and if she didn't reply, he would leave.

Or go inside and finish painting.

Or start setting up for the party.

He thought about the party and once again questioned his own judgment on agreeing to go along with it. Maybe it would be a better idea to let everyone know he hadn't created it. Let everyone know there was no party.

* * *

"He threw my phone into the street!" Samantha said, showing him the phone.

"Yeah, he'll do that," Deputy Hawkins said while the dispatcher tried to get Sheriff Burke on the radio. "He hates cell phones."

"But he can't just destroy people's property," Samantha said.

"It's a private establishment," Deputy Hawkins said, palm pointing up toward the ceiling in a half-assed shrug.

Samantha shook her head, an overarching sense of exhaustion making it so she didn't want to begin the process of explaining how ludicrous that "private establishment" excuse was. Instead, she simply wanted to use a phone at the station to finish her conversation with Detective White. Before she could do that, however, she needed his phone number, which, hopefully, was something the sheriff had on file given that the two had spoken.

"He isn't responding right now," the receptionist, who looked to be about ninety years old, said. She gave an apologetic smile. "Do you want me to leave him a message to call you?"

"What good will that do?" she asked, voice elevated. "I don't have a phone!"

The old woman didn't reply, just stared.

Samantha felt guilt creeping in but rather than dwell upon it asked, "Are you able to look up the phone number for the Elm Grove Police Department?"

"Yes."

"Okay, can you call them and see if Detective White is available?"

Without a word, yet managing to show displeasure at being ordered to make the call, the old woman pulled up some information on the computer and then dialed a number. "Yes," she said a moment later. "This is Becky Palmer over at the Rockwood Sheriff's Department. Is Detective White available?"

Samantha waited as Becky sat there in silence, seconds ticking by until a minute came and went, and then two minutes.

"Okay, yes, that's correct," Becky said with a nod. "Thank you." She hung up the phone.

Samantha stared.

"They're going to have him give us a call once they can reach him." She motioned toward a chair beyond the desk. "If you like, you can have a seat and wait. We have coffee, tea, and a vending machine."

"Thanks," Samantha muttered and took a seat, hand instinctively pulling out her phone to check if she had any messages or updates in her social media feeds, the broken screen mocking her. *Fuck.*

The sound of keys clicking on a keyboard began to echo.

She looked up and saw that Becky's eyes were going back and forth between a file and the computer screen.

"Excuse me," Samantha said, standing.

"Yes?" Becky asked.

"You wouldn't happen to have the case file of the murders from ten years ago on hand, would you? I'd like to familiarize myself with it again given recent events." She had never actually seen the police report, but she figured making it sound like she had would help make it seem like showing it to her was okay.

"I'm sorry, that file is not available right now."

"Oh?"

Becky didn't seem to want to elaborate upon that and simply turned back to her computer screen.

"Why not?" Samantha asked.

Becky hesitated and then said, "You'll have to talk to Sheriff Burke about that." She didn't look away from her screen while stating this and, without elaborating upon her statement, went back to typing, the clicking of the computer keys echoing once again.

* * *

HEY, ARE WE STILL GETTING TOGETHER? Steve asked.

Hanna didn't reply.

Five more minutes, he said to himself.

Nothing.

Fucking bullshit! he silently shouted, hand slamming against the steering wheel.

The horn beeped.

Questions on why she'd done this echoed.

No answers followed.

Now what?

He looked at the house, thoughts of going inside and painting unfolding. He then thought about how his father had been this morning and said, *"Fuck it!"* while switching on the ignition and shifting to drive.

* * *

Renee watched from the trees as Steve pulled away from the Harper house, frustration and an odd sense of disappointment at the fact that she didn't see Hanna anywhere getting the better of her.

Maybe he isn't fucking her.

But then why did he come here?

If it were to work on the house for his father, then he would have actually gone in and done some work. Instead, he had just been sitting there in the car, waiting, the engine running so he could have the heater on. Why?

Obviously, it was to meet up with someone.

Hanna?

Who else?

Someone his father hired to work on the house?

No, the only thing left to do is painting, and Steve obviously didn't go inside to do that.

So...

A moment of indecision gripped her, but then she pushed

it aside with a decision to head back to her car and see where he was going.

Or not going, she said to herself since she wasn't going to be really following him, but instead simply heading to his house to see if he went there.

Where else would he go?

Hanna's place?

Would he be that obvious?

No answer.

Shivering a bit, Renee pushed away from the tree and started toward her car but then stopped and ducked back behind it when she saw a figure approaching the house from behind the McKenzies' place.

Who is... she started but then stopped when she realized she had on a Santa hat.

And a Santa coat!

One that looked out of place without the fatness everyone associated with the jolly old elf.

No beard either.

The girl who escaped?

Oh my God!

She pulled out her phone but then hesitated, uncertain about who she should call. Was this something for 911?

Would she get in trouble if it weren't?

She stared at her phone for several seconds, cold fingers ready to press the digits.

Call the sheriff instead.

But...

She had no idea of the number, though she figured she could easily Google it.

Fuck it! She pressed the three digits and put the phone to her ear.

"*Nine-one-one, please state your emergency.*"

"Yeah," Renee whispered. "I'm at the Harper house, and I just saw someone dressed like Santa prowling around it."

She looked up to see if she could add anything more, but the Santa figure was no longer there.

"*You said you're calling to report a prowler dressed as Santa at your house?*"

"No, not my house, the Harper house."

"*And what is the address of that house?*"

"What?" Renee said, startled. "Don't you have it on your screen?"

"*No, ma'am. You're calling from a cell phone and I can see your location as being in the Rockwood area, but I will need you to tell me the exact address so we can contact local law enforcement and have an officer dispatched.*"

"I just told you, it's the Harper house!"

"*And what is the address of the Harper house?*"

"I don't know—" Renee started and then spun around when she heard a crunch.

Santa was coming up behind her with an ax.

"HELP ME!" she screamed.

* * *

"Whoa, whoa, whoa," Richard said, palms up. "You're reading way too much into it."

"Really?" Samantha asked, crossing her arms. "Then tell me, what other files disappeared during the last ten years?"

"I..." Richard started and then stopped.

Samantha waited and when he didn't continue said, "So

you think it's simply a coincidence that ten years later, after two copycat murders take place and the only surviving girl of the original murders disappears, the file on that case has vanished?"

"Yeah, I do," he said, though he wasn't really sure if he did. "And the reason is because I'm sure there are other files that have vanished as well, ones that we would only know about if we actually had to go find them for a case that was reopened."

Samantha shook her head.

"I hate to admit it, but stuff like that happens in every department from time to time."

Samantha just stared at him.

"But it seems you think it's more likely that someone broke in here and stole it so that we wouldn't have access to it during a series of copycat murders," Richard said. "Tell me, honestly, do you think that's more likely than to have had it misplaced?"

"I think it's disconcerting enough that you should look into who might have taken it so that you can see if there are any other strange things going on with their life, things that might paint a picture that leads to them being involved in the recent murders."

Richard agreed but didn't want to admit it.

The emergency line rang.

Becky picked it up, listened for a moment, and said, "That was a nine-one-one dispatcher over in Russellville, says they received a call from a cell phone in this area that said someone was prowling around the Harper house in a Santa suit. The call then ended abruptly after a scream."

"Have all units head toward the Harper house right now," Richard said and then turned to head toward his vehicle.

Samantha was right behind him.

"I can't have you come with me," Richard said.

"If Michelle is there, you need me," Samantha said.

"If things get dangerous," he started and then, realizing he didn't want to argue, "fine, but don't get out of the vehicle until I give you an okay to do so."

"Fine," she said.

A moment later, the two were in his SUV, heading toward the Harper home at about sixty miles an hour, lights and siren going.

* * *

Renee reacted just in time, her body dropping down as the ax cut the air above her head and embedded itself into the tree she had been leaning against.

A frustrated grunt escaped her attacker, who then cried out in anger as she struggled to get the ax free from the tree.

Renee ran.

Not toward the house, due to the tree and the killer, but away from it, deeper into the woods, her body plowing through the overgrowth blindly as her arms shielded her face from all the branches and vines that had gone untouched for years.

And then it happened: something tangled her foot to the point where it felt as if a hand had reached up from the earth and yanked her ankle out from under her. She went face-first toward the ground, an upright stick gouging her cheek just as her forearms broke the fall. An inch to the right and she would have lost an eye.

Where is she?

Nothing but the sound of her own breathing reached her ears.

She twisted over and looked toward the woods she had just run through.

No one was there, and no sounds of pursuit echoed.

She's not chasing you.

Why?

No answer followed, nor was there any certainty that she was correct that she wasn't being chased.

She's sneaking up on me!

With this thought, Renee began fighting with the vines that had caught her ankle, silent curses echoing as thorns snagged her clothing and pierced her flesh.

And then she heard it, the sound of someone carefully coming through the brush, almost as if—

There!

Though quite faded, the red of the hat and coat still stood out against the gray tones of the wintertime forest, the killer's movements easily visible.

She's looking for me.

Don't move.

But...

If the girl came upon her while her foot was entangled, there would be no escape, and while it was obvious the girl didn't know where Renee was at the moment, Renee wouldn't be difficult to spot once she was closer.

She had to free herself.

Eyes on the killer, Renee carefully shifted her hands back to the vines, the thorns piercing her skin every time she attempted to pull.

The killer got closer, yet the vines didn't get any looser.

You have to yank it! she told herself, knowing the pain from the thorns would be intense yet nothing compared to the horror of the ax chopping through her chest.

Do it!

Gritting her teeth, she grabbed the vine and pulled with all her might, her skin tearing as the thorns staked their claims within her flesh, right leg kicking to try to help free itself.

The killer turned, eyes looking her way.

Renee froze.

She can't see you, not through the brush.

The eyes stayed on her.

Don't move!

Don't breathe!

Don't—

The killer turned and continued through the brush, passing Renee by about thirty feet.

Renee let out a deep breath and quietly went back to freeing her leg, the initial pain from the thorns dulling as the nerves across her palm and thumb began to accept all the rips and tears.

Her foot came free.

She shifted herself so she could climb back onto her feet, face wincing as she pressed her chewed-up palm against the frozen ground.

Crunch!

She looked up and to her horror saw the killer breaking through the brush and coming straight for her, ax held high above her head and ready to come crashing down into her body once the distance between them was erased.

* * *

"Stay in here until I come back," Richard ordered, his tone making it clear that he wasn't going to take no for an answer.

Samantha nodded.

He stepped out from the SUV and started toward the

house, gun drawn.

Behind him, another siren echoed.

Richard circled the house as the siren approached, eyes scanning everything before he returned to the front and greeted the first deputy on the scene. It was Beverly Crawson.

"What we got?" Deputy Crawson asked.

"Not sure. Girl called in saying there was a prowler dressed as Santa."

"Prowler dressed as Santa?" Deputy Crawson said, voice asking if he was serious.

"Yeah."

"Okay," Deputy Crawson said.

Though she didn't say it, Richard could tell she didn't think this was something they should have responded to. However, he also knew, now that they had responded, that she would take the situation seriously and do her best to make sure the place was secure.

Nothing seemed amiss.

Another deputy arrived as Richard was checking the doors. Both were locked.

"Windows are secure," Deputy Crawson said.

Richard nodded and took a look at the garage.

Once again, nothing seemed amiss.

Deputy Milner came around the house and asked what the trouble was.

Richard explained.

"Probably kids messing with you," Deputy Milner suggested.

"Even so, we need to make sure that's all it is. According to the nine-one-one dispatcher, they heard a girl scream into the phone and then the phone went dead."

"Do they know who called?" Deputy Crawson asked.

"Not yet, but they're looking into that," he said. "It was a cell phone."

Both deputies nodded, their time upon the force having taught them all too well how unreliable cell-phone-location information could be when out in the countryside.

"Crawson, I want you to patrol the area and see if you can spot anyone dressed as Santa prowling around. Someone like that should stand out."

"Yes, sir."

"Milner, I want you to take a look into the woods a bit, not too far, and see if you can find anything."

Deputy Milner nodded.

"I'm going to go see if the McKenzies have noticed anything." His statement wasn't really necessary, but being in charge, he always liked his personnel to know that he was doing his part, not just delegating from above.

Samantha was standing outside the vehicle as he came back around the house.

"You find anything?" she asked.

"No, nothing," he said, holding back a desire to chastise her for leaving the vehicle.

"Now what?" she asked.

"I'm going to go talk to the McKenzies," he said.

She started to follow.

He stopped and said, "This is an official investigation, and—"

"You said earlier that I'm a part of this official investigation."

He stared at her a moment, frustration growing, and then shook his head with a sigh.

Two minutes later, they were standing outside the McKenzies' front door, waiting for an answer to the bell.

"So, this is the family that discovered everything," Samantha noted as they waited.

"Yep," Richard said, aware of the fact that someone could come to the door at any second and hear them speaking. "You never met them?"

"No, speaking with them would have been beyond the scope of what we do. Our focus was solely on Michelle and trying to break down the walls her mind had created."

Richard nodded and turned to the door, a mental frown present. He rang the bell again.

No response.

"They're not home?" Samantha asked, glancing toward the cars that sat in the driveway.

"Those're their cars, so…" He didn't finish, finger ringing the bell a third time. He followed it with a firm knock that couldn't go unheard.

"Maybe they went somewhere with someone?" Samantha suggested.

"Without their cars?"

"Rental vehicle, for a Christmas vacation?" she asked, voice carrying a tone that suggested she didn't think this was the situation at all but offered it up anyway.

"I don't know, maybe, but…" He didn't have anything to add after the *but*. "I just don't know."

He looked at the cars, trying to remember how many they had. Two for sure, but maybe a third now that the kids were of driving age.

They could have gone somewhere with the third car.

Maybe out of town to get away from the horrible reminders of that Christmas nightmare all those years ago.

Have they done that before?

He would have to ask around, his knowledge of the family and their actions during the last ten years pretty much nonexistent.

* * *

Renee was lost, though she didn't really want to admit it to herself, her aimless flight from the Santa-dressed killer having brought her deep into the woods rather than toward the house as she had hoped.

Does she know the woods?

How could she if she's been in a mental institution all these years?

Is it really the girl from the mental institution?

No answer arrived.

All she knew was the girl had dark red hair, hair that had fallen over her face after she had tripped over the same vines that had snagged Renee's own foot, the Santa hat falling as she crashed face-first to the ground.

Get the ax! Renee's mind had urged.

Instead, she had run.

Now, leaning against a tree, she tried to catch her breath while her right hand pressed against a sharp cramp that had developed from running, one that reminded her of the pointless cross-country mile runs they were forced to complete in gym class every month or so. During them, she hated everything about them, but now, having fled the ax-wielding manic, she wished that was the situation she found herself in rather than the current one.

I'll run that cross-county mile every day without complaint for the rest of the year if it means getting out of this fucked-up situation.

Seconds turned to minutes as she leaned against the tree, the cold air starting to bite.

You need to keep moving.

But which way?

Though the woods were large, she knew they didn't go on forever, and if she kept walking in one direction she would come upon a town, road, or farm. That said, she also knew she couldn't stay out after dark, not in this cold and not with a snowstorm coming.

She went to check her phone to see what time it was and once again was reminded of the fact that she had dropped it.

You have three hours, four at the most, she told herself.

The sun would be setting sometime between four and five and last she had checked, it had been one o'clock in the afternoon.

She had to start moving again.

Crunch!

She froze, looking toward the trees on the right.

She couldn't have followed me this far.

Could she?

Heart racing, she held her breath and waited, cramp intensifying.

Someone was watching her. She could feel it.

Run!

She did, as fast as she could, arms once again fighting off every branch, twig, and vine that tried to stand in her way, the sleeves of her favorite leather coat suffering tear after tear as she plowed through the brush, cold air stabbing her lungs with every breath she took, legs struggling to keep her upright as each step landed upon an uneven, sometimes shifting surface.

* * *

Though he knew it would be a pointless endeavor, Steve couldn't help but stop by Hanna's place on his way home, memories of doing somber, sometimes tearful drive-bys after the breakup last year echoing through his mind as he pulled up in front of her house.

Back then, she was all he could think about, and each time he drove by, he had hoped she would come running outside, his desire to get back together erasing all the horror of the breakup. These days, she was barely a blip on his radar, even when bumping into each other at school, yet despite this, all the emotion came flooding back to him, her texts having rekindled a coal of desire that had been hidden beneath the ashes of their extinguished relationship.

Don't, he told himself as he started to pull over and park. *Just go home.*

He ignored the suggestion and got out of the car, his need to find out why she had messaged him and then stood him up too much to ignore.

No one was home.

He rang the bell five times and knocked twice.

Following that, he walked around to the side of the house to peer into the attached garage to see if their cars were there. Only one was, that one belonging to Hanna's mom.

Why didn't she answer the door?

Did the two go somewhere?

In Hanna's car?

No, if they went somewhere, they would have taken her mother's car, given that it was nicer and fit in with the standard mode that parents and children operated in when going out to-gether.

His phone rang.

He didn't recognize the number.

"Hello?"

"Steve, this is Sheriff Burke."

"Oh...um...hi," he muttered, unsure what to say.

"Hey, I've been trying to reach your father but can't get ahold of him. Someone called in about a prowler at the house to-day, and I'd like to check it out to see if they did any damage in-side."

"A prowler? When?"

"About twenty-five minutes ago."

"I was there twenty-five minutes ago."

"You were?"

"Yeah?"

"And..."

"And no one else was there."

"What were you doing there?"

"My dad wants me working there, painting and stuff."

"Speaking of painting, did you drop a can of paint on the back porch the other day?"

"What? No."

"Then do you have any idea how a giant spot of paint got on the back porch?"

"No."

"Hmm...okay. So no one was prowling around while you were there?"

"No one."

"Any idea why someone would call in and say there was

and then scream into the phone as if they were in trouble?"

"Um..." He hesitated, wondering if maybe Hanna had gone to the house to wait for him and something had happened. After all, someone had broken in not too long ago and vandalized the place.

"Steve?" Sheriff Burke asked.

"No, I have no idea why anyone would do that."

"Okay."

Steve waited.

"Has there been anything going on at the house that I should be aware of, things that your father may not want you to tell me for fear that it will hurt the chances of a sale?"

"No, nothing," he lied.

"Okay, well, if you think of something, please don't hesitate to tell me."

"I won't."

"Also, remind your father that he is required by law to disclose stuff that has occurred within the house to potential buyers, so if something has happened and he hides it, it could result in legal actions further down the road."

Steven nodded as if they were talking face-to-face and then said, "I'll be sure to tell him."

"Okay, good. And you'll come by with the key so I can take a look inside."

"Um...I need to wait and see if that's okay with my father."

The sheriff didn't say anything, yet Steve could sense frustration at his reply oozing through the phone.

"Sorry," Steve added. "If it was up to me, I'd let you in without a thought, but you know how it is."

"I do. Please have your father call me as soon as you hear from him."

"I will."

"And, Steve?"

"Yes," he said, growing weary and wanting to end this conversation.

"You sure you were alone at the house today?"

"Positive."

"Okay, well, again, let me know if anything odd happens."

"Yep."

"Thanks."

With that, the call ended.

* * *

"It may have been a prank after all," Sheriff Burke said while putting his phone away, dismay present within his voice.

"What makes you say that?" Samantha asked.

"Steve was here moments before the call about a prowler was placed and says no one else was here."

"Huh."

"Yeah."

"And you asked him about the paint," she said.

"Yeah, and he says he didn't drop it."

Though she had known this would be the case, Samantha still dwelled upon it for several seconds, her mind trying to come up with something useful.

Nothing arrived.

Richard turned and looked at the house.

Samantha followed his gaze.

"You said a little while ago that you confirmed with Detective White that Michelle Harper had a boyfriend," Richard said.

"Yeah, maybe."

"Maybe?" he questioned. "You seemed certain of it while driving here."

"Certain that someone was messaging her as if he wanted to be her boyfriend," Samantha said. "Whether or not he actually was looking to be a boyfriend...that remains to be seen."

"You think it was someone who was using her?"

"I don't know, and that prick smashed my phone before Detective White could tell me anything more."

Sheriff Burke nodded. "I'll have a talk with him about that and get the diner to buy you a new phone."

"I can get my own phone. Tell the guy who owns that place that you'll arrest him if he does anything like that again."

"He has a No Cell Phone sign up—" he started but then stopped when he caught the look she was giving him.

Silence settled.

"Sir," a voice called.

It was the deputy Sheriff Burke had sent into the woods.

"Yeah?" Sheriff Burke called as they started walking toward him.

"Didn't find a thing in there, but given how tangled up it is, someone could easily go to ground if they knew what they were doing, and we'd never find them."

"Someone with a red coat and hat on?" Samantha asked.

The deputy gave the sheriff a questioning look before glancing back at her.

"Deputy Milner, Dr. Loomis."

"Oh, you're the one who let the girl out," Deputy Milner said.

"No one let her out. She was in a children's home getting treatment, which came to an end," Samantha said.

"Yeah, a home that she had been placed in after slaughtering her entire family, and now she's—"

"Deputy," Sheriff Burke snapped, holding up a hand. "We don't know what happened with Michelle Harper, but if she is here and we do eventually have her in custody, Dr. Loomis will be invaluable in understanding what is going on with her and why she is doing the things she's doing."

"Like trying to understand a rabid dog," the deputy muttered.

The statement was like a slap in the face, one Samantha was about to respond to, but the sheriff said, "Enough!" He then followed that up with instructions to the deputy on staying at the house for the rest of his shift to keep an eye on things.

"You want me to just sit in my car and watch a house?" he questioned.

"No, I expect you to get out and patrol the property as well, so you can make sure nothing is going on in back or near the garage."

"But—"

"I'd say at least twice, maybe three times an hour."

The deputy looked dumbfounded.

"I'll let you know who is to relieve you once your shift ends."

"Waste of tax dollars," Deputy Milner said.

"Tell me about it," Samantha said. "I can't believe they pay people like you to be on the force."

The look on the deputy's face was priceless, and if it hadn't been for the sheriff escorting her away from the young man,

Samantha had a feeling things would have gotten ugly.

"What a prick," Samantha said once they were back in the SUV.

Sheriff Burke didn't say anything.

"What?" Samantha asked.

"Deputy Milner grew up here, which means he grew up hearing about how Michelle Harper slaughtered her family and then carried a head to the McKenzies' house."

"Yeah, because Detective Hines wouldn't accept any other possibilities."

"It wasn't just because of Detective Hines," Sheriff Burke said. "You know as well as I that the media also pointed a finger at her, and even if they didn't come right out and say she was responsible, they worded their stories to make everyone think she was."

Samantha conceded the point with a nod.

The media had been bad and probably would be again now that the story was spreading.

"What Would Turn an Eight-Year-Old Girl into a Butcher?"

"Are the Parents to Blame?"

"Where Was Her Father?"

"Why Would Michelle Harper Slaughter Her Family?"

"An Exclusive Look at Michelle Harper's Childhood Before the Murders!"

One would have to pay close attention to realize that the headlines weren't saying Michelle was responsible, just asking why someone like her would do such a thing. It was tricky and one of the problems with the media these days. They didn't report straight facts and instead relied on sensationalism to draw in viewers and get website clicks. It was sad and somewhat destructive to the population, as people became less and less informed without even realizing it.

"So what were you saying about the boyfriend?" Sheriff Burke asked.

"What? Oh, um, just that something doesn't seem right about that situation." Samantha explained how the two had been messaging each other like crazy up until the murder and then it stopped.

Sheriff Burke nodded. "I get what he's saying: if the two didn't meet that night, he would want to know why she stood him up. But if they did meet, that means he may have been present during the murder, or responsible for it, or have been killed during it."

"Exactly."

"And it seems really odd that someone would start talking to her online right after she moved in with her uncle."

"Not if she put up a profile online on some dating site," Samantha said.

"What do you mean?"

"From the minute their profile goes live, women will be bombarded by people trying to get in their panties."

"Oh, really?"

"Yeah."

"Well then, maybe the boyfriend aspect is nothing but coincidence. Maybe the guy was talking to other people too, and when she stopped responding he moved on."

"We need to speak with Detective White, find out if he knows anything more on that."

"Go ahead," Sheriff Burke said, handing her his cell

phone. "I have his number in there."

Caught off guard, Samantha stared at the phone for several seconds before she got control of herself and hit the call button while on the contact screen for Detective White.

"Sheriff Burke," Detective White said after two rings.

"Hi, actually, it's Samantha," she replied. "I'm using his phone since mine was busted."

"Ah, okay. What's up?"

"You learn anything else about the possible boyfriend?" Samantha asked.

"Actually, yeah. Were you aware that Michelle had a pen pal while in the children's home?"

"Yeah, lots of the children did. It was an encouraged activity, one that many of the local schools helped with by having their students write letters to our children."

"And the letters that Michelle received, did you read any of them?"

"Me, no, though there was some screening by the staff to make sure nothing inappropriate was being discussed."

"So you had no idea that Michelle's most frequent pen pal was the same young man she was talking to online?"

"Like I said, I didn't read any of the letters, and it wasn't something she ever chose to talk about with me." She could tell he was getting at something and wished he would just come out and say it instead of asking questions.

"Well, it seems she saved all the letters in a box and—"

"You found something within them that's important, something that you should stop hinting at and just tell me," she said, cutting him off.

He was silent for a moment, somewhat taken aback, it

seemed. Then, "It wasn't the content of the letters but the envelopes, which she kept the letters in. Her pen pal, who then started talking to her online and became her boyfriend, lives in Rockwood."

"Wait, what?"

"The envelopes, they're stamped as having originated in Rockwood, Illinois, and we've narrowed down the IP address for the email account of the person who was messaging her to Rockwood as well."

Samantha didn't know how to reply to that, her mind and body at a complete loss for words.

"Do you know of anyone there named Steve that might have seemed overly interested in Michelle Harper and what happened ten years ago?" Detective White asked.

* * *

The cat that came into the attic reminded her of Popeye as he crawled into her lap and started purring. With him came memories, ones she had not looked upon for years, the worst of them involving Mrs. Palmers' black-and-white cat, the burlap sack, and the fireworks. His name had been Charles because Mrs. Palmers thought it sounded distinguished and matched up well with his black-and-white tuxedo appearance. Following the fireworks, Charles hadn't looked very distinguished.

Tears arrived.

She had never really liked the games, not after they had actually hit Popeye in the face with the bottle rocket. But at least in those early days, the cats and dogs had been able to run away. Once the rope and burlap sacks came out, the animals had no chance to escape the torment. Such restraints had also allowed them to be close enough to hear the screams, which she didn't like.

And then seeing what had happened with Charles…

She pushed the thought away in horror as she watched the new cat carefully explore the attic, his nose eventually bringing him face-to-face with the severed head.

"No, no, kitty," Michelle said as he began to paw at the head, her mind not wanting to think about what she had done to quell her hunger. "Leave that be."

The cat didn't listen.

"Hey!" she snapped.

Startled, the cat looked at her for a moment but then went back to playing with a strand of hair as if it were string on the end of a ball.

Michelle sighed and went over to pick up the cat so she could sit with him. Panicked, he tried to get away, but then, as her one hand gently stroked his back, he began to calm down. Purrs followed as she carried him to the window to look outside.

The deputy was still there, sitting in his car, the others having left sometime earlier.

"Santa isn't going to like him being here," she muttered, the cat looking up at her and putting a paw to her mouth.

Michelle smiled.

"It's okay. She's not here and can't hear us right now."

The cat began to squirm.

She tightened her grip.

He squirmed even more, his back claws tearing into her stomach while his body snapped backward in what had to be a painful arc.

Michelle let go, right hand going down to the new wound without much thought, eyes following the cat as he hurried toward the stairway.

"Don't go," she said. "You're supposed to stay up here."

The cat didn't listen and went down the stairs.

"Please don't let Santa find you," she said, the sadness of that summer returning.

Fresh tears began to fall.

She went back to the brick column and sat down against it, her mind drifting back to Mrs. H. and her brother and the things she had seen while spying on them that warm summer day.

* * *

Nathan Milner stared at the clock in his cruiser, frustration getting the better of him as he counted down the minutes until seven thirty when his shift ended, anger toward the sheriff and the Samantha bitch oozing from his pores.

She should be held accountable, he said to himself. *Prosecute them both for the murders and lock them away in a cell together for the rest of their lives.*

Such action, while harsh, would make doctors like her realize that they couldn't simply release patients on a whim. In fact, it might put a stop to the pointless attempts at treating people who should simply be removed from society by either imprisonment or a death sentence. No one wanted to admit it, but some people just didn't belong in this world and needed to be cut free like an infection before it spread.

The ancient world knew this.

They didn't waste time trying to rehabilitate people who did despicable things. They acted. Swift punishments in public that were painful, ones that made everyone else think twice before they engaged in similar acts.

The people of today's world, well, those of the civilized parts, were too soft. They all wanted a kumbaya utopia that simply wasn't possible. Sure, it would be great if everyone could get along, but that wasn't the reality of the world. Never had been and never would be, and attempting to make it so just brought disaster.

But no one will listen to you.

Or anyone else who explains how the world really works.

They were all in denial and didn't want to hear the truth, and anytime anyone tried to tell them the truth they put their fingers in their ears and screamed that they were racists, bigots, or right-wing Christian gun nuts. It was sad.

Nothing you can do.

Just hunker down and let them destroy themselves so that you and everyone who knows better can rebuild things once they're gone.

The radio came to life. It was Becky.

"Milner here," he said.

"We just got a call from the McKenzies," Becky said. "They saw someone prowling around their yard and going over toward the Harper house."

"I'll check it out. Over."

If this is just some punk kid trying to scare up trouble, they're going to get a nightstick in the side of their head as a lesson! he said to himself while getting out of the vehicle.

He started toward the McKenzies' place, deciding to wrap around so that he would end up alongside the woods of the Harper house, thereby cutting off whoever it was so she couldn't go running for a vehicle parked somewhere beyond the McKenzies' place.

What if it really is the Harper girl? he asked himself as he rounded the far side of the McKenzie home, a moment of apprehension shortening his steps.

He reached down and gripped his Glock, a realization

that he could put an end to this once and for all appearing within his mind.

Avenge Hines!

Put to rest the trauma that had driven the man to the bottle as his failure to close the case got the better of him.

Avenge all of us who have been faced with progressive lib-tards who pass rules and regulations binding our hands and making it impossible for us to do our jobs.

With this thought, he pulled the gun, which he had only ever fired on the range and at stray cats lurking behind his house.

No one was in the McKenzies' backyard.

He crossed over into the scrubland between the two properties and started toward the Harper home, shadows growing quickly as the winter sun set in the west, his breath visible in the cold air as he made his way across the frozen ground.

His fingers started to stiffen within his gloves, especially the one within the trigger guard, one that was ready to squeeze should the Harper girl make her presence known.

He crossed over onto the Harper property, memories of his childhood and the stories of Mr. McKenzie coming here ten years earlier to return the cat that Michelle Harper had systematically mutilated, first with the eyes and then the whiskers and ears, echoing within his mind.

Supposedly, the cat had still been around during those days, and he and his friends had tried to find the cat but never saw it.

Now he was sure it was gone. Five years ago, they might have seen it, but after ten years, no way.

No one popped out at him.

In fact, the entire area was completely quiet, almost deserted.

The McKenzies wouldn't have called unless there was someone out here, he said to himself, eyes scanning the house.

He looked at the back door.

What if they're inside?

How would they get a key?

Maybe it's unlocked.

Less than a minute later, he was back in the yard, a test of the door having proved it was locked.

Into the woods then, he decided. If the prowler had gone anywhere else, he would have seen her for sure.

Maybe she'll freeze to death.

Once summer arrived, they would find a girl dressed in a Santa suit, body rotting, animals having eaten the best parts. Though anticlimactic, such an end might be for the best since it would prevent people like the Samantha bitch from trying to fix her.

* * *

Michelle watched as the deputy headed back to his car, a desire to pound on the window to get his attention present yet going unrealized as she simply watched, knowing that if she did get his attention in such a way, Santa would be mad and punish her.

Cut out my tongue!

And my eyes.

She could still feel the knife after all these years, the point having left an invisible mark upon her skin below her eye. And the icy chill of the razor upon her tongue.

You should have told Dr. Loomis about her, she said to herself, the memories of that summer having never gone away.

Fear had prevented it.

Fear of Santa and the power she had.

Fear of that night and the fact that she couldn't find her.

You shouldn't have said anything.

She warned you.

But—

Her brother had seen what they did to Charles and told on them.

Outside the deputy started to get into his car.

"No!" Michelle screamed and finally pounded on the window, consequences be damned.

He looked up toward her.

She tricked me.

Not Samantha, but the girl who had said her name was Steve, the one who had been writing to her for years as if she were a nice boy who wanted a relationship.

* * *

Nathan heard an odd thumping sound as he opened the driver's side door on his patrol car, and he looked up at the house, his bowels nearly releasing themselves as he realized someone was looking down at him from the attic window.

Holy shit! his mind cried.

From within the car, a hand grabbed the front of his belt and pulled.

What the—

A sickening pushing sensation arrived as something cold entered his lower stomach, his bowels releasing themselves for real this time as the blade was buried to the hilt.

It jerked to the left, his flesh and organs yielding to the razor edge.

Blood spurted from his lips as he cried out in pain, the

scream nothing but a wet-sounding *"Umph"* that barely reached his own ears.

His legs gave out, the hand releasing his belt as he crumpled to the ground.

He saw steam rising from his belly.

A chill followed, the frozen ground sucking all the warmth from him.

He reached for the radio on his chest, his hand fumbling it from the Velcro patch to the ground, where he blindly searched for it by patting the pavement.

There! he silently cried, the triumph short-lived due to the pain.

He brought the radio to his lips, thumb pressing against the broadcast button.

"No you don't," a voice said, a hand reaching out of nowhere and snatching it away.

A horrific spasm raced through his abdomen at that moment, and he felt an odd relief as something squeezed itself from within.

"You just shit yourself," the voice said, an odd astonishment present. "From your stomach!"

He refocused his eyes and saw that she was lying across the front seat of his squad car, body perched so she could look down upon his crumpled form, smiling.

"Why?" he muttered, recognizing her, the blood in his mouth and throat making the word heavy.

She grinned and then, without saying a word, reached down into his wound, causing unbearable pain as she dug around within his bowels before finding a chunk that she could grip and pulling at it.

Unable to heave properly due to the damaged muscles and pain, Nathan began choking on the bloody vomit that tried to come up, his hands clawing at his throat in an attempt to clear his airway, all while she continued to pull chunks of his bowels from his body, a playful laugh echoing in the cold winter air.

* * *

"Please, he didn't do anything!" Michelle cried as the girl held up the squirming cat by the scruff of the neck, his claws lashing out in an attempt to free himself while he let out hisses, all to no avail.

"You tried to warn him," she said.

"No."

"He saw you at the window. That's why he hesitated getting into the car."

"No. I didn't go to the window until I heard him scream and looked outside."

"He never screamed!" she shouted and with one quick motion cut the cat's throat.

Michelle screamed in horror and then jumped back as the girl threw the twitching cat at her, the chain catching on the corner of the brick column and yanking at her throat.

"You butcher your entire family yet are horrified by the slaughter of a stray cat," she said with a shake of her head, hand wiping away blood on the pant leg of her Santa suit.

"I didn't kill them," Michelle said, holding the chain that leashed her to the brick column. "It was…" She was going to say Santa but knew that wasn't right. She had just been dressed as Santa. Because it was Christmas Eve.

"Let me guess, it was Santa Claus."

"No," Michelle said.

This seemed to startle the girl. "Oh?"

Memories of that night began to surface once again and caused her to drift, the horror of watching from her hiding spot as Santa and her elf cut them up too much to bear, her mother screaming the entire time but unable to do anything.

Santa slapped her.

No, not Santa! The girl who'd pretended to be Steve. This girl!

"Admit it, you killed them!"

"No!"

The girl yanked on the chain, pulling her forward, the links digging into her throat.

"Say it! You killed them."

"I didn't!" she screamed back, knuckles turning white as she continued to hold the chain, anger growing. "You killed them!"

She didn't reply.

"You killed my uncle and Lucy!"

She grinned.

"And my brothers and sister."

The grin grew into a smile.

"You killed them, while dressed as Santa, because I told about Charles and all the other animals." A huge sense of relief filled her mind as the words left her mouth, this being the first time she had ever been able to say what had happened that night. "No, you weren't dressed as Santa. Your mom was. You were dressed as an elf."

"Well, well, guess you aren't as crazy as everyone seems to think," the girl said and came at her, knife gleaming.

Startled, Michelle backed up as far as the chain would let her and then tried to sidestep away as the girl came at her with the knife, her foot twisting out from under her as it came down onto one of the severed heads.

She felt a crack as her head hit something and saw a flash of yellow sparks, followed by darkness.

* * *

Shivering uncontrollably, Renee finally emerged from the forest into what appeared to be a field, her eyes able to make out a light in the distance, one that looked as if it were positioned high up near the roof of a two- to three-story box-like building. Beyond that were even more lights, the square shapes looking as if they were the windows of a house.

Snow began to fall.

And then a gust of wind caused her to lose her footing, crying out in agony as she fell upon the frozen ground.

"Get up!" she said, the sound of her teeth chattering filling her head.

She didn't move, body scrunching itself into a fetal position.

You'll die!

Despite the urgency, she decided to close her eyes for a moment while curled up so as to wait out the relentless wind gusts that were cutting across the field.

Just for a second.

Gotta get my strength back.

Above her, the wind continued to howl.

* * *

"I'm telling you for the hundredth time, I never wrote any letters or spent time emailing that girl," Steve said, looking down at his hands, which were fumbling with the empty Styrofoam cup that had once held water.

"Steve, tell them the truth," his mother said.

"I am telling the truth!" he snapped, anger toward her for

siding with the sheriff wanting to burst free.

His mother looked at the sheriff, who then looked at Steve.

Steve looked back at him for a few seconds and then went back to looking at the Styrofoam cup.

Tell them about the party.

No, they'll just think you're making that up too.

"Steven," the sheriff said. "Where were you Monday night?"

"Um...at home."

"Are you sure?"

"I was sleeping!" he said.

"That wasn't one of the nights you snuck out to be with that girl?" his mother asked.

"What? Mom! Stop." *Why is she trying to help them?*

"Honey, it's better if you tell the truth."

"I didn't go out that night!"

Silence settled for a moment, then...

"Earlier today, what were you doing at the Harper house?" the sheriff asked.

"My dad wants me painting."

"And yesterday, when you were there, Renee was helping you paint?"

Steve didn't reply to that.

"Why weren't you and Renee together today?" the sheriff asked.

"We had an argument yesterday."

"About?"

Steve stared at the cup.

"According to your brother, you were with a girl today,

but not Renee."

Steve continued to stare at the cup.

"Who were you with today?"

"No one."

"So your brother was lying?"

"I got stood up!" Steve snapped.

"By who?"

"By Hanna, my ex-girlfriend. She told me she wanted to get together at the Harper house, so I went there. But she never showed up, so I went back home."

Steve caught a startled look from Sheriff Burke, one that he quickly masked.

"Have you heard from Hanna at all since she contacted you this morning?"

"No."

"What about Renee?"

"No."

"I'm sure I don't have to tell you it doesn't look very good that you were interacting with two girls who now can't be found."

"What?" Steve asked.

"Renee has been missing since leaving her house this afternoon, and Hanna and her mother are both missing." He shook his head. "No one knows where they are. And Molly Mason has been missing since yesterday. What do you know about that?"

"Nothing!" he cried.

Sheriff Burke turned to Steve's mother. "We're going to hold him overnight until we can verify that his computer wasn't the one used to send those messages."

"Hold me!" Steve said. "But I didn't do anything."

"I'm going to send a deputy by to get the computer and

anything else we need from his room."

Steve thought about everything that was on his computer, all the sites he had visited, and the pictures he and Renee had taken, and the ones Hanna and Sarah had taken, and without warning, he burst into tears, the sudden onset of emotions too much for him to control.

* * *

"Do you really think he's the one?" Samantha asked.

"Hard to say," Richard said. "We'll know more once we look at his computer."

"But why would he have messaged her? And then killed her family?"

Exhausted, Richard simply shrugged.

"Sir," Becky asked. "Who did you want relieving Deputy Milner?"

"Have Kemper do swing-bys every hour," Richard said, thinking that he didn't actually need someone sitting outside the house all night. "That'll make the McKenzies feel more secure." He thought for a moment. "What ever happened with that prowler they reported?"

"Nothing, it seems."

"Did Milner report anything unusual at all while there?"

"No."

Richard thought about this for several seconds.

"Maybe because you have Steve in custody," Samantha suggested.

"That's what I was thinking, but…"

"But what?"

He shook his head.

"You don't think it was him," Samantha said.

Richard didn't reply.

"That's it, isn't it? You don't think he did it at all, but you're holding him anyway."

"Honestly, it isn't that I don't think he did or didn't do it," Richard said. "It's that I don't fully understand what it is that he did or didn't do." He looked over to make sure no one else could hear him and then, voice low, asked, "What the hell is going on here?"

It was Samantha's turn to shake her head and say, "I don't know."

He sighed.

"Sorry," she muttered.

He waved that away and said, "For nearly ten years you've been convinced that she didn't kill her family, and more recently that she didn't kill her uncle. Why? What did she tell you to convince you of this?"

"Nothing."

"Nothing," he repeated.

"Nothing," she said again. "I just know."

"How?"

"Because to do something like what happened that night, one needs to get a true sense of enjoyment out of what they are doing—not just the act of killing but the mutilation of the bodies and the writing on the walls. Michelle never behaved like someone who would get such enjoyment, and despite what many have said, there is no way she would have been successful in suppressing it or hiding it during her years at the children's home."

"But she is the one who wrote 'Santa took them' on the wall."

"Yes, because she was trying to convey a message, one

that rings true with the bits and pieces she was able to recall from that night, that someone dressed as Santa was responsible for the murders."

"Why not just write the name of the person who was dressed as Santa?" Richard muttered. "That would have been a bit more helpful, don't you think?"

Samantha stared at him for several seconds and then said, "Imagine that you were eight years old, and that you hid after your mother went to bed so you could try and catch a glimpse of Santa coming down the chimney and putting toys out for Christmas. Then imagine falling asleep while in that hiding spot and waking up to seeing someone dressed as Santa butchering your family and putting the heads by the chimney." She paused for a moment. "What do you think that would do to your eight-year-old mind?"

Richard thought about what she said, and while he understood what she was getting at, he still thought it was possible that Michelle had been responsible. Not that she *was* responsible, but the possibility existed. Debating that wasn't something he was going to get sucked into, however, so he said, "Let's say that she didn't do it and that someone dressed as Santa was responsible. Why kidnap her, kill her family, and come back here? And if it is Steve, as the name on the letters and messages suggests"—*would you have suspected him if it wasn't for his involvement with that house?*—"what is his motivation? Do you think he was the one who dressed up as Santa all those years ago and slaughtered her family?"

"No, obviously not," Samantha said, a pissy tone present in her voice.

"Then who was it back then, and who is it now? I find it highly unlikely that a completely different individual would strive to commit the same type of murders, but then if it was the same individual, why did they wait all this time to do it again?"

"Maybe the murders themselves weren't the purpose of the homicide, at least not in a thrill sense that you get from a person who gets pleasure from such acts. Maybe there was a reason that the family was murdered, one that the Santa elements were added to as a distraction, one that wasn't a complete success since Michelle survived, and now that individual is trying to finish what was started."

"Why not simply kill her then?"

"Because that may draw attention to the fact that she wasn't responsible for the murders ten years ago and cause people to dig a bit deeper into it. With her disappearing after her family was murdered and then making it look like she came back here, if that is what is taking place, people will just focus on her and the fact that she shouldn't have been put back into society."

"Sounds way too elaborate," Richard said, though at the same time he heard a ring of plausibility in what she was saying. "And let's not forget that we haven't actually seen any 'Santa took them' style murders here."

"No, you haven't, but this is where the letters and messages to Michelle came from, and you now have several people unaccounted for as well as prowler reports that feature someone dressed as Santa around the house where the murders took place."

Richard thought it was a stretch to imply that several people were missing, though the term *unaccounted for* was accurate. He knew the word *missing* was what she wanted to say but couldn't because then the only one she could use as an example for that comment would be Molly Mason, who had no connections to the Harper house at all.

But Sarah does, and Hanna, both of whom haven't been seen or heard from since this morning, and someone had sent him that photo.

"So if Michelle was brought back here, where is she?" Richard asked, pushing aside his thoughts on Sarah and Hanna.

"At the Harper house would be my guess, or somewhere near there."

"This entire time?" he asked, his mind unable to accept her answer. "Without anyone realizing it?"

"Well, you just booked the one person who has had the most access to the house. In fact, he is the only one who has really been inside it, so if he is responsible, which you obviously feel is a possibility since you have him locked up, then he could easily have been keeping someone prisoner there without anyone else knowing."

"His father was there too, and Renee."

"Both of whom are among the ones that can't seem to be located…" She raised an eyebrow while saying this in a "you want to explain that?" way.

"You really think she's there?" he asked, a large part of his mind thinking that she might be correct.

"Logically, I think it's worth checking out."

"Well then, let's check it out."

"What?"

"The house," he said, enjoying the surprise her face showed. "I have a key now, thanks to Steve being in custody, and I think a look inside the place is long overdue."

"But his father?" Samantha asked.

"Isn't responding to any calls and looks to have stepped out on his wife again for the evening."

Samantha nodded.

* * *

Was getting hold of the key the real motivation for booking Steve? Samantha wondered as they navigated the dark snowy streets toward the Harper home. *Was having the same name as the person who sent the messages enough for such action, even with the connections to the house?*

No answers arrived.

"What was she like?" Sheriff Burke asked.

"What do you mean?" Samantha asked back.

"Michelle," he said, eyes watching the street. "As a kid, what was she like?"

Samantha thought about this for several seconds, questions on what his motive was for asking entering her mind. Most wanted to hear how horrible and demonic Michelle was and what Samantha's own feelings were when sitting across from someone who was pure evil. *Could you see it in her eyes? Were they black and void of life? Was she always thinking of ways to kill you while you sat there?* Her answers always disappointed them, especially when she revealed that the two would often leave the office and walk around the gardens and stream behind the children's home, picking flowers or throwing grapes to the ducks. *She got upset with me once for bringing bread because she had read that it was actually bad for the ducks and they would be in pain if they ate it.*

"You never met her?" Samantha asked, refocusing the question.

"No," he said, turning the wheel. "She was already gone by the time I arrived at the house. All I remember was seeing what had happened, the heads by the fireplace, the mother dead in her own excrement, the children's bodies, and the writing on the wall."

"I'm guessing it was pretty horrible."

"Yes, it was."

"And I'm also guessing that right away you were told that Michelle was responsible."

He didn't reply.

"I was told she was a psychotic killer who had slaughtered her family before I met her, and I had heard news stories," Samantha said, remembering sitting down with the file and seeing some of the photos of the scene. Not the really graphic ones, but ones that were graphic enough to cause a feeding frenzy among the media.

"And did you believe them?" he asked.

"It wasn't a matter of believing or disbelieving them. My job was to talk to her and find out why she had killed them and what the best course of action would be from that point onward."

"And it was during that process that you came to believe her to be innocent?"

Samantha nodded.

A gust of winter wind hit the vehicle, and for a moment, she thought she could feel the chill of it enveloping her.

Or was that just in my mind?

She shivered.

"Her appearance wasn't what I expected when I first met her. She was well put together, wearing a blouse, sweater, and skirt, the outfit surprising me because many of the children wore clothes that were pretty tattered and threadbare. They had full wardrobes, but most of it was from donations or bought at Goodwill by the doctors when the donations ran thin, so it was all pretty worn. Occasionally, some also had items from their families, which, interestingly, was the case here. Her uncle, despite only being sixteen years old, had gone out and gotten her clothes. She had an entire closet and dresser full of clothing, all of it bought with the income he had made from a part-time job."

"He was the one who was murdered the other night?"

"Yeah." She waited a moment and then, when he didn't ask anything else, continued. "What piqued my interest right away was when I learned that she had dressed herself without prompting. According to the staff, she was catatonic. Fully functioning but wouldn't communicate with anyone and would pretty much stay in the same place all day long unless prompted to move. Yet she dressed herself for our first session together, and I think she chose her clothing because she wanted to present herself to me in a way that would knock away any preconceived notions I had about her."

"An eight-year-old?" he asked with a sound of disbelief. "No offense, but I think you're reading too much into things."

"Maybe, but even if she didn't do it on purpose, even if it was just a random collection of clothes she put on—her Sunday best as it were, since that is what she wore to the church services at the home as well, without prompting, mind you—it did the trick. When I walked in and saw her, I removed my initial thoughts on her being a killer, which put my mind at ease, and I just viewed her as a little girl who needed my help."

"So you did think she was a killer when you first met her."

Samantha sighed. "Yes. I had heard the stories and saw the file and was a bit apprehensive about seeing her for the first time."

"Like Jodie Foster meeting Hannibal Lector?" he asked.

"She was eight years old."

"An eight-year-old who had been painted pretty harshly

by everyone."

"Yes, and many thoughts were racing through my mind before I went to see her, especially considering that I had never dealt with anyone who had been accused of such horror before."

"What were the typical children cases that you were handling at that time like?" he asked.

"I can't discuss that," she said. "Patient-doctor confidentiality."

"Yeah, yeah. I know she was one of your first patients, that you had only been out of school for a short period of time, and that one of the reasons you got that case was because no one else wanted it for fear that it would turn into an anchor weighing them down from climbing higher on the ladder of the career field that you all work in."

Samantha felt anger rising at the statement but then pushed it aside. He wasn't being mean; he was just stating a fact, one that did nothing but highlight that she had been inexperienced at the time and stuck with a case no one else wanted.

"I also know that being young and fresh means you probably handled things a bit differently than most would have, and that might have been exactly what Michelle needed."

Samantha nodded.

"So what I want to know is, was it her outfit that told you she wasn't a killer, which, honestly, wouldn't amount to much in the way of persuading me or anyone else, or was it your time with her? What did she do that proved to you she wasn't a killer and made it so you decided to race out here once you felt this was her destination? Like you're her guardian, so to speak, so that once she's apprehended you can be there for her and protect her."

"Honestly," Samantha said, "I don't know. I wish I could

tell you something that would convince you of this, but I can't."

You have to give him more!

But there isn't anything more.

* * *

Renee felt as if a warm blanket had been put over her, one that was actually making her sweat.

She tried throwing it off.

Confusion followed.

No blanket was upon her.

I'm on the ground!

In a field.

Gotta get help.

She tried to stand, but her legs wouldn't move, and her arms wanted to stay folded beneath her.

NO!

Pain erupted as she forced her arms out from under her, the blood racing back toward her fingers, her teeth grinding together against the pins and needles.

A minute passed, then two before the pain began to subside, tears freezing to her cheeks during the process.

She began to crawl, her legs slowly but surely coming alive once again.

And then she stood.

The wind tried to knock her down.

She fought against it, somehow knowing that if she lay down again she would die. She had to stay on her feet and move toward the lights. She had to get help.

Something appeared before her.

It looked like a giant rectangular frame of some kind, one that was stuck in the middle of the field.

Confused, she continued toward it, the snowy darkness yielding more of its shape as she got closer and closer.

A goalie net!

Only the net was gone, taken inside the field house where it would stay until spring, the frame itself left outside since it could endure all kinds of weather without a problem.

She was on the soccer field, the one the school team practiced on, which meant the building in front of her with the light on the corner was the school.

And beyond that, where the square of light was earlier, a house!

All she had to do was keep walking through the field, about a quarter of a mile, and she would be at the main entrance of the school, able to cross the road that led into the neighborhood beyond it.

"Just keep moving!" she said, head angled downward as she walked to keep her face from being pounded by the wind. *One step after another.*

* * *

"Wait here," Richard instructed as he opened the door and began to step out, the sight of the empty patrol vehicle making him uneasy.

"Maybe I should —" Samantha started, hand on her door.

"Stay in the vehicle!" Richard snapped.

A gust of wind hit, knocking the door against him.

"Fuck," he muttered, not in pain but simple frustration, hands thrusting the door back open.

Cold snowy air enveloped him.

Samantha said something that he couldn't hear, the wind having grown too fierce.

A moment later, the door shut.

Is he actually checking out the house? Richard wondered as he neared the patrol vehicle, doubt at the possibility arriving instantly. And then he saw what looked to be blood on the pavement near the driver's side door, the wind having kept the snow cover thin enough for it to be seen.

He peeked into the window of the vehicle.

No one was inside.

He tried the handle.

Locked.

A voice reached his ears.

He turned back toward his vehicle.

Samantha was standing between his vehicle and the patrol car, body braced against the wind, shouting to him.

He couldn't make out what she was saying, but seeing her out and about after he had told her to stay inside frustrated him.

"What?" he asked, moving closer.

"Did you" — a gust of wind cut her off — "find anything?"

"No, nothing," he shouted. "Now wait in the vehicle while I check out" — more wind — "the house!"

"I think I should come with!"

"No!"

"But—" she started.

"NO!"

With that, he turned toward the house, keys from Steve ready to be used, mind noting the exact position of his sidearm, even though he doubted he would need it.

The front steps groaned with his weight, the cold having stiffened the wood. The porch also didn't like his presence.

Why did Henry ever think he could flip this place? he asked himself. *Why couldn't he have just left this place alone?*

The questions echoed through his mind as he fumbled with the key, his fingers completely frozen despite the gloves he wore.

The key didn't work.

What the fuck?

Back door?

He started around to the back, wincing as the icy wind battered his face, snot running from his nose through his mustache and onto his lips.

A swipe with his sleeve did little to clean up the mess. It also revealed that parts of his mustache were beginning to freeze, any warmth the snot had held when leaving his nose fading fast once it was within the facial growth.

The back porch did not groan as he climbed up the steps, but the lack of sound might have only been due to the wind, which was now producing a constant howl.

This time the door opened without a problem when he put the key into the lock.

He stepped inside, the warm windless air a huge relief. Exhaustion hit, a yawn actually stretching his face.

Once it passed, he stood in the middle of the back room, listening, but the only sound was that of the wind battering the house.

Feels empty, he noted.

Even so, he started into the main room to look around, flashlight guiding the way until he found a light switch.

* * *

Samantha didn't like being left in the SUV and still felt a sting from the way Sheriff Burke had snapped at her. The lack of a phone or any way of communicating with him also concerned her.

What if someone dressed as Santa appears?

What if they go inside?

She would have no way of warning him.

Unless…

She looked at the radio setup and wondered if it was possible to contact Sheriff Burke directly, or if she would have to contact Becky at the station—or whoever was there during the night—
who would then contact him. If the latter, the message relay could
prove costly if the warning didn't get to him in time.

*There has to be a way to send a general broadcast out, one that
he would be able to hear.*

Thinking about movies she had seen, she picked up the
handset on the radio and pressed the button on the side, a statement of "Test, test, test" going out.

Nothing.

She released the button and then pressed it again, but if it
did anything, she couldn't tell.

Next, she fumbled with some of the buttons, but nothing
that she twisted or pressed seemed to have an effect.

A realization arrived. She hadn't heard the radio at all
while they had been driving here. The one he wore on him, yes,
but the car one, no. And earlier, when driving, she had heard this
one, because she remembered him switching it off to cut the chatter
while they were speaking.

How do you turn it on?

She started looking for a switch but then stopped, a light
from the house catching her off guard. The entire first floor was
now illuminated.

Seeing this, she looked out toward the McKenzies' house,
thoughts of how they had called earlier to report a prowler while

she had been at the station arriving in her mind. She also remembered Richard making a statement on how they didn't seem to be home even though their cars were in the driveway.

No lights were on there.

If they were, she should have been able to see the glow, even with the distance and the storm.

Maybe not...

Go check.

Hesitation arrived.

She looked at the Harper house and saw movement by the window as the sheriff passed through the front room. He seemed to be heading toward the stairs. Room by room, he was being methodical, which probably meant she would have time to check out the McKenzie place and see if anyone was home.

Or have him check it out once he gets back.

The hesitation continued.

She knew he would be pissed at her if she did it herself, but at the same time, she didn't like just sitting in the vehicle, especially when there was no way for her to communicate with anyone.

Anger toward the owner of the diner appeared once again. Adding to it was the knowledge that nothing would change. Whatever the malfunction was that drove him to act that way when frustrated would likely continue. He needed help, mentally, but it was doubtful he would ever get it. That was the problem with the world they lived in. Most would rather live with their mental issues than risk the stigma that could arrive from seeking out help.

Light appeared in the middle window of the second floor, and though she had never been inside, she was familiar enough with the layout to know that it was the second-floor landing light that had been switched on. The window she could now see was set in the wall between the two bedrooms at the front of the house, one being a standard bedroom, and the other being the master bedroom, which had its own bathroom and stairway within the closet that went up into a small semi-attic space. Two more bedrooms were at the rear of the house, along with a bathroom. It was in the far rear bedroom where the children's bodies had been found, the bloody "Santa took them" message on the wall. The closet in that room also had a stairway up to the main attic, which had been used as a playroom when the children were young, given that it had a floor and quite a bit of space to scatter things around on.

The light in the master bedroom went on.

Samantha turned her attention back toward the McKenzie home.

Just do it, she said to herself and started to step out of the vehicle, her hands having to push the door with all her strength as the wind tried to close it on her.

And then she had no door between her and the relentless wind, her hands making fists in her coat pockets as her body hunched against the bitter onslaught.

"*No, no, no,*" she said after four steps, a realization that she could not walk in these conditions hitting home. She would wait for the sheriff to come back and share her suspicions.

She hurried back to the vehicle and grabbed the handle.

Locked.

NO!

Struggling to stay upright, she ran to the driver's side and tried that handle. It too was locked.

FUCK! FUCK! FUCK!

Shivering, she looked at the house, willing the sheriff to

come back. Instead, the ground-floor lights went out.

* * *

Once at the school, Renee discovered that the building shielded her from the wind, which was coming from her left. This was a huge relief, though one that would be short-lived as she stepped out of its protection and crossed the front lawn of the school and then the road and then the backyards of the homes that backed up to the school, her hope being that she could find an opening in the wooden fences that shielded those houses from the road.

Or get into the school.

The reality of this happening seemed unlikely, however, her frozen hands discovering every door to be locked as she gave each a yank while passing them.

And then the school building ended and she had nothing but a field to cross before she came upon the road, which hadn't had a single car passing by this entire time.

She didn't want to go out there.

The wind was too strong, and the snow it carried felt like tiny pins hitting her face.

You can't stay here, she told herself, her body huddled beneath the overhang at entrance one, which was where the buses dropped everyone off, the overhang protecting against rain when it was falling. *But not against wind or the cold.*

If she stayed here, even hunched up against the wall, she would die.

You made it this far.

Through the woods, through the sports fields, and alongside the school...

All she had to do was cross the second field, which was probably only a third the size of the previous field, and then the road.

Now or never, literally.

She took a deep breath, then a second and third, and then pushed herself from the wall and left the protection of the building, body being knocked to the ground by the wind.

* * *

Richard had considered calling for backup while still on the ground floor, his eyes staring at the word *Santa* written in what appeared to be blood on the hallway wall, an arrow beneath it pointing to the front living room where an oddly placed, unlit Christmas tree was standing.

Instead, he'd left the radio alone and drawn his gun, a decision to sweep the second floor and attic by himself unfolding, a decision he now regretted as he lay on his back, stomach and chest opened from the repeated chops from the ax, organs visible, blood flowing through a gap of torn flesh and shattered ribs on his right side.

"*Why?*" he asked, voice wet with blood.

She didn't answer, just looked down at him.

He gagged, a combination of blood, bile, and shit coming up from his lower body to trickle from his mouth, his stomach unable to spasm properly to get any force behind it.

His throat felt clogged.

Several more gags erupted, but none of them were strong enough to clear his airways.

Panic set in.

He lifted his right hand, fingers working at his throat to try to move everything up to his mouth.

It didn't work.

He needed air.

She stepped into view, the end of the Santa hat swaying toward him as she leaned in.

Please! he tried to say, his vocal cords failing to generate any sound.

She took a deep breath and lifted the ax high above her head before bringing it down into his stomach, a wet splash echoing before the *thunk* as the blade landed upon the liquidy mess of exposed organs, clumps of blood flying up at her and the walls.

Though he didn't hear it, a horrific crunch echoed within the room as the blade crushed through his lower spine and into the hardwood floor beneath him.

* * *

Unable to get back to her feet, Renee crawled to the road, her gloveless hands completely numbed from the cold and feeling like nothing but rubber lumps each time she put one on the ground to hold her weight while the other reached forward.

And then came the pavement, the frozen sharpness of the torn-up shoulder bringing a bit of life back into her left palm via the pain that raced through it as jagged edges cut the flesh.

Lights!

A car is coming.

She tried to stand up but couldn't and instead braced herself on her knees and waved her arms in the air, wind trying to force her back down.

The car drew closer.

And closer...

And closer...

And then passed her without slowing, her face bombarded by unknown particles that flew at her from the vehicle as it sped by.

Tears burst from her eyes, the feeling of defeat too much for her to continue onward.

She was going to die.

Freeze to death on the side of the road, fifty feet from salvation.

* * *

Sitting up against the wall, a hand to her head where the windowsill had cracked it in her fall, Michelle tried to understand what it was she had just heard down below, the commotion having yanked her from the unconsciousness that had plagued her ever since the fall.

It had sounded like screams from a man, but she wasn't sure, each one punctuated by the sound of a heavy wet *thump* before all went silent.

She vomited.

It hit without warning, the horrific bile and chewed-up tongue concoction ripping at her throat as it spewed forth upon the attic floor, the lifeless eyes of the girl's severed head looking up at her with what would have been disinterest if she still had been alive.

Footsteps—*hurried ones*—came up the stairs, and suddenly the Santa girl was there, fleshly bloodied, coming toward her, pausing only to lean the ax against the brick column.

"Everything's fucked," she said, right forearm wiping at her face, smearing blood. "You were supposed to kill everyone tomorrow night at the party, but now"—she grabbed the chain and pulled—"we'll have to rewrite things a bit."

Michelle grabbed the chain herself, trying to prevent it from cutting into her throat again.

The girl pulled harder.

Rather than resist, Michelle came to her feet and then, seeing the slack in the chain as she stumbled forward, had a sudden idea.

She charged.

Startled, the girl took a step back and turned to reach for the ax.

Michelle looped the chain around her throat before she could get to it and pulled.

The sound the girl made as she was yanked backward was incredibly pleasing, and for the first time since the night of her abduction, Michelle felt as if everything was going to be all right. All she had to do was keep hold of the twisted chain until the girl stopped kicking and—

Stars erupted as something hit her in the face, and then she felt the chain slide through her loosened fists.

NO!

Another blow landed, this one even harder than the first one, and she fell to the ground, her legs simply unable to support her weight.

Coughing, the girl stumbled away from her, and while Michelle couldn't see her due to focusing on her own situation, she pictured her with a hand to her throat, moving toward the ax.

Get up.

Get to it first.

A hand was on the chain.

She focused her eyes and saw the girl standing over her, hand working at the chain.

CLICK!

The sound echoed in her ears.

The chain fell away.

What?

She freed you.

The girl stepped back.

Michelle stared at her and then looked at the ax that stood between them, and then back at the girl, who had also looked at the ax.

Confusion paralyzed her.

Why did she do that?

Was she planning to free me all along?

The girl started toward the ax.

* * *

Arms struggling to hold in warmth, Samantha hurried from the front door of the Harper home, which was locked, to the back door, which, to her surprise, was standing open.

An invitation to come inside?

Like a lamb to the —

NO!

She cut the voice off and stepped through the door, heading to the left to where she knew a wall would be, her back pressing against it while her eyes tried to focus on the dark room and see if there were any immediate threats.

Nothing.

The room was empty.

The house wasn't though, sounds of movement directly above her passing through the floor.

That's the bedroom with the stairway attic.

Is that Sheriff Burke moving around?

She considered calling out to him, the sound of his voice something that she wanted to hear to set her mind at ease, but didn't. Fear of what it could do to him if he was still alive—or what it would do to her if the killer were lurking just beyond the door— kept her foolishness at bay.

More sound echoed up above.

Though she liked her position near the door, she edged herself closer to the hallway and then into it, guided by thoughts on how she might be able to get a better grasp of what was going on up there if she was closer to the actual stairway. It was also warmer in the hallway than it was in the back room, and if something happened where she had to race back out into the cold, it would be better to do it once her body had warmed up a bit, thus giving her a chance to make it to the road and beyond.

Something wet touched her neck.

Startled, she pushed away from the wall and spun around, her eyes just barely able to see that something was written there.

Her hand found a light switch.

Hesitation arrived.

Darkness is their ally, not yours.

She flipped the switch and gasped. "Santa" was written in blood, an arrow beneath it pointing into the family room.

Go back, wait by the door, and then run to the McKenzies' place once you're warm.

But Sheriff Burke is up there!

He WAS up there.

How she knew something had happened to him, she did not know, but her gut was telling her it was so and that nothing good would come of investigating further.

She retreated into the back room but then sidestepped into the kitchen, a sudden desire for a weapon guiding her to the drawers where she hoped to find a knife.

Nothing.

Judging by the freshness of everything, the kitchen had been remodeled recently, which meant even if everything had been left behind after the murders ten years ago and somehow stayed inside the house after all the break-ins and souvenir hunts, it would have been tossed out during the gutting process.

But what about tools!

If the place was still in the process of being remodeled, which was what it seemed like based on everything she had heard, then why weren't there any tools left here?

Because of the break-ins.

But maybe...

She approached a door in the kitchen, one that stood next to the pantry, her hand quietly twisting the knob and pulling.

A dark stairway into an even darker basement loomed before her.

Would anything be down there?

Don't!

Just go to the McKenzies'.

Break in and use their phone to call for help.

Leaving the door open, she backed out of the kitchen and started toward the back door but then stopped, the wind outside sounding stronger and more intimidating than it had been when she came around the house.

You might not even be able to make it to the McKenzies'.

But you can't stay in here.

Indecision plagued her.

* * *

Renee felt hands upon her body and, thinking it was the Santa killer, started kicking and screaming, her feet landing a good solid blow, one that caused a cry to escape from her attacker.

And then she was being hoisted up into the air, her physical protests no match for the strength in the arms that lifted her.

Warmth followed as she was set down upon a soft, slanted surface, one that felt familiar yet couldn't be placed within her frozen mind.

Unconsciousness returned.

* * *

Seeing the girl go for it, Michelle lunged for the ax herself, noting at the last second before grabbing it that the girl had stopped after just a step or two and waited.

Ax in hand, Michelle stared at her.

What is she doing?

She could have easily gotten it first.

The girl took a step back toward the stairs.

Michelle matched it.

Something's wrong.

Don't follow her.

The girl took another step.

Michelle stayed where she was.

A final step put the girl near the stairs. It was at this point that Michelle realized the girl was not wearing her Santa clothing.

The girl turned and headed down the stairs.

Michelle followed, memories of going up and down these steps as a child dominating her mind, especially the ones when she had crept down to spy on her brother and Mrs. H. making their little movies.

At the bottom she stepped through the closet door, ax ready, eyes looking for the girl.

A body was lying on the floor, one that had a coat with a

patch on its sleeve.

>*Sheriff's department.*

>*His gun is gone.*

Movement.

Michelle looked up.

The girl was standing in the doorway, gun in hand, the barrel pointing directly at her.

* * *

Outside, the wind continued to howl, the gusts so strong that they were shaking the house. Uncertain about what to do, Samantha stayed huddled in the corner, ready to dart out through the door should anyone start down the hallway toward the room.

While huddled, she kept thinking about Sheriff Burke. Something had happened to him. Of this she had no doubt. What concerned her now, however, was whether he needed help or was beyond being helped. What if he was slowly bleeding to death from some injury and could be saved if help arrived in time? What if her hesitation was killing him?

>*What if someone is up there waiting for you to try to help?*

Heroism and stupidity often went hand in hand, and in this situation the latter would be the dominant player if she went up the stairs.

>*The best thing you can do is go call for help.*

To do that she would need to get to the McKenzies' and, if they didn't answer the door, which she didn't think they would do, break inside somehow and use the phone.

She went to the back door, cold air engulfing her as it battled the warm air inside for dominance.

>*What if you can't get inside?*

>*You can't stay here.*

Eventually whoever was upstairs would come down to get her.

Do they know I'm here?

She turned toward the hallway, which was still bathed in light.

They know.

Go!

She turned back to the doorway and was about to go through it when she heard a new noise upstairs, one that sounded like heavy footsteps.

She looked up at the ceiling.

A sudden scream for help echoed, followed by several gunshots and a crash of something heavy.

* * *

Realization of the trick entered Michelle's mind seconds before the first impact, her ears not hearing the blast until after the bullet struck.

Several more shots followed, some of them hitting her, some not, the ax eventually falling from her hands onto the floor.

Somehow, she was still standing, but that didn't last, her legs eventually giving out and causing her to crumple next to the body near the stairs, a coppery taste mixing with the bile in her mouth.

Questions started to appear but went unasked.

She then started to lose her grip on consciousness, the last thing she saw being the Santa girl sans the Santa suit leaning against the corner of the room, body slowly oozing down, gun still pointed at her, tears bursting forth from her eyes.

December 24, 2015

Samantha got back to her motel room around four in the morning, the wind having finally died down to the point where the snow was able to fall with a picturesque Christmas-card style.

Exhaustion enveloped her, and while she wanted to take a shower, she couldn't bring herself to even take off her coat and fell asleep on top of the bedsheets.

Flashes of the horror that had unfolded mixed with fabrications from her mind and plagued her dreams, making her sleep restless and disjointed, her eyes opening several times in a panic before closing again and forcing her back into the semi-reality-based netherworld.

And then there was a heavy knock on the door that pulled her from sleep. It was the motel manager. He had gotten a call from Detective White asking if he could pass on a message that he was heading into town and would like to meet up with her.

* * *

Forty minutes later, showered and somewhat presentable despite the exhaustion that plagued her mind and body, Samantha greeted Detective White outside her door, her parted curtains having allowed her to see him pulling into the snowy parking spot next to her car.

"Looks like we'll have a white Christmas," he said in greeting.

"Yeah," she replied, the word punctuated by a yawn.

"When did they finish with you?"

"About three thirty this morning."

"Yikes. Well, my treat if you're hungry for breakfast."

Sleep followed by a drive back to her home was the only thing she was really craving right now, but she nodded anyway and let him drive her into town, which, thanks to the unplowed roads and the snow that was still falling, took another forty minutes.

Five minutes after arriving in town, they were seated at a booth in Kathy's Place, the owner's protests about having her back in his restaurant cut short by the badge that Detective White shoved in his face. "It was me she was talking to yesterday when you ruined her phone, and because of that, a killer was able to roam free longer than she should have been able to."

"I-I—"

"Apologize profusely and gladly provide fresh coffee and breakfast on the house so as to minimize our desire to highlight the role you played in this serial killer's reign of terror when *Dateline* decides to do a special on it."

The owner stared at him for several seconds and then nodded, his hands fumbling with two menus that he handed over to a young waitress who had overheard everything, a statement about getting them whatever they wanted leaving his lips.

"Thought you said this was going to be your treat," Samantha said, a smile breaking out.

"It totally is," he said. "Who else but I could have charmed him like that into giving us free food?"

"Charmed him so much that everyone in back will probably shoot snot wads into our food."

"Welcome to the world of law enforcement." He paused

while the waitress came over with a pot of coffee and filled their mugs. "Enduring such treatment is one reason why those on patrol should never, ever order from a drive-through."

"Really?" she asked, grimacing.

"Sadly, yeah, and after all the recent media coverage on shootings and cops behaving badly, it's now a risk more than ever before."

"Ugh, sorry."

He shrugged and opened the menu, looked at it for a moment, and then put it back down. "So what the hell happened last night?"

"You don't know?" she asked, her question genuine.

"No. The local law enforcement is in complete chaos now that the sheriff is dead, and their line is clogged with media calls." He took a sip of his coffee and winced at the heat. "I woke up this morning without knowing a thing about what had happened, even though I should have been notified right away, and then saw a *Breaking News* alert when I turned on the TV. The media doesn't really know much either, but they're going with a story on how an escaped mental patient, aka Michelle, killed her family—uncle and his girlfriend—and then chopped her way through several local teens, some adults, a deputy, and the sheriff before she was shot to death by her next potential victim, a seventeen-year-old girl named Hanna Hines, who, coincidently, was the daughter of the detective who got the original case all those years ago."

"That about sums it up," Samantha said with a sigh and started adding sugar to her coffee. A careful sip followed.

Detective White eyed her during this and then said, "No, I don't think it does."

"Why not?"

"Because you still don't believe Michelle was the killer."

"She was shot to death while going after a teenage girl with an ax."

"A teenage girl who, for some reason, was kept prisoner all day when others were simply killed, one who then somehow got hold of the sheriff's gun and then shot Michelle to death as she came after her with an ax."

Samantha didn't say anything.

"How long were you inside the house before Michelle was shot?" he asked.

"Um...I don't know, ten, maybe fifteen minutes."

"And you didn't hear the fight at all?"

"No, not until they were on the second floor right above my head. But with the wind outside"—she shook her head—"it was the only thing you could really hear, especially with that door open."

Detective White thought about this for a moment and then looked as if he was going to say something but stopped as the waitress came by to take their orders, a whispered "Thank you for putting the owner in his place" leaving her lips before she headed back to the kitchen.

Detective White gave her a smile and, once she was out of earshot, turned back to Samantha and said, "I don't think we have anything to worry about with our food being defiled."

Samantha nodded and then quietly asked, "You really don't think Michelle was responsible for all this?"

"I don't, and I know you don't either, which is why I came out here."

Samantha didn't reply.

"You didn't fuck up," he said. "I know it, and you know

it. Something more was going on here than Michelle simply coming here to kill people after all these years." He took a sip of his
coffee. "Unfortunately, I'm guessing we're the only two who think
that. I'm also fairly positive that you're going to get dumped on by
the media, especially once the desire to lay fault upon someone
appears."

"Yeah." She gave a weak smile. "They always have to find
someone to be angry with, and since her parents are dead and she
wasn't one to play video games…"

"Exactly." He took another sip of his coffee. "Making
things worse, they're all going to want to believe that she was responsible, which will nullify any doubts they have when it comes
to Hanna's story."

"But why would someone bring her out here and try to
make it seem like she was responsible?" Samantha asked.

"That is the million-dollar question, one that won't get
answered by those who think everything is now packaged up in a
Case Closed box."

* * *

Panicked at the unfamiliar surroundings and thinking the Santa
killer was going to get her, Renee tried to get out of the bed she
found herself in, a sharp pain erupting within her arm as she
twisted to the left.

An IV, she said to herself, watching as the needle swayed
in the air beneath the bag that had been pumping some sort of
fluid into her, fluid that was now dripping onto the floor.

Blood bubbled from her arm.

She clamped a hand over the tear and looked around for a
call button, which she found on a control sitting on a table that
could slide out over her should a meal be brought.

Or my computer, she thought to herself.

Will I be here long enough to where I need it?

A nurse came in while she was thinking this, gave a brief rundown of why she was there—someone had found her freezing to death on the side of the road—replaced the IV, and then said her mother would be there shortly now that she had woken up.

"Did they catch the person who was chasing me?" Renee asked as the nurse was starting to leave.

"Who was chasing you, dear?"

"That girl dressed like Santa."

The nurse's face changed and she suddenly said, "I'll be right back," and hurried down the hallway.

Confused, Renee stared at the door for several seconds and then, just as she was about to figure out how the TV worked, watched as the nurse returned with another nurse, this one seemingly in a position of authority.

"You say you were being chased by the Santa killer and that's why you ended up nearly freezing to death?" the new nurse asked.

"Um…yeah," Renee said. "She chased me into the woods. I tried calling for help, but the idiot nine-one-one person couldn't figure out where I was, and then I got lost for hours."

"And eventually came out by the high school."

Renee nodded, memories of the cold and the wind causing a shiver to race through her.

"Okay, you're going to need to talk to the police."

"What happened?" Renee asked.

"Let's wait until the police get here."

"But—"

The new nurse left, the original nurse following in her

wake.

Confused, Renee stared at the door and then went back to trying to figure out the TV, which, as it turned out, was fairly simple given that there was a TV button at the top of the remote she had used to call the nurse.

* * *

Even though she was the one who had reminded the sheriff's department to release him now that the real killer had been found, Steve wouldn't talk to his mother and did nothing but stare out the window as she drove him home.

"The police took your computer," Kyle said after coming into Steve's room.

"No shit, Sherlock," Steve said, hand motioning to the empty spot on his desk. Then, seeing the hurt on his brother's face, he sighed and apologized.

"Hanna killed the killer."

"I heard." They had been talking about that at the station. And the fact that Sheriff Burke was dead. They also had found severed heads, one of them belonging to their father.

Steve wasn't sure how to feel about that.

Though the man had been a prick, there were still good memories of them together, memories that he couldn't help thinking about now and wishing they could relive.

Downstairs, the doorbell rang.

News people? Steve wondered. Several reporters had been outside the sheriff's department, though not as many as he had expected given all the excitement about cameras and reporters from the deputies.

"Steve," his mother called, no explanation following.

Steve left his room and went to the top of the stairs. From

there he could see two people in the entryway, one of whom was the lady from the other day who had been with Sheriff Burke.

"Hey, Steve," the man said. "I'm Detective White with the Elm Grove Police Department. Mind if we talk for a bit?"

Steve didn't want to talk with anyone but said, "Fine," and started down the stairs.

"Somewhere private," Detective White said.

"I'd like to be present," his mother said.

"I don't want you there," Steve said to his mother.

Shocked, she looked at him and started to say something but then stopped and simply walked away.

With that, the three went into the family room, which, while not really all that private, seemed to work for them.

* * *

"Any idea why someone would want to make it seem like you have been sending messages to Michelle Harper?" Detective White asked, a question that made Samantha wonder if the detective had pinpointed this as being the actual address where the letters and emails had originated.

"No, and I didn't send them myself," Steve said, seemingly exhausted.

"I know you didn't, which is why I want to know why someone would want us to think you did. Any idea on that?"

"No," Steve said, "but..."

"But what?"

"Nothing," Steve said.

"I think there's something."

Steve looked back and forth between the two of them several times, sighed, and said, "Someone hacked my Facebook yesterday, or really the night before, I guess, and made it look like I was having a party at the Harper house tonight."

"Why?"

"You're the detective," Steve said, tone bitter. Another sigh. "Sorry. Last night..." He shook his head. "Is that going to be on my record, the arrest?"

"You weren't charged with anything, were you?" Detective White asked.

"I don't know, was I?"

His question seemed directed at Samantha. "I don't know," she said. "I wasn't involved in that, just there at the station."

They both seemed to want more.

"I think he was just holding you since everything seemed so focused on you, the letters, the emails, and the fact that you had access to the house." She looked at Detective White. "I really don't know."

"So it's all because I was working on the house. That's why she sent letters and emails and made it look like I was hosting a party." He paused and gave them a puzzled look. "Wait, why would that girl do all that? Was she upset that I was spending time in her old house? How would she have even known I was there if she had just gotten out of the mental place?"

"Now you see our dilemma," Detective White said.

Steve didn't reply to that.

"Steve, do you know of anyone in town who would have wanted to make it look like Michelle Harper came back to town to go on a killing spree, someone who would have used your name in those letters and your Facebook to create a party?"

"No, no one," he said.

"Think about it. Is there anyone out there who seems conniving enough to do something like this, someone who would have begun doing it a few years ago?"

He shook his head. "No. Um. Renee maybe...no...never mind, not her. She's spontaneous when angry, but..." He shook his head again. "I can't really think of anyone."

"Renee is one of the girls who's missing," Samantha said to Detective White. Then, to Steve, "That's who you were with the other day when I was at the house, right?"

"Yeah."

"Did you see her at all after that?"

"Um...no. I took her home, which pissed her off because she wanted us to spend the day together, and then the next thing I knew, she was text-bombing me about the party."

"The one you didn't create."

"Yeah. Whoever put it together didn't invite her but invited my ex-girlfriend, who Renee has always felt insecure about since she broke up with me rather than me with her. I actually had to block Renee from all the pictures of us together because she would obsess over them, even though they were almost two years old."

"So whoever hacked your Facebook didn't realize you were dating Renee?" Detective White asked.

"Um...no, they must have known because they also took away our relationship status on there, making it look like I dumped her."

Samantha and Detective White exchanged glances.

"But you have no idea who would do something like this?"

"No, I mean, if I had dumped Hanna rather than her dumping me, then maybe she would have just to stick it to Renee, but—"

"Your ex-girlfriend is Hanna Hines?" Detective White asked.

"Um...yeah."

Detective White looked at Samantha with a "did you know this?" stare. She shook her head and turned back to Steve. "Why did you two break up?"

"I have no idea. One day she just ended it. Things were going great and then *BAM*, she totally blindsided me. Said it was over."

"Was this right after her father's death?" Samantha asked.

"No, I mean, well, later that year, but"—he hesitated—"I don't think that had anything to do with it."

"And then you started dating Renee."

"Yeah, but now...I don't know. Did they find Renee at that house?"

"If they have, they haven't released that information yet," Detective White said.

Steve nodded.

* * *

"What'd they do with Hanna last night?" Detective White asked once they were back in his vehicle, wipers having to clear the freshly fallen snow from the windshield before they could start driving.

"I think they took her to a hospital to be checked out," Samantha said. "Her throat looked pretty bad from being nearly choked to death, and given how hysterical she was, they couldn't tell if the blood on her was from a wound or just splatter."

"Did she say anything to you?" he asked.

"Yeah, though it wasn't very coherent." Images from the

night began to play out within her mind's eye, the memories of the wind and the bodies causing gooseflesh to spread along her arms. "She was in a type of shock when I found her after the gunshots, sitting in the corner of the room, finger still trying to pull the trigger, blood all over her. She tried to shoot me at first but then realized I wasn't a threat."

If the gun hadn't been empty…

Samantha shivered.

"Then what?" Detective White asked and then fought against a skid as they made a turn on the snowy road.

"I saw Michelle crumpled on the floor, the ax next to her, and put two and two together." *It really was her!* she had thought, dismay and sadness echoing. "And then I tried calling for help with Sheriff Burke's radio, but it had been damaged by the ax, so I had to pull out his phone." The memory of reaching into his pocket, which was sticky with blood and bits of tissue, was too much for her to bear, and she shouted for him to pull over, which he did with a skid, her hands getting the door open just in time for her to puke up the breakfast she had consumed.

"You okay?" Detective White asked.

Samantha didn't reply, fear of what would happen if she opened her mouth overwhelming her.

He got out of the car and came around.

She vomited a second time just as he neared, his reflexes not quite quick enough to get his feet out of the blast area.

"Sorry," she muttered afterward, a sense that it was safe to talk arriving.

"It's okay," he said while twisting his foot around at an awkward angle to scrape the vomit residue off onto the frozen ground. "Not the first time and probably won't be the last that my shoes have endured such trauma."

She smiled with embarrassment and then looked around for something to wipe her mouth with. Nothing was present, though, so she decided to wait until they arrived at their next destination, where she would duck into the bathroom to freshen up.

Speaking of their next destination, "Where're we headed?"

"I was thinking I want to speak with Hanna and find out what happened while she was kept prisoner at the house."

"Will they let us?" Samantha asked.

"I'm an official part of this investigation, so…" He left it at that.

* * *

"But I thought you said you didn't get a good look at her face," the deputy said, voice somewhat condescending.

"I didn't, but I saw enough of it to know that *that* wasn't her."

The deputy followed her finger, which was pointing at the TV screen where a holiday-themed car commercial was playing. He gave her a quizzical look.

"The girl they keep showing on the news," Renee said before he could say something about the commercial. "The one they say escaped the mental institution. She wasn't the one who was chasing me."

The deputy smiled and stood up. "I think maybe we'll wait until you've recovered a bit before we take an official statement." He turned to the nurse, who had been present during the interview, and must have mouthed something silently with his lips because she nodded in reply before showing him to the door.

"I know what I saw," Renee said when the nurse returned.

"Honey, you've been through so much, you're probably just confused right now."

"Honey," Renee said back, "I'm not confused, and if *you* had come face-to-face with that lady while she was trying to kill you with an ax, you would also know that the one they keep showing on the TV wasn't her."

The nurse smiled again and said, "Well, once you're rested and recovered you'll probably see things in a different light." With that, she left the room.

Frustrated, Renee reached for the phone on the nightstand-like table but then, unsure who to call, left it where it was and grabbed the TV clicker to unmute the TV so she could follow any new developments that arose. As before, however, once the news touched on the story, they simply showed a picture of Michelle Harper that had been taken while she was in the mental institution, a picture that did not at all resemble the person who had chased her through the woods.

* * *

"My name is Detective White and this is Dr. Samantha Loomis," Detective White said to the young woman sitting behind the desk in the nurses' station, which was decked out in Christmas decorations. "We'd like to speak with Hanna Hines."

"Okay, let me just make sure she's awake," the nurse said and got up to go down the hall and check on her.

Samantha followed the nurse with her eyes as she walked down the hallway, so she could see which room she went into.

"Detective," a voice called.

Samantha turned and saw a deputy walking up to them, a cup from the cafeteria in hand.

"Yes?" Detective White asked.

"Are you here to talk with Renee? Because if so, I'll tell you she isn't making much sense right now."

"No, Hanna Hines," Detective White said, an odd look coming over his face.

"Ah, okay." He sipped from his cup.

"You said you were here to speak with Renee?" Samantha asked.

"Yeah, girl they found near the school last night, nearly frozen to death. She claims she was attacked by the killer yesterday and fled into the woods." He took another sip. "Don't know if she's bullshitting us for attention, or if she really was attacked, but if so, she's totally going to muck things up since she claims it wasn't that Harper girl that attacked her." He sipped again. "Anyway, hope you're able to wrap up what you need to do and get back home for the holiday."

"Thanks, you too," Detective White said.

The nurse who'd gone to check on Hanna returned. "Okay, she's awake and you can go talk to her. Room two seventeen."

"Thanks."

Samantha waited until they were away from everyone and then said, "Did you know Renee was here?"

"No. You?"

"No."

A nurse came walking by them on her way down the hall.

"Excuse me," Detective White said.

"Yes?" the nurse asked.

"Can you tell me what room Renee is in?"

"Renee?" the nurse questioned. "Are you family?"

"No." He held out his badge. "We're here to speak with her about what she witnessed."

"Oh, room two twenty-four."

"Thanks."

The nurse walked away.

"Now what?" Samantha asked. "They just told Hanna we would be speaking to her."

"That's why I'm going to go speak with her and you with Renee."

"Oh?" She paused. "Can I do that?"

"It's unorthodox and won't be official at all, but given what that deputy just said, I don't think they're going to be taking anything she says as official anyway, not if it brings doubt to the conclusions they already have made."

"Okay, good point."

With that, she started toward Renee's room while Detective White headed toward Hanna's.

* * *

Steve felt naked without his phone and computer and grew more and more irritated at the lack of progress he was making in trying to get the sheriff's department to give them back. Fear was present as well, fear of the embarrassment that would arrive once they came across the pictures and videos, ones of him, Hanna, and her mother. Why he had allowed them to talk him into the odd three-somes was something he would never understand, and then letting them take videos of them, that was beyond stupid.

* * *

"Renee?" a voice called into the room.

"Yeah?" Renee asked, turning toward the door.

"Mind if I talk to you for a moment?"

"Who are you?" Renee asked, unable to attach a name to the familiar face, even though she knew she had seen her before.

"My name is Dr. Loomis, Samantha Loomis. We met briefly the other day when you were with Steve at the Harper house."

"Oh, yeah." It all came back to her. "You're the doctor for the girl they say did this, even though that wasn't the girl who attacked me."

"And that's what I wanted to talk to you about." She took a seat. "You're sure it wasn't Michelle who attacked you?"

"Yeah, positive. Not that anyone cares since they all think I'm full of shit."

"I don't."

"Why?"

"Because I spent several years with her and know she isn't a killer. She didn't kill her family ten years ago, or anyone else this year, but everyone thinks I'm full of shit. So if you could tell me everything you know about the person who attacked you, maybe we can help get this all straightened out."

"What does it matter?" Renee said.

"It matters a lot, because if like you said, Michelle wasn't the one that attacked you, then the person who did is still out there and may come after you in the future."

Renee hadn't thought about that and now, realizing it was true, felt a shiver race through her.

"So what can you tell me?"

"Not much, just that she had red hair, like you."

"Like me?" she asked.

"Yeah, but a bit darker."

"Okay."

"That's all really," Renee said, frustration appearing.

"Oh."

Renee saw disappointment on Samantha's face and added, "It didn't look natural, not like yours, so I'm guessing it probably was a dye job. You know those cheap ones you can get at the grocery store. I think she probably used one of those."

"Okay."

"But that's really it, sorry."

* * *

Getting nowhere with securing his computer and not wanting to sit around the house, Steve drove over to Hanna's house to see if she was there.

"Who is it?" a voice called from within after he rang the bell, a voice that he knew belonged to her mother, Sarah.

"It's Steve," he said.

Sarah Hines opened the door and smiled. "Long time, no see," she said. "What brings you here?"

"Was just wondering if Hanna was okay," he said, feeling a bit awkward. "I heard about last night and well, you know…"

"Ah, she's fine but, as you can imagine, quite shaken." She opened the door wider. "Come on in."

He hesitated. "Is she home?"

"No, still at the hospital, but I was actually going to head that way in a bit to pick her up."

"Okay, maybe I'll stop by once she's back," he said.

"Oh, you sure?"

He wasn't.

"I could make us something to drink if you like, let you warm up a bit, and then we could go pick her up together. I know she really wants to see you."

"Um..."

"Come on." She took him by the hand and pulled him inside, an odd tingle racing through his skin at the memories of things that hand had done with him. "It's been so long. We should catch up a bit before we leave."

He didn't resist and let her guide him into the house, which he hadn't been in since a night two years earlier, a night when she and Hanna had talked him into wearing her late husband's police uniform.

* * *

"You were here in town earlier today, before you came and picked me up at the motel," Samantha said once they were back in the car.

"Yes," Detective White admitted.

"Why'd you lie to me?"

He didn't reply right away.

She waited.

"I wanted to talk to you myself before I came to certain conclusions."

"Conclusions?"

"About whether or not you were involved in the murders."

"Involved?" Then, realizing what he was saying, "You think I'm the killer?"

"Me? No. But some in my department think you are, and it will only be a matter of time before authorities here think it as well."

"What! Why?"

"Because someone is trying to make it look like you and Michelle were in cahoots."

Samantha thought about this for several seconds and then

realized there had to be more to it than simple suspicions. "You found something?"

"Evidence that you were obsessed with Michelle, the murders, and Detective Hines to the point of it dominating your life. Your home was filled with documents about all of them, as well as—"

"My home!" she cried. "You went into my home?"

"There was a call about suspicious activity at your home yesterday afternoon, and the local police found the door standing open when they arrived. No one was inside, but they found documents about Michelle on the kitchen table as well as notes written down about her uncle and when he would be home and what had been observed about him from day to day, as if you had been watching him. They also found a Santa hat with blood on it, which is undergoing DNA tests, a box of latex gloves, pictures of the Harper home, and a police file on the murders themselves that Sheriff Burke confirmed was missing."

"So Sheriff Burke thought I was responsible?" *Is that why he let me tag along, to keep an eye on me and see what I would do?*

"Not quite. He and I both agreed that it seemed like someone was trying to frame you and Michelle, though I got the feeling that he was less convinced about that than I was."

Samantha didn't know what to say to this and, not for the first time that day, felt as if her emotions were going to get the better of her.

Someone was in my house!

Going through my things!

Planting evidence!

She felt completely violated.

You were violated.

The realization hit hard, but rather than drag her down, it sent a jolt of anger through her system.

"So someone out there is trying to make it look like Michelle and I were working together, or that I was guiding her. Why?"

"Obviously someone who has something to gain by all this."

"Or *feels* like they have something to gain," Samantha said, an idea forming. "And it might not be something you can see or touch."

Detective White thought about this for several seconds and then asked, "What?"

"Revenge."

"Revenge? Against you? For what?"

"For being a thorn in her father's side for years."

"Whose father?"

"A young lady who has expressed anger toward me in the past, someone who is very connected to everything that is going on and was very much unaccounted for during all this."

He looked at her but didn't say anything.

"And you have even expressed doubt about her story."

"Hanna," he said.

"Hanna," she confirmed.

"But why?"

"Because she blames me for her father's death, his obsession with the case, and his drinking. Pretty much everything negative that happened to him following the murders."

"That doesn't make much sense."

"To you and me it doesn't, but to her, it might make perfect sense. She believes, as her father did, that Michelle was the killer ten years ago, but he was unable to prove it, which led him to obsess over the case to the point where it dominated his mind. During this, he probably expressed frustration and anger about me and my treatment of Michelle, because my reports always stated that I didn't think she was responsible and that her condition was trauma-induced from witnessing what happened. Unable to solve the case, he started drinking and, well, the rest is history."

Detective White didn't say anything, his hands firmly on the wheel as they drove back into town, snow still falling, the flakes heavy.

"So?" she asked.

"I don't know. I can see her blaming you for her father's death. People link things together like that all the time, especially young people. But to go so far as to kill people in hopes of implicating you and Michelle, that's a huge leap." He paused. "There has to be something more."

"But there may not be. I'm sure you've seen plenty of situations during your time where people have resorted to violence over something ridiculous, something that most people would simply brush off."

"You're right; I have, but not like this."

"What do you mean?"

"The situations you're talking about, at least the ones I think you're talking about, are usually spontaneous reactions, spur-of-the-moment things that they later regret—killing a spouse because he took the last pickle, killing a mother because she was grounding him over grades, killing a wife because she liked a photo of her ex on Facebook or because she was simply interacting with a guy on Facebook—things like that." He stopped talking while making a turn. "This was cold and calculated, planned out over time."

"Planned out and yet it didn't go according to plan," Samantha said.

"Wait, what?"

"Think about it. She obviously wanted a party at that house, one where Michelle would slaughter several local teens, almost like the bloodbath at the end of a slasher film. Who better to host such a party than Steve since he had access to the Harper house, thanks to his father? Only it didn't quite work out, probably because Steve wasn't actually the one planning the party, and because the two were no longer dating. She had to hack his Facebook to set it up. Actually, she might have simply known the password. People leave phones and laptops open all the time and rarely change them, and since they had been dating...she probably knew what it was long before she planned on killing a bunch of people." She waved a hand. "Anyway, things weren't working out, and by the time the sheriff was killed, she knew she couldn't stick with the plan any longer and decided to end things right then and there. Michelle was dead, she looked to be the killer, and Hanna was the surviving hero who had ended things."

"But you're still alive."

"Maybe killing me wasn't always a forgone conclusion, especially if she made a call about the suspicious activity at my place. All that stuff was found yesterday, and the party wasn't going to be until tonight."

"We're assuming she made the call."

"Huh?"

"The suspicious activity may have been just that, a neighbor saw someone at your house who wasn't you and called the police. Hanna, or whoever is behind all this, may have been hoping all that stuff would be found after the fact."

Samantha nodded. "Another aspect that didn't work out as planned."

"Quite a few: no party, you're alive, and a survivor says it wasn't Michelle who was trying to kill her."

"Yeah," Samantha said, a part of her wanting to actually laugh at the incompetence. Given everyone that had died, however, she didn't cross that line. And then a thought arrived. *"Oh my God!"*

"What?"

"It couldn't have been Hanna."

"But a minute ago you—"

"Yeah, I know, but Renee and Hanna knew each other, so if Renee saw enough of the killer's face to know it wasn't Michelle, she would have seen enough to tell us it was Hanna."

"So then, if not Hanna..."

"Someone who might have just as much anger toward me and Michelle for what happened to Detective Hines, more even since the fact that he was drinking and driving might have hindered any benefits she would have gotten after his death."

"And if they proved Michelle was the killer, mostly by making it look like she was responsible for everything this time around, and if Hanna was the lone survivor during the Christmas party massacre, they might profit big time by sharing their story with the media."

"Money and revenge," Samantha said. "Is that motive enough for you?"

"Yes, but only if we can prove it, and..." He didn't continue.

"And what?" she asked.

"I find it really difficult to believe a mother and daughter would work together in such a way like this. I mean, I'm not saying it couldn't happen, just that the likelihood of it occurring is rare."

"But not beyond the realm of possibility, and if Hanna grew up being told over and over again that Michelle was the killer and I was to blame for her not being prosecuted, and then her father died in an accident that could be linked to his agony over not being able to solve the case, which they could twist around so I was blamed for that as well—I can see her being edged into helping her mother take revenge against me, especially if it would then help solve their monetary problems."

* * *

"Steve?" a familiar voice called out as he and Sarah Hines emerged from the second-floor stairwell and began crossing the small lounge area toward the nurses' station.

Steve turned and saw Renee's friend Maggie, who had gotten up from her chair upon seeing him.

"Hey, what're you doing here?" he asked. *Is she friends with Hanna?*

"Came to see Renee, but right now she's arguing with her mom, so…" She shrugged. "Katie and I are just waiting out here until they finish." She pointed to Renee's little sister, who was sitting in a chair, eyes focused on an iPad that she held.

"Renee's here?" he said, a bit startled.

"Yeah, you didn't know?"

"No, I came to see—" He stopped and instead asked, "Is she okay? What happened?"

"Yeah, she seems fine. Guess someone found her on the side of the road by the high school, nearly frozen to death. She was attacked and chased by that girl at the Harper house, only she is pretty adamant about it not having been the mental patient that everyone says is the killer."

"Seriously?" Steve asked. "Shit, I had no idea."

Sarah made a sound, which initially made Steve think she was trying to move him along so they could see Hanna, but then she asked, "Did you say she says it wasn't the Harper girl who was after her?"

Maggie looked at Sarah and then back at Steve, face seeming to ask who she was, but then, before Steve could introduce her, said, "Yeah, guess she came face-to-face with the killer and it wasn't the girl everyone thinks it is." She shrugged. "Of course, the police say she's mistaken, but she's pretty adamant, especially about the hair."

"Hair?" Sarah asked.

"Yeah, she says it was like dark red, an obvious dye job."

"What color did the mental patient have?" Steve asked.

"Not red, that's for sure."

Steve didn't know how to reply to this.

"Her doctor had red hair," Sarah said. "Maybe the two were in cahoots."

"Maybe," Maggie said, voice making it obvious that she was ready to move on from this topic. She looked at Steve. "I'm going to go back and see if they've settled down. Want to come with me?"

"Um..." Steve looked between Maggie and Sarah. "Not right now. Her mother doesn't care for me. I'll visit her later."

"Okay."

"And do me a favor. Can you keep it between us that I'm here right now? I honestly had no idea she was here and don't want her to think I'm ignoring her in favor of"—he didn't say her name—"well, you know how she is. Best not to upset her while she's trying to recover."

Maggie nodded. "It's cool. I won't say anything."

"Thanks."

Steve turned back to Sarah, who started leading him down the hall but then stopped and said, "She's in two seventeen. Why don't you go on ahead? I want to talk to her nurse for a bit and just make sure it's okay for her to come home today."

"Okay," he said and continued down the hallway, eyes on the lookout for room 217.

Hesitation gripped him at the door.

What if she doesn't really want to see me?

What if she blames me for what happened?

Red hair.

The last thought knocked the other two away, mostly because Sarah had brought up Dr. Loomis.

Could she really have chased Renee into the woods?

Twice he had spoken with Dr. Loomis, and both times she had seemed like a perfectly normal human being, one who, unfortunately, had to deal with the mental defects of society on a day-to-day basis.

Would that make her crazy too?

Day in, day out?

No answer arrived and rather than dwell upon it, he willed himself to take the plunge and stepped into the room.

* * *

"So now what?" Samantha asked as they arrived back in town, the road they were on better than it had been earlier, thanks to a plow having gone by at some point.

"Have you ever met Hanna's mother?" Detective White asked.

"Actually, no."

"Me neither," he said. "I think I'd like to change that."

Samantha thought about this for several seconds and then asked, "You know where they live?"

"Yep."

Nothing else was said as he guided them toward her house, Samantha's thoughts starting to ponder what coming face-to-face with the woman would be like, especially if she truly was working with her daughter to frame Samantha and make everyone believe she and Michelle were responsible for everything.

* * *

"Steve!" Hanna called from the bed, voice a mix of surprise and happiness.

"Hi," he said, smiling.

"What are you doing here?" she asked, sitting up.

Gauze covered her throat, and a huge bruise dominated the side of her face. Most disturbing of all, however, was her left eye, the ruptured capillaries having stained the white areas with blood.

"That bad, huh?" she asked after a moment.

"Sorry…it's just…what happened?"

"That crazy girl was holding me prisoner in the attic, and I decided to make a stand and jumped on her. She then started choking me with the chain that she had locked me up with. I fought back, knocked her in the face with my elbow, got the key, freed myself, and then hurried downstairs, got the gun from Sheriff Burke, and shot her as she tried to kill me with an ax."

"My God!"

Hanna smiled.

Steve tried not to look away, the smile somehow making her bloodied eye look worse. "Are you okay?" he asked.

"Yeah," she said, "just really sore and my throat is killing me, but don't tell my mom, because—"

"Don't tell me what?" Sarah asked, stepping into the room, arms crossed.

"That I feel really good, in perfect health, but will fake being in pain so that you'll pity me and bring me my favorite foods and drinks whenever I ring my bell."

"You want a bell? You got one right there on that control, one that you can ring to your heart's content for the next week while you recover."

"Fuck that. I'll walk around the house getting my own food."

Sarah laughed. "Thought that would change your tune." Then, more seriously, "Do you really think going home is a good idea? I mean, you look—"

"I'm not staying here for Christmas," Hanna said, voice raised a bit.

"Okay, well, I just spoke with the nurse, and they're getting your discharge papers together so we can head out."

"Good." Then, after a moment, "You two don't have to just stand there until we leave. You can come in and sit down." She motioned to the chairs.

Steve stepped forward and started to take a seat next to the bed.

"What, no hug?" Hanna asked, a pouty look appearing.

"Oh, um, wasn't sure if—"

"Seriously, I'm fine!" she said and opened her arms to

him.

He opened his own arms and leaned in.

The embrace lasted longer than he expected it would, and during it, she pressed herself into him, the thin hospital gown doing little to buffer her nipples, which he could feel poking him.

"I missed you," she said into his ear. "We both have."

"Me too," he said, his mind a mess of questions that he decided not to ask.

The hug ended.

She leaned back against the bed.

No one spoke for several seconds.

"So," Hanna said. "Still need my help getting ready for the party?"

He chuckled, even though he didn't think that was funny. "I think we'll have to cancel it."

"Pity. Well, maybe we can have our own private party, right, Mom?"

"Of course," Sarah said. "That'd be fun."

Steve, unsure how to respond to this, stayed silent. Something was off about her, something he hadn't noticed when simply passing her within the hallways at school and in various businesses around town.

"What's wrong?" she asked.

"Nothing," he said. "Just overwhelmed by everything that happened."

"Yeah, me too, but we're safe now. That bitch won't be able to hurt anyone ever again. I made sure of that." She touched her throat again and swallowed, a momentary look of pain spreading across her face.

"You sure you're okay?"

"Yeah, just really—"

"*Renee! Stop!*" a voice echoed from the hallway.

"*Steve!*" Renee shouted.

Panic began to rise, and his heartbeat quickened.

"Is that—" Hanna started.

Renee stepped into the room, body clad in normal pajama-like clothing rather than a hospital gown, her face going from inquisitive as she looked to see who was in the room to angry once she spotted him.

"So you come to visit *her*, but not *me!*" Renee shouted.

Maggie, Renee's mother, and a nurse came in behind her, the nurse trying to step between her and them, while her mother actually grabbed her by the arm.

"Renee, come on, leave them—" Maggie started.

Renee pushed by the nurse and came closer, started to say something about Hanna being a whore, and then stopped, face looking puzzled for a moment, then a bit horrified. "You!"

"Me?" Sarah asked, puzzled.

"You're the one who attacked me!"

"I beg your pardon?"

"You're the one who killed everyone, not the crazy girl!" She winced as her mother grabbed her arm and pulled. "Steve, listen to me. It's her!"

"Young lady, I don't know who you are, but my daughter just survived a harrowing ordeal, and if you don't stop right now, I'm going to call the police!"

With that, Renee's mother, Maggie, and the nurse were able to get Renee pulled from the room, the nurse saying something about keeping her another few days for observation, all while Renee cussed everyone out.

Silence settled for a moment and then Sarah said, "I'll be right back," and followed the group out.

"That was fucked up," Hanna said once her mother was gone.

"I guess she was attacked and nearly killed too," Steve said, trying to make sense of what had just happened. *She thinks it was Sarah?*

"Serves her right for spying on you."

"What?"

"You don't know, do you?" Hanna said. "She was spying on you at the house yesterday, when you and I were supposed to meet. The crazy girl saw her lurking around and chased her into the woods."

Steve didn't know what to say.

"Honestly, I thought that was a good thing. Not that she was trying to kill Renee, but that she left me all alone there, because I knew you were going to be showing up, which you did, but then you just stayed in your car and didn't come inside. I was pounding and pounding and pounding while chained up in the attic, but you never heard me."

"I'm sorry."

"Watching you leave was one of the worst moments of my life. I-I-" Her bottom lip began to quiver.

"I didn't know," he said. "If I had…"

"I know," she said, rubbing at her eyes.

"Where was your car?"

"What?"

"Your car," he said. "If I had seen it parked somewhere near the house, I would have known you were there. That's why I never went in."

"Oh, Michelle moved it somewhere. I don't know where. Every time she killed someone, the first thing she did was take their keys and go hide their car."

He nodded but then wondered why she hadn't killed Hanna.

"She's gone," Sarah said, returning to the room.

A nurse followed, an apology echoing.

"Why wasn't she restrained?" Sarah asked.

"She had just been released," the nurse said.

"Well, obviously she shouldn't have been, a mental case like that. Makes me think you have a bunch of amateurs running this place."

The nurse was taken aback a bit but then, a moment later, said, "I have the discharge papers. All you have to do is sign them." She handed over a clipboard.

Sarah and Hanna signed the necessary areas while Steve watched, his mind continuing to process what had just happened and the fact that Renee seemed adamant that Sarah had been the one who attacked her.

Red hair?

But Sarah's hair is black.

Too black.

It used to be brown.

Did she dye it recently?

Black to cover up the red?

Where was she yesterday?

Neither was home, but Sarah's car was there.

"*Finally!*" Hanna said, springing from the bed, stripping off her hospital gown so that she could change, her nakedness yanking Steve's thoughts back into the room.

"Ready?" Sarah asked a minute later, Hanna having donned a shirt, jeans, socks, and shoes.

"Yep, let's roll."

With that, the three left the hospital, Sarah getting behind the wheel while Steve and Hanna sat in back, Hanna only breaking her hold on his hand in order to get into the car, at which point she snuggled up against him.

Steve didn't say anything as she did this, his sense of awkwardness continuing to grow, and though he was enjoying the renewed closeness Hanna was displaying, something about it felt completely off, almost as if she was pretending.

Renee says it was Sarah.

Hanna says it was Michelle.

Hanna has choke marks and was held prisoner for nearly a day, while Renee was running through the woods.

"She moved my car before you got there."

"And then went after Renee."

"I was trying to get your attention."

"What's wrong?" Hanna asked.

"Huh?"

"You're so quiet."

"Just thinking," he said and smiled. "Everything that has happened, it's pretty overwhelming."

"Yeah," Hanna agreed.

"Did you know they arrested me last night?"

"What?"

"Yeah, you and Renee had both disappeared, and they found letters and emails to that girl that they thought I had written, and I since I had keys to the house…it was crazy."

"And then there was the party, which probably added to

their suspicions," Hanna said. "Did you tell them you didn't create that and you had been hacked?"

"No," he said after several seconds of hesitation, "they never even asked about that."

"Well, don't worry. They'll get everything all straightened out now that she's dead."

"Yeah," he said, his arm tightening around her as she tried to snuggle in closer.

A chill arrived.

I never said anything to her about being hacked.

* * *

No one was home at the Hineses' residence, so rather than wait there, Samantha and Detective White headed to the Harper house.

While heading that way, Samantha continued to ponder the possibility that Hanna's mother was responsible for the murders, a possibility that she was growing more and more certain of despite having no evidence whatsoever.

And then they were outside of the Harper home.

"Media must have grown weary of sitting outside an empty house," Detective White said.

"Either that or something snagged their attention," Samantha said.

"True."

On cue, his phone rang.

"My lieutenant," he said to her and then, into the phone, "Detective White."

Samantha could hear but not make out the words that were being spoken, but she grew concerned when she saw him look her way with dismay and then say, "Yes, sir, I understand." He listened. "No, sir, I don't believe it at all." He nodded. "Yes, sir,

I know and I will."

The call ended.

"What?" Samantha asked.

"The local sheriff's department has announced to the media that you're wanted for questioning."

Her heart sank.

"Because of the things found at my house?" she asked.

"No, your motel room and car."

"My motel room!"

"Seems the hotel owner took a peek inside and found quite a bit of blood in the shower. They also found a set of keys that belonged to Molly Mason, who went missing the other day, her head being one of the two found in the attic. And then, when the police popped the trunk of your car, they found wrapping paper that matches the paper that was used to wrap the gifts that were under the tree in there." He pointed toward the Harper home. "Eight gifts to be precise, each one holding a severed head, four of them belonging to the members of McKenzie family."

Samantha was speechless.

"Making matters worse, they know you're with me, and I've been ordered by my lieutenant to escort you to the local police station."

"But you know I didn't do it," she said. "Someone is setting me up."

"Your prints were also found on the gifts, on the paper used to wrap them, to be exact, which means you will be arrested once you're at the station. They haven't released that yet to the press."

"How would my prints be on those gifts? I never touched them."

"Easy. The wrapping paper was yours to begin with, and whoever planted the stuff at your house grabbed it so they could add to the evidence against you."

Samantha couldn't believe this was happening.

"What about Renee? She knows I wasn't the one chasing her!"

"Yeah, but you heard the deputy earlier. Everyone thinks she's full of shit."

"But she isn't, and if we show her a picture of Hanna's mother, maybe she can confirm to us that it was her, which then can help in making sure the truth is known."

He nodded but then said, "I've been ordered to take you back to the local station, so from this point on, I can't be seen with you, which means we can't go back to the hospital together." He sighed. "And if I don't bring you in, I'm going to be in serious trouble."

Samantha stared at him.

He stared back.

"You know it wasn't me."

"I know."

"But…"

"But nothing, I'm not taking you in. However, like I said, we can't be seen together either, or else we'll both be in trouble and prevented from finding out the truth."

"So what are you suggesting?"

He told her.

* * *

"Honey, you're just confused."

"I'm not confused!" Renee shouted, anger toward her mother, the police, the hospital staff, and everyone else who didn't believe her beginning to dominate her mind. Most of all, she was pissed at Steve and the fact that he was with *her*. "She is the one who attacked me!"

"Her daughter killed the girl who attacked you, and now the police are looking for her doctor, who may have been helping her."

"It wasn't her doctor," Renee said.

"You're just confused," her mother said again.

Renee wanted to scream, but instead she simply turned and looked out the window, her head eventually resting on the glass.

"Mom, is Renee going insane?" Katie asked.

"Katie, knock it off."

"But the nurse said something about moving her to the crazy floor."

Renee closed her eyes and took a deep breath, fogging up the window.

"Honey, just play your game."

Silence arrived.

Why was Steve with them?

This question had been in her mind ever since Katie had blurted out that Steve was with Hanna, her actual words being, "Don't you want to go tell Steve we're leaving?" as they were walking toward the exit, which, Renee had known, meant he was with Hanna.

Hanna's presence in the hospital had not been a secret, the staff acting as if they had a celebrity on the floor rather than a whore who had gotten lucky when being attacked.

If I had somehow gotten a gun and shot her...

Or bashed her head in with a rock when she fell...

I'd be the town hero now instead of her.

But no, everyone viewed her as a stupid teenager who was confused, one who may or may not have been chased into the woods by an ax-wielding Santa-suited killer.

Not Dr. Loomis, she said to herself.

She most certainly was not the woman who had attacked her.

Nor had it been the Harper girl.

Hanna's mom.

Of this, Renee had no doubt.

But they all thought it was the Harper girl and, if what her mother had read in the text was true, that Dr. Loomis had helped her.

And Steve doesn't believe you either, an inner voice said.

I don't care!

It was a lie. She did care. Not only that. She was worried. Hanna had always had an odd type of power over him, one that Renee could never understand or match, and now, with her being a hero, that power was even greater. So great, in fact, that he wouldn't realize it was all a lie. Hanna was not a hero. She was an accomplice. With her mother being the killer, that was the only plausible explanation. They had worked together to frame Michelle and, if the text her mother had gotten was true, her doctor.

And Steve is with them.

He doesn't know.

Nothing else followed for several seconds, and then, without warning, a thought arrived that chilled her to the core.

They know that I know!

She had made that pretty clear while in the hospital room, and while no one else really believed her, Hanna and her mother knew she was telling the truth, which might be enough for them to want to silence her.

But if they do, everyone else will then realize you were right.

Unless they make it look like an accident.

Or worse, that Dr. Loomis was to blame.

* * *

Samantha stared at the two tape outlines on the floor, blood marking where their wounds had gushed, the sight somehow more disturbing than the actual bodies had been the night before.

She left the bedroom and went back into the hallway, a creak from the landing echoing throughout the second floor and sounding louder than it really was.

This was a bad idea, she said to herself.

I should have just gone to the station with him, gotten taken into custody, and let them figure everything out.

Instead, she was stuck in the empty house, standing around a crime scene with no phone and no radio, her hands gloved so she didn't leave prints, waiting for Detective White to return.

Useless.

She had failed Michelle while she was alive and now had no way of helping her after her death. Everyone thought the girl was a killer and would go on thinking it unless she and Detective White could prove otherwise.

And I can't help to prove anything while stuck in this house.

Then again, she wouldn't be able to help if she were outside the house either, because being out there meant being stuck in a different location, one that had bars.

I'll probably end up there anyway, she told herself.

Should have stayed home.

Should have —

Something clicked.

How did they know I would come out here?

They couldn't have.

Which means —

They had probably been planning to abduct me too!

She had no idea why, but this realization caused her to shiver, as did the added speculation that if they had been planning to abduct her, then they had probably been watching her as well.

But why not take me that night when they got Michelle?

Did something go wrong?

Did they misjudge something?

She suddenly wished Detective White were there so she could bounce some ideas off him because there was an element they were missing. *Something important.*

She went to the window and peeked out at the empty street, the snow having accumulated to the point where one couldn't differentiate between the road and front yard.

No one had been by to plow.

In fact, the only indication that a road was even present was the tracks that Detective White's vehicle had left, and those wouldn't be visible for much longer.

She was alone, not just in the house, but the entire area.

They're all dead.

Everyone who had been able to call this house home, and the one next door, had been killed.

Why?

Why were the McKenzies killed?

Was it simply so they wouldn't be able to interfere in what was happening here, or because they knew something?

Samantha dwelled upon this for several minutes before deciding to go over to the McKenzie house to look around, her thinking being that the police had probably not really done a thorough investigation, not when their only goal had been cataloging who had been killed.

* * *

Steve nearly sighed with relief as Sarah pulled the car into the garage, the anxiety and terror that had developed following his realization that Sarah was the killer and Hanna an obvious partner difficult to mask while sitting there with Hanna's head in his lap. Sarah's repeated glances at him within the mirror had been worrying, his mind repeatedly warning him that she had caught Hanna's slipup about the party and now suspected that he knew Renee had been telling the truth.

But now all that was at an end.

All he had to do was get into his car and head home or, better yet, to the police station, so he could tell them that Renee was right, Sarah was the killer.

The garage door started to close before they got out of the car.

Is she blocking me from my car?

"Oh my God," Sarah said, looking at her phone.

"What?" Hanna asked and then reached for her own phone as a musical note echoed from her pocket.

How does she still have a phone if she was held captive?

Hanna read her message, an odd look coming over her face. She then looked up at her mother and said, "Really?"

"Yeah," Sarah said.

"Fuck." She turned to Steve and glared.

"What is it?" he asked.

"You weren't going to say anything, were you?" Hanna said, voice carrying a tone of accusation.

"What're you talking about?" he asked, hand reaching for the door.

Sarah opened her own door and stepped out of the vehicle.

"You know!" she said.

"Know what?" He pulled on the handle, but the door would not open.

"Child lock," Hanna said. Then, "I fucked up, didn't I? About the party. You never said anything to me about being hacked."

"Huh, what? I figured the police—" he started but then stopped, his mind asking what was the point of feigning surprise when they obviously knew that he knew. Instead, he asked, "Why'd you do it?"

The passenger door was yanked open from the outside before Hanna could reply, Sarah standing there, a gun in hand. No, not a gun, a—

He felt the jolt just as his mind registered the word *Taser*, his bladder suddenly releasing itself, the words *pissed himself* registering within the pain his body was experiencing.

And then he was being pulled from the car, his useless legs hitting the concrete with a *thump* that he heard more than felt.

"What're we going to do?" Hanna demanded, stepping out over him.

"I don't know," Sarah said.

"We have to do something!"

"Let me think about it."

"What about Renee?"

"No one believes her."

"You don't know that!"

"We can't kill her!"

"We have to."

"No!"

Steve felt his limbs start to come to.

Just have to get up and get to my car.

Without warning, Sarah zapped him again, and this time with a charge that knocked all sense from him.

* * *

COME ON, MAGGIE, YOU OWE ME! Renee typed into the Facebook messenger on her computer, the lack of a phone making it really difficult to communicate.

Thankfully, Maggie had been online when her first message had gone out; unfortunately, her friend was being lame.

OWE YOU? Maggie typed. FOR WHAT?

FOR NOT TELLING ME STEVE WAS THERE!

YOUR REACTION ONCE YOU DID LEARN HE WAS THERE SHOWED WHY I DIDN'T TELL YOU.

COME ON, ALL I NEED YOU TO DO IS PICK ME UP AND TAKE ME TO MY CAR SO I CAN BRING IT HOME, Renee typed, ignoring Maggie's last comment.

HAVE YOUR MOM TAKE YOU.

SHE WON'T!

AND NEITHER WILL I.

YOU'RE A BITCH, YOU KNOW THAT!

WHY DON'T YOU LOOK IN THE MIRROR!

FUCK YOU!

Maggie didn't reply after that, but that was okay, because at that very moment, a message from Steve popped up, one that apologized for the drama at the hospital and then asked if she really thought it was Hanna's mom who was responsible.

YES! she typed. I CAME FACE-TO-FACE WITH HER WHEN SHE FELL IN THE WOODS. HER HAIR WAS RED AT THE TIME, WHICH MEANS SHE DYED IT SINCE THEN, BUT I STILL KNOW IT WAS HER.

No reply.

I'LL NEVER FORGET HER FACE, Renee added.

Several seconds passed, then, I BELIEVE YOU.

YOU DO? she typed and hit send, his words stunning her.

YEAH, he said.

WHY?

I JUST DO. MOM IS CRAZY.

*HER MOM.

HA! MINE TOO, THOUGH NOT LIKE HANNA'S.

Nothing.

HEY, CAN YOU DO ME A FAVOR? CAN YOU PICK ME UP AND TAKE ME TO MY CAR?

OF COURSE. THAT WILL BE GREAT. IT'LL GIVE US SOME TIME TO TALK AND MAKE UP A BIT. I FEEL REALLY BAD ABOUT EVERYTHING THAT HAPPENED.

GREAT! JUST PULL UP OUTSIDE AND I'LL COME OUT. DON'T COME TO THE DOOR BECAUSE MY MOM IS BE-ING RIDICULOUS.

OK! PERFECT.

Renee waited to see if anything else would follow, and when it didn't, she quickly changed from her pajama-like lounge-wear to something a bit more socially acceptable and then waited by the window in her bedroom with her shoes and coat on. This way she could just head down and out once he got there rather than waiting down in the entryway, which would cause her mother to question what she was doing and get upset.

Minutes ticked by, her eyes staring at the street through the cold glass, watching as people came and went, none of them being Steve.

What's taking so long?

Is it a trick?

Could he and Hanna be teasing me?

Could it have just been Hanna?

The thought threatened to plague her mind, but then she watched as Steve's car took a slow turn down the street, a slight fishtail occurring. He then made his way to her house, moving at something like one mile an hour, if that.

Once his car was there, she slipped out of her room and headed down the stairs, opening and closing the front door without a sound.

With luck, no one would even realize she had left.

Once outside, she hurried to the car, the cold urging her along at a speed that was reckless given the frozen ground, face looking down due to the snow.

Warmth hit her as she opened the passenger door and got inside, her hand pulling it shut as soon as her butt hit the seat in an effort to preserve the warmth.

"Thank you so much—" she started to say while turning toward Steve.

It wasn't Steve.

Hanna!

Renee reached for the door just as something was pressed into her side, pain unlike any pain she had ever felt before hitting her ribs.

It didn't paralyze her, however, and her hand still got the door partially open.

The next zap, which caused her teeth to clamp down like a vise as the shock shot up through the underside of her jaw, did the trick, her body going limp in the passenger seat.

* * *

Both doors of the McKenzie house were locked, and since Detective White wasn't there with a key to let her in (*does he even have one for this place?*), she decided to break one of the basement windows and crawl inside.

Though muffled by the snow, the sound of the glass shattering seemed excessively loud, and for a moment, Samantha stood completely still, waiting for someone to come confront her.

No one came.

No one was around.

No one to hear you scream!

The thought somehow found an area within her body that could still be chilled.

Using a piece of firewood to clear the glass, Samantha made sure the window was safe to reach through and then flipped the latch so she could push it open, the rectangular window narrow to the point where she knew the extra inch of window frame would catch her up if she tried to slip through.

Less than five minutes later, Samantha was in the cellar of the McKenzie place, the dry musty smell reminding her of the cellar at her grandparents' house back when she had been a kid.

Not wanting to get sucked into a nostalgic moment, Samantha focused herself upon the stairway and carefully made her way to it, having to navigate around several random box stacks and what appeared to be a dumping ground for old wooden chairs. Beyond that, on the opposite side of the stairway, was what appeared to be a teen hangout area, one that had a big TV, gaming system, battered couch, some reclining chairs, and a scarred coffee table.

Chris and Paul, Samantha noted.

A Christmas tree was present as well, one that was pretty run-down and would probably never work as the main holiday display in a family room but was perfect for a teen hangout that was already comprised of secondhand items.

Sadness arrived.

As children, the two had survived the horror of Michelle bringing a severed head into their family room, only to have their own heads boxed up as Christmas gifts ten years later.

Why?

Was it really an attempt to bring closure to the case that Detective Hines failed to solve?

Or was it something else?

Could Hanna and her mother have a different reason for making it look like Michelle came home to continue what was started ten years ago?

Something was missing, something that wouldn't be revealed simply by pondering the questions.

Will it ever be revealed?

She climbed the steps while thinking this, the silence of the house a bit overwhelming. Eerie too, given that four people had been killed here.

Why?

Had it been an attempt to make it look as if Michelle was finishing something that she never actually started, or had there been a different reason?

Sheriff Burke had mentioned something about the family always going out of town for Christmas, so if using the house as a type of lookout or base given its proximity to the Harper house had been the goal, killing them would have been unnecessary because they could have simply waited until they left. Plus, killing them would have been a risk, given that they would have had to do it several days before the planned Christmas Eve slaughter, and if the bodies were discovered, it would have ruined everything.

Then again, their plans for a Christmas Eve slaughter didn't exactly work out, so…

She let her thoughts on the why of everything fade as she explored the house, her mind once again accepting the fact that there really wouldn't be any solid answers within her head. They would need to be found.

And you might not find them.

Sometimes the why of things always remained a mystery.

Sometimes—

A car drove by the front windows and came to a halt outside the Harper home. A second car followed, this one pulling into the driveway and disappearing behind the pine trees.

A woman got out of the first car and started walking toward the driveway, body eventually disappearing behind the pine trees.

Was that Sarah Hines?

If so, what was she doing back at the house, and who had been in the other car?

Go and see.

The pine trees would shield her upon her approach, just as they were now shielding the second car.

Decision made, she grabbed a fire poker from the rack by

the fireplace and headed to the back door, her feet once again forced to endure the cold deep snow as she tramped through it toward the Harper home, body angled in such a way that she was coming at it from the rear of the McKenzies' yard.

A shout echoed.

Though risky, Samantha quickened her pace, her hope being that any sound she made would be muffled by the snowy landscape and the drama that was now unfolding in the Harper driveway.

"Mom, grab him!" someone shouted.

Samantha got to the pine trees and peered around just in time to see a young man sprawled face-first on the driveway, his hands cuffed behind him, twisting as the woman, who was also on the ground, held on to his left foot.

"Hanna, zap him!"

Hanna, who was near the opened trunk of the first car, hurried toward where the young man had fallen, an unrecognizable object in hand.

She reached toward him.

He kicked, catching the object square and launching it into the snow beyond the driveway. Stunned, Hanna twisted toward the area of snow it had flown into, indecision evident.

A scream echoed from the woman on the ground.

The young man struggled to his feet, the hand that had been holding him now being cradled by the woman's other hand, the young man having probably brought his foot down onto it, crushing the fingers.

Springing to action, Hanna grabbed him as he got to his feet, but she couldn't seem to get a good hold against his bulky winter coat and quickly lost her grip as he twisted away from her.

He ran behind the Harper home and straight into the woods, a trail of cut-up snow marking his path.

"Fuck!" Hanna cried. Then, "Where's the gun?"

Standing up, her mother pulled a gun from beneath her coat.

"Why didn't you have it out?" Hanna demanded.

"And what, shoot him if he struggles?" she demanded back. "That would fuck everything up."

"It's already fucked up." She reached for the gun.

Her mother pulled it back, out of reach of her daughter.

"Give it to me!" Hanna shouted.

"No, you bring her into the house. I'll go get him."

"No, you tried that yesterday with her and she got away. I'll go after him." With that, she took the gun from her mother, spun around, and started following the tracks the young man had left.

Meanwhile, Hanna's mother went to the passenger side of the car and opened the door.

"Get out," she said.

Nothing.

She reached inside, struggled a bit, and eventually yanked someone from within, throwing her to the ground to end their struggle.

Two kicks followed, each blow hitting the handcuffed girl square in the ribs, cries echoing out with each impact.

Following this, she reached down and took hold of the girl's hair, yanking her to her feet, and then switched over to holding her by an arm so she could start walking her to the back door of the house.

Renee, Samantha's mind shouted. *If they kill her...* She

nearly charged forward with the poker but hesitated, knowing she would not have any surprise on her side given the distance that still remained.

Go back to the McKenzie house and call the police.

Was there a phone?

She couldn't remember seeing a landline anywhere, but if they had all been killed there, then chances were there was a cell phone lying around somewhere.

Unless the police took them all?

Go check.

With that, she turned and started running back to the McKenzie house, lungs aching as she sucked in cold air with each breath she took, legs on fire from having to cut through the snow with each step.

* * *

Blood. He could taste it in his mouth as he ran, the face-first fall onto the driveway, though slightly cushioned from the snow, having still exacted a toll on him.

And then he hit a tree, chest first, the hard thump causing him to gasp as all the air was forced from his lungs.

Stay up!

Though he wanted to lie down, he kept his body leaning against the tree as he regained his composure, several slow and deep breaths helping to calm his lungs and slow his frantic heart.

"*Steve!*" Hanna called.

He didn't reply, working himself around the tree so he could peer back toward the house, startled to see that he couldn't actually see it or anything but the snow-heavy trees.

And then Hanna appeared, her head swiveling back and forth, trying to spot him, all while her legs struggled against the snow.

Gun!

He could see it in her hands, the distinctive outline impossible to mistake.

A gust of wind tore through the trees, causing clumps of snow to rain down from the branches, whiting out the area.

Steve bolted.

No shot followed.

He went to the right rather than deeper into the woods, his goal being to stay along the edge so he could be near the house, guided by his unfamiliarity with the woods coupled with his knowledge that Renee was being held captive.

Something caught his leg.

He went down face-first just as a gunshot echoed.

Fuck!

Though he didn't actually know the path it had traveled, his mind pictured the bullet passing directly over his head, the fall having saved his life.

Get up!

He shifted himself around and peered toward where he figured Hanna would be.

Nothing.

Was the shot toward me?

Maybe the gun simply went off by mistake.

Keeping low, he carefully scanned the area she would have been in and then, once he was certain she wasn't anywhere near him, rose up and continued along what he hoped was the path that ran along the edge of the woods.

* * *

"Why are you doing this?" Renee demanded, her body in the corner of the kitchen, wrists hurting where the cold edge of the hand-cuffs cut into her flesh, her ribs aching where she had been kicked. Her muscles also felt exhausted, almost as if they had been repeat-edly used and abused during one of those stupid gym periods where Miss McHaily forced them to use the weight room.

No answer.

Hanna's mother didn't even look at her, just stared out the window toward the woods.

"You could have left me alone, you know," Renee contin-ued, needing to speak. "No one believed me when I told them it was you."

This earned her a glance but no reply.

She's worried, Renee realized.

About Hanna?

About being caught?

"Hanna fucked everything up, didn't she?" Renee said, shifting herself a bit. The movement aggravated the burn on her throat where the Taser had been pressed, her lips momentarily squeezing tight in an effort to keep herself from showing pain.

Nothing.

"You wanted everyone to be killed at the party tonight, but instead Hanna lost control of things and had to kill Michelle Harper a day early, didn't she?"

Hanna's mom turned and looked at her again, one hand making a fist while the other simply stayed open, fingers dangling.

She's hurt, Renee realized.

How badly?

Is it enough for her to be unable to use that hand in a struggle?

If push came to shove, she would focus her attention on it and see what happened.

"Hanna always was a fuckup. Probably why your husband started drinking so much and eventually wrapped his car around that tree."

Rather than being set off, Hanna's mother laughed and said, "My husband started drinking because he couldn't stand the thought of his precious daughter becoming a serial killer. Bad enough he fell in love with one, but then for it to have been passed down, that was just too much for him to stomach."

Renee didn't know what to say to that.

"Of course, we were going to kill him eventually, the plan always being to make it look like an act of revenge from Michelle after she was released from the home—a full circle type of thing—but then he decided to wrap his car around that tree, not only ruining our plans but fucking us over with the lack of a pension and life insurance payout."

She took a step toward Renee.

"It was so effective in screwing us, a part of me almost wonders if he did it on purpose, but given how weak he was, I think it was just a fuckup on his part. I mean, he didn't even have the balls to talk to me about what we did here ten years ago, but I always knew he knew."

She took another step toward Renee.

"Did you know that Hanna and Michelle used to play together?"

Renee hadn't known that.

"They became friends during first grade, and by the time summer rolled around they were almost inseparable—that is until one day in mid-July when Hanna led Michelle into a small clearing in the woods where she had a burlap bag filled with firecrackers and a cat." She sighed. "Several pets went missing that year, but apparently Michelle wasn't as into the games as Hanna thought she was, and she eventually told her brother about all the horrible things Hanna was *making* her do with the animals. Naturally, her brother told her mother, who then called me and, well, the rest is history."

"You killed them," Renee said.

"I suppose other mothers would have been horrified hearing what their daughter had done and, admittedly, given my love of cats, I was pretty upset. But another part of me was intrigued." She paused. "Have you ever heard those mothers who talk about the moment they just knew their son was gay, how it just clicked?"

Renee nodded.

"That's how it was for me. Hearing about the animals and remembering all the different things I had done to the kids I babysat while growing up, things that I grew more and more excited about as the night to babysit grew nearer and nearer, it all clicked. Hanna was just like me, only she started with animals rather than toddlers. And just like with me, I knew her actions would grow more and more extreme, eventually involving people, so Michelle's family had to go. If they didn't, they would have drawn a connection between her and whatever future events unfolded."

She took another step toward Renee, paused a moment to look out the back door, and then knelt down so she was face-to-face with her.

"Have you ever watched an eight-year-old try to chop off a person's head with an ax?"

She waited, face leaning in closer.

Renee simply stared back at her.

"Remember the scene in *Titanic* where Rose needs to free Jack from the pipe he's handcuffed to? It was kind of like that. She couldn't hold it properly, given the weight, and kept missing the mark, so I eventually let her use a hatchet, which was much easier."

"You brought Hanna with?" Renee asked, finding her voice.

"My husband was working that night. Didn't even have the balls to tell them no. So I decided it was time to finally put an end to the threat of them revealing what Hanna had been doing with Michelle, and since I couldn't really get a babysitter—I mean, hello, it was Christmas Eve, and that would be a huge red flag in wondering who had killed the family—I decided it was time to see what she was capable of and move her along to people so she'd stop with the poor animals."

She touched Renee's face, causing a shiver to race through her.

"Your skin is so soft. If we didn't have to try to keep things in sync with the other murders, I'd peel it from your face while you were still alive." She traced a line with her finger just below Renee's left eye. "I'd make the cut here. The bottom half would simply fall away from your mouth, dangling beneath your chin, but the upper part would need to be worked away from your eye sockets and nose." She smiled. "Very painful."

The hand moved down and pressed against Renee's right breast. She then unzipped Renee's coat and reached inside to cup it.

"Did you let Steve touch you like this?" she asked. "Did you enjoy having his hands on your body? I bet you did." She removed her hand and stood back up to look out the window. "I wonder if he enjoyed you as much as you enjoyed him. After being with me and Hanna, I bet there was a serious lack of excitement and adventure." She turned back to face Renee. "Did he ever tell you the things the three of us did together?"

Renee shook her head.

"It's always amazing what a horny teenager will let you do, though I think Hanna may have gone overboard one day when pushing his face down in my pussy while I was menstruating. That, and the time she shoved his jizz-filled condom up his butt with the nightstick." She shook her head while grinning. "That was a bit extreme, something that I think got to him after the fact. Not sure. He actually came a second time that night while we were playing with him, but afterward"—she shook her head—"I think he was upset by it."

Renee was about to say something, but then Hanna appeared at the back door, gun in hand.

Her mother unlocked the door and let her in.

"You get him?"

"No," Hanna said, frustrated.

"There's snow on the ground. He's leaving tracks!" she said.

"Yeah, well, it's hard to tell in the woods. Snow keeps falling from the trees and making it look like tracks are going every which way!" She set the gun down on the counter and rubbed her cold hands together. "But with the snow still falling out there and given how cold it is, I don't think he'll last very long."

"That's what I thought about her!" her mother snapped, pointing at Renee.

"Yeah, but he's handcuffed and has been Tasered several times. His body can't last out there."

"Give me the gun," her mother said, hand out.

"What?" Hanna asked.

"Give it to me. I'm going to go get him myself."

Hanna looked as if she was going to protest but then, without a word, handed the gun over.

Gun in hand, her mother stepped out through the door and onto the porch.

Hanna slid the door shut, locked it, and turned to Renee, a terrifying look on her face. "Get up," she said.

Renee didn't move.

"Get up!" Hanna shouted and started to reach for her hair.

A knock on the glass door caused her to spin around with a yelp.

Hanna's mother was back.

"What is it?" Hanna asked while opening the door.

"Did you go that way at all when looking for Steve?" She pointed toward the house next door rather than toward the woods.

"No."

"Fuck!"

"What?"

"Someone else is here, and they went to the McKenzies' house!"

* * *

No phones. Samantha searched all the likely places where a land-line would be, but every jack was empty. There also didn't seem to be any cell phones, and even if there had been, chances were a screen lock would have foiled her attempts at making a call.

You have to go get help, a voice instructed.

The nearest house was half a mile away, a distance that wouldn't have been a problem for her on a warm sunny day, or even a cold rainy day, but in the snow, which was still falling and piling up...she didn't know if she could make it.

You have to try.

If you don't—

She heard someone downstairs. It was just a slight sound, as if someone was carefully moving around, but it was enough to make her realize she was no longer alone in the house.

* * *

Kneeling within the trees, staring at the back of the Harper house, Steve was gripped by indecision on what to do next, the pain from his frozen hands urging him to head toward the back door while his mind cautioned him due to the fact that Hanna was still in there.

And with my hands behind my back—

He was useless.

Hanna wouldn't even need a weapon to subdue him, just her own hands.

She couldn't grab you on the driveway.

Running away was one thing; going in there to try to get the upper hand and free Renee—that was another thing altogether.

Go get help instead, he told himself.

But they may kill Renee before you can get to anyone.

They'll probably kill both of you if you go in there.

* * *

"Your mother told me all about you and her," Renee said, trying to block her senses as the lingering smell of piss, shit, and decay within the attic assaulted them. "And about how you killed the Harper family."

She grinned. "Doesn't surprise me. They don't make 'My child is a successful serial killer' bumper stickers, so she can only brag to those we are going to kill."

"You're not worried that Steve will go get the police and you and her will go to jail for the rest of your lives?"

"Nope," Hanna said.

Renee could tell this was a lie. Hanna was worried. More than worried. She was terrified. The pacing back and forth between the two attic windows to look outside proved it.

"You do realize everyone is going to know it wasn't Michelle. Killing us is going to do nothing but help prove that she was simply a victim and point the finger elsewhere."

Hanna stopped pacing and looked at her. "Maybe I just want to kill you to kill you."

"Then why take us here to this house?"

Hanna didn't reply to that.

"You two thought you were really clever, didn't you? Planning all this out so that it would look like Michelle came back and went on a killing spree."

"Shut up."

"How long did you plan it all out?" Renee asked, unsure why she was trying to antagonize her.

Hanna didn't reply.

"Your mother made it sound like it was quite a while," Renee continued. "What's that like? To plan something for so long and have it all crumble around you. I've never failed at something so spectacularly, but I bet it just destroys you."

Hanna went back to the window.

Renee shifted herself, maneuvering into position so she could slip her wrists beneath her butt and past her feet. Once her wrists were in front of her, she would stand a better chance at subduing Hanna.

"Fuck it," Hanna said without warning and turned back

toward her.

For a moment, Renee thought she was going to come over and kill her, but instead she crossed over to the stairway and started down.

What the—

Rather than dwell upon the unexpected departure, Renee lay back, lifted her butt off the ground, and slipped her wrists beyond it. After that, she scrunched her legs tight to her chest and stretched her arms as far as they would go, hands fisted as she strained to get the cuffs beyond her heels.

It wasn't working.

The link in the chain was too short to allow both her feet through it at the same time.

One foot at a time, she told herself.

Pain erupted as her heel actually caught on the chain and seemed to press against it, her wrists, arms, and shoulders all feeling as if they were being stretched beyond the breaking point.

And then the pain went away and her wrists were now between her legs.

Hanna was returning.

She could hear her stomping across the landing below and then on the stairs leading up to the attic.

* * *

Oh fuck! Steve's inner voice shouted as he watched Hanna emerge from the garage with a red gas can and head back inside.

She was going to torch the place.

With Renee inside!

He had no choice. He had to go after her.

Without any further hesitation, Steve stood up from his crouched position and hurried through the snow toward the back door.

* * *

"Well, look at you," Hanna said.

Renee stared at the red gas can Hanna was holding.

"Did you get stuck?"

Renee tried to finish what she had started as a reply to Hanna, but she couldn't get her wrists beyond her second foot.

"Pathetic," Hanna said, the smell of gasoline entering the attic as she uncapped the can.

Renee continued to struggle, her wrists finally slipping beyond her foot just as Hanna splashed her with gasoline.

* * *

Steve was in the hallway of the house, making his way to the stairway, when he heard someone on the landing above.

He stopped.

The sounds of fluid splashing upon the floor reached his ears.

He waited.

Hanna started down the steps, the smell of gasoline reaching him before she emerged.

He charged her.

Startled, she swung the gas can at him, hitting him just seconds before he crashed into her, their bodies going down onto the dining room floor as the force of his chest hitting her caused her legs to tangle.

Gasoline poured over both of them before she let go of the can and tried to fight him off with her hands.

Eyes burning from the fumes, Steve did the only thing he could think of as her hands tried to get hold of him. He reached for her throat with his teeth and sank them into her once he felt flesh.

She screamed and clawed at his face, her nails tearing at his flesh as he held firm and twisted back and forth like a dog with a chew toy, tasting blood once again, only this time it wasn't his own.

* * *

Barely able to breathe from the gasoline, and her eyes unable to stay open for long periods of time, Renee made her way down the attic steps and into the bedroom.

Downstairs she heard a struggle and then screams, the latter possibly coming from Hanna.

Not wanting to waste any time, she forced her eyes to endure the burning sensation so she could hurry down the steps, emerging upon the first level of the house.

What she saw on the floor of the dining room was something she would never forget.

Steve was on top of Hanna, his mouth clamped onto the left side of her jaw, twisting back and forth, all while she was shredding the flesh from his face with her nails, neither one seeming to have the upper hand, her screams filling the air.

Gasoline pooled around them, the can on its side, most of the fluid having oozed out.

Help him!

How?

She looked for something she could grab as a weapon, but nothing was available, so rather than stand there helplessly, she hurried into the room, got down behind the two, and grabbed Hanna by the hair.

"Steve, I got her!" she cried.

Steve didn't let go.

"Steve!" she screamed.

This time he heard her and let go, his mouth bloody.

Hanna screamed, the left side of her face a mess of chewed flesh and blood, cheekbone momentarily exposed before more blood pooled around it.

Horrified, and hoping to silence her, Renee lifted Hanna's head by the hair and smashed it back down against the hardwood floor, a sickening crack echoing.

It wasn't enough.

Stunned, but still conscious, Hanna reached for her.

Renee smashed her head again, and then again, the third time finally causing Hanna's body to go limp.

Steve looked at her, and she back at him.

She then stood up; handcuffed hands helping him get to his feet.

Nothing was said as they left the dining room and headed to the kitchen, Renee going right for the sink.

At first, nothing but a wretched gurgle echoed from the faucet, but then the pipes kicked into gear and water began to flow.

She splashed her face, the water feeling good against her skin but doing little to remove the burn from her eyes. She then helped Steve put his face in the water, his hands still bound behind him.

* * *

Clenching the fire poker, Samantha waited near the door of the bedroom she was in, her heart racing and sweat oozing from her pores.

Downstairs, she could no longer hear the person, but she knew she was still there, her careful movements likely that of someone who also knew she was not alone and was methodically searching the place.

Why?

How did she know I was here?

Had she not known, she wouldn't be trying to stay so quiet, of this she was certain.

My tracks!

Once the realization clicked, there was no denying it. She had left tracks in the snow, and one of them had simply followed them to the house. And no other tracks would be showing that she had left the house, at least not in a way that would signify she was seeking help.

Are they both here?

Or is Hanna still going after Steve?

Or did Hanna come back, see the tracks, and just come out this way?

Do they have a gun?

No answers were available.

And then she heard a creak on the stairs.

Her grip on the fire poker tightened.

* * *

Having water splashed on him was a huge relief, but one that wasn't fully enjoyed because Steve knew they were not out of the woods yet and that at any moment Sarah could return with the gun. And with his hands still behind his back, and with Renee's cuffed in front, they wouldn't be much of a match against her.

Renee went back to the sink and started dousing her entire body.

"Renee, we gotta get out of here!"

The smell of gasoline was growing stronger and stronger as the fumes saturated the air.

"Not yet!" she said, continuing to splash herself.

Worried, he turned to the window to look out, eyes scanning the area.

No Sarah.

Nothing but falling snow.

He heard a click and a tiny *whoosh* sound behind him.

What is she—

"Renee, don't!" he shouted as she twisted back toward the hallway, and Hanna, with a lit lighter.

"She was going to burn us alive," Renee shouted back and started toward the hallway. "We'll burn her instead."

"Renee, the fumes!"

* * *

Another creak echoed, this time on the landing of the second floor just beyond the open door that Samantha was standing behind.

Her grip on the fire poker grew even tighter.

She held her breath.

Walk past the room.

Please!

If she did, Samantha would be able to step out behind her and hit her in the head with the poker.

If not...

She sensed and then heard the movement of the person passing the door.

Relief filled her.

Another creak echoed, this one louder than all the rest.

NOW!

Samantha stepped out though the bedroom doorway into the hallway, poker ready, and came face-to-face with Mrs. Hines. She was holding a gun, pointed at Samantha's chest.

"Drop it," Mrs. Hines said.

Horrified, Samantha lowered the poker but didn't release it.

"Should have wiped your feet before coming inside," Mrs. Hines said, grinning. "Your prints led me—"

A huge *whoosh* echoed followed by a flash.

Startled, Mrs. Hines twisted a bit toward a bedroom door, the windows within obviously giving a view of whatever had happened.

Samantha lifted the poker and brought it down toward Mrs. Hines's head just as Mrs. Hines caught herself and pulled the trigger.

The bullet hit Samantha's shoulder just as the poker cracked Mrs. Hines's head, spinning her around as Mrs. Hines's face went slack.

Samantha stepped backward against the wall, a hand going to her shoulder, the initial shock of the bullet entering her flesh and tearing through the muscles quickly wearing off and allowing the pain to register.

Mrs. Hines dropped to her knees, stunned, but still conscious.

The gun was still in her right hand.

Unable to use the poker again given her shoulder, Samantha took a deep breath against the pain and stepped forward, foot swinging back and then forward, connecting with the hand that held the gun.

Mrs. Hines screamed as her fingers were smashed, the gun bouncing across the floor, coming to rest next to the banister that overlooked the stairway.

And then with a cry Mrs. Hines was launching herself from the floor, hands grabbing Samantha by her coat and arm, pain echoing as her shoulder was yanked.

The two tumbled against the wall, Samantha's back to it, family pictures flying as she struggled against Mrs. Hines, the edge of something small yet wicked catching her neck and tearing the flesh.

"We were going to burn you all in the house," Mrs. Hines said, breath hot on her face, before jerking her away from the wall and then slamming her back into it, her head cracking the drywall. "But it looks like Hanna started without us, so I'll just take you to the cabin and have fun with you instead." She slammed her again, Samantha's head actually going through the drywall.

"Then they'll know it wasn't me!" Samantha said, words somehow audible. She felt tears forming from the pain and squeezed her eyes against them.

"They'll never find your body." Mrs. Hines slammed her again. "It'll look like you fled the scene and disappeared."

Samantha opened her eyes once again, each jolt from being slammed into the wall having brought anger with the pain, and now she'd had enough. Equally infuriating, she saw a grin on Mrs. Hines's face, one that almost looked orgasmic.

"Fuck you!" Samantha cried and head-butted her square in the face, her goal being to knock away the grin.

A serious crunch erupted against her forehead, which she later realized was Mrs. Hines's nose.

Grabbing her face, which was oozing blood, Mrs. Hines let go of Samantha, who quickly squirmed to the left away from her and the wall and then turned back to face her.

Blood was everywhere, along with snot, her hands now reaching for Samantha once again.

Samantha knocked them away and body-slammed her,

knocking her back against the far wall. She then reached down for the gun but only managed to knock it between the railing supports.

It fell to the floor down below, bouncing off three steps before settling next to the front door.

With a scream, Mrs. Hines was on her again, knocking them both to the floor.

Blood dripped onto Samantha's face.

Unable to win a wrestling match with just one arm, Samantha squeezed her good hand up between them and grabbed Mrs. Hines's nose.

The wet scream that followed was unlike anything Samantha had ever heard.

Attempting to get away from the pain, Mrs. Hines rolled away.

Samantha turned over, pushed herself to her feet, and hurried to the top of the stairs.

Mrs. Hines followed.

Samantha lost her footing near the bottom of the steps and went down the last three on her butt, pain vibrating through her spine and into the shoulder wound.

Get it!

Behind her, she could feel Mrs. Hines getting closer.

Ignoring the pain, her fingers closed around the gun and brought it around just as Mrs. Hines was atop her once again, screams and blood flying.

She pulled the trigger.

The gunshot was muffled by Mrs. Hines's stomach.

She pulled it again, and again, and again, losing count of the shots, watching as Mrs. Hines's eyes first showed pain and then dulled out into a lifeless stare.

* * *

After finding himself in the melting snow, the heat from the burning house keeping him warm, Steve wasn't sure if he had lost consciousness or if he had simply been stunned by the blast to the point of being unable to register anything. One thing he did recall was going through the sliding glass door. It was like he had been pushed, not thrown, his feet never leaving the ground, his body simply hurried along as he registered what was about to happen, thanks to Renee's foolishness, and tried to flee.

And then he saw the burning figure and heard the screams, which, thankfully, only lasted a second, either because she was dying or because he stopped registering things.

He sat up, pain making itself known, his hands feeling cooked and the back of his head and part of his scalp feeling singed. His chest also hurt, probably from the impact of the glass door that he had gone through, and the right side of his face felt wrong, almost as if it were—

He couldn't reach it with his hands, which were still cuffed behind him, the slight movement causing him to fall back and groan.

A few seconds later, he was able to sit up again.

Gunshots echoed.

He turned to the right, movements slow enough to prevent the pain from taking control once again.

Five or six?

He wasn't sure if he had counted the first one, but either way, the gun was silent now, the bullets either used up or the effect of the ones that were used having satisfied whoever was pulling the trigger.

Sarah went that way.

She had the gun.

If she was the one pulling the trigger...

Panic building, he tried to stand but couldn't, his legs too wobbly and the pain from the attempt too much.

* * *

Samantha stayed under the body of Mrs. Hines for several minutes, her mind and body simply too overwhelmed to do anything but stare into and beyond the dead eyes that were frozen upon her.

Disgust was the first thing that finally registered and forced her to act, her hands shoving the body from her own and rolling away from it.

She tried to vomit, but there was nothing within to expel, so she simply heaved a few times, spittle eventually dripping from her lips.

She spat and stood up, her good arm wiping her mouth, which was when she realized the gun was still in her hands.

It was empty.

She tossed it down with the body and stepped out onto the front porch, legs growing more and more secure with each step.

The Harper home was on fire, as were the pine trees near the driveway.

Some smaller fires were burning in the front yard but wouldn't go anywhere.

"We were going to burn you all in the house."

Did Hanna do this?

If so, she might still be lurking around, ready to finish Samantha off, unaware that her mother was lying dead in the McKenzie home.

Why would she stick around?

The fire is bound to attract attention.

From who?

Had it been night, those in the nearest occupied house might have seen it, but during the afternoon hours, with the sun still keeping the land bright, no one would see a glow, and the blast hadn't really been a blast, more of a sudden brightness.

No, no one would come unless she called them or unless Detective White decided to make a return visit to check on her.

Go the other way.

You need help.

Though she knew it was the intelligent thing to do, she didn't turn and head toward town and the nearest house but instead headed toward the burning Harper home.

* * *

Steve saw the figure coming toward him and thought it was Sarah, his body trying but failing to crawl backward through the snow that hadn't melted yet.

And then she was standing over him.

It wasn't Sarah.

It was—

He couldn't remember who it was but recognized her as being on his side.

"Renee's dead," he said, his voice weak.

"What?"

"Burned."

"Come on, get up. We need to get you help."

This time, with her help, he was able to stand; however, he couldn't make it very far once the snow became solid again beyond the heat of the flames.

"Can you make it to the McKenzies'?" she asked.

"I think so," he said.

He made it about fifteen feet before falling into the snow.

After that, she left him for a moment to tramp a path through the snow, going back and forth several times between him and the back door, her exhaustion evident when she returned to help him back up, one hand cradling her shoulder.

With the path she had made, he was able to get to the McKenzie house. Even better, she was able to free his wrists with a handcuff key, one that he wondered about for several seconds, because she obviously hadn't had it when meeting him in the backyard.

"Stay on the couch," she said after brining him a glass of water, one that his hands couldn't hold, the flesh on top of each badly singed from the blast. "I'm going to go get help."

He nodded and, eventually, passed out.

* * *

"They only found one body in the house, and given what Steve has said, that likely belongs to Renee," Detective White said, sitting by her hospital bed.

Samantha didn't reply, her mind a bit foggy from the pain medication that was being delivered through an IV, her shoulder completely patched up, the bullet apparently having gone straight through the muscle and out the back.

Part of me is lodged into the wall of the McKenzie home, she thought to herself.

"You said that they planned on burning all of you in the house," he said, not as a question but a statement.

"Yeah," Samantha said.

"Doesn't make much sense. Something's off about that."

"Yeah," Samantha repeated, though she wasn't fully sure

what he meant by *off*. Later, once the fogginess cleared, she would understand it all better.

"How would they know you were there and could be burned with them?" he asked. Then, before she could answer, "If what Steve says is true, there is no way they could have known you were there. And it seems like they were going to make it look like he and Renee had gone to the house on their own. That's why they went in two cars and only parked on the driveway." He shook his head. "We're missing something."

"They had a cabin," Samantha said.

"What?"

"A cabin," Samantha said, feeling her eyes growing heavy. "She said something about taking me to the cabin." She closed her eyes for a moment, and when she opened them, Detective White was gone.

December 25, 2015

The tires of Renee's Saturn were bad and the car fishtailed several times as Hanna headed north to the cabin, her hands instinctively controlling the skids without any thought from her mind, which had pretty much shut itself down hours earlier, before the midnight hour had arrived, before the 93.3 station had cut out, leaving her without any Christmas carols for the rest of the journey.

The cabin was cold, yet cozy, the McKenzies always keeping it in livable condition for their holiday and summer visits.

No Christmas tree.

The McKenzies would have cut one down and decorated it on the first day after their arrival, Paul having talked about their family tradition in an essay last year for an English class assignment.

Hanna thought about this for a while, curled up on the sofa she had uncovered, a warm blanket wrapped around her body.

I should make a fire.

Wood and paper were in abundance by the fireplace. All she would have to do was place it within and light it. Doing that, however, after everything that had happened that day, seemed too much for her, and she simply stayed curled up on the couch.

Need to clean the bite, she told herself, the inner words doing little to motivate her.

Sleep seemed like a more pressing issue at the moment.

Need to find out if they're looking for me.

Need to find out what happened to Mom.

Nothing else followed as sleep took hold, the pain that should have registered from her bite wound as she turned over no match for the exhaustion that needed to be sated.

* * *

"Merry Christmas," Detective White said to her upon entering the room.

Samantha had just finished her breakfast.

"Heard you were awake and figured you might be a bit more conscious today."

She smiled and then asked, "Don't you have a family to be with today?"

"Not this year," he said, a sad look coming over him. He shook it away. "I did some research about what you said yesterday about Sarah Hines mentioning a cabin, but so far we haven't been able to find anything showing they own one, and if what everyone says about their financial troubles is true, they probably didn't have one."

Samantha thought about this but couldn't think of anything to say. Sarah Hines had talked about a cabin and they obviously had a place to go, but—

Doesn't matter. They're dead.

Are they?

Sarah Hines was—there was no doubt about that.

"Have they found Hanna's body yet?" she asked.

"No, nothing so far, but given the damage to the front of the house, and how unstable it is, they haven't been able to do a thorough search yet." He paused a moment. "They'll find it."

Samantha thought about that and then, after a few minutes, said, "I still don't understand their motivation. Why kill so many people and try to make it look like Michelle?"

"With them dead, we may never know," he said, shaking his head. "Sadly, this happens more often than you would think with cases."

* * *

The bitch burned, Hanna said to herself with a smile after seeing a news report on the McKenzies' cabin TV, which showed a class photo of Renee while delivering the news of her death to an uncaring viewership.

Her own mother was dead too, and while it had not happened in the way Hanna had envisioned, it had still brought about the results she had hoped for.

Still, she wished things had gone according to plan, her mother burning to death in the house with Steve and Renee, a smile from her daughter as she dumped the gasoline all over the attic being the last thing she saw before the flames cooked her eyeballs.

Oh well.

Her mother was dead, Renee was dead, and the officials were pretty sure Hanna was dead as well, though that might change in the near future once they realized her body was nowhere to be found.

But that was okay.

All she had to do was stay low for a while, get rid of Renee's car, which they probably didn't even realize was gone, given that it had been left on the road leading to Route 8, and find a new place to stay, preferably an isolated house where the people living inside wouldn't be hesitant to open the door to a poor teenage girl who was having car troubles down the road.

She smiled, already anticipating the horror she would bring to the unsuspecting family once she had them subdued.

And, when the time is right, to Samantha Loomis.

Printed in the USA
CPSIA information can be obtained
at www.ICGtesting.com
LVHW052354050124
768169LV00032B/1030/J